3800 17 0061966 5

HIGH LIF

D0835663

Pieces of Happiness

Also by Anne Ostby

Town of Love

Pieces of Happiness

A Novel of Friendship, Hope and Chocolate

ANNE OSTBY

Translated from the Norwegian by Marie Ostby

HIGH LIFE HIGHLAND LIBRARIES	
38001700619665	
BERTRAMS	06/06/2017
GEN	£14.99
AF	

WITHDRAWN

Doubleday

LONDON · TORONTO · SYDNEY · AUCKLAND · JOHANNESBURG

TRANSWORLD PUBLISHERS

61–63 Uxbridge Road, London W5 5SA
www.penguin.co.uk

Transworld is part of the Penguin Random House group of companies
whose addresses can be found at global.penguinrandomhouse.com

First published in Great Britain in 2017 by Doubleday
an imprint of Transworld Publishers

© Anne Ch. Ostby 2016
English translation © Marie Ostby 2017

Anne Ostby has asserted her right under the Copyright,
Designs and Patents Act 1988 to be identified as the author of this work.

This book is a work of fiction and, except in the case of historical fact,
any resemblance to actual persons, living or dead, is purely coincidental.

Every effort has been made to obtain the necessary permissions with
reference to copyright material, both illustrative and quoted. We apologize
for any omissions in this respect and will be pleased to make the
appropriate acknowledgements in any future edition.

The quotation from Epeli Hau'ofa comes from *We Are the Ocean, Selected Works*
(Honolulu: University of Hawai'i Press, 2008).
Grateful acknowledgement is made to Faber and Faber Ltd for permission to reprint
lines from the poem 'The Schooner *Flight*' by Derek Walcott in *The Poetry of
Derek Walcott 1948–2013* by Derek Walcott (Faber and Faber, 2014).
The translation of the Fijian farewell song 'Isa Lei' comes from Rod Ewins,
'ISA LEI (Fijian song of sad farewell)'.

A CIP catalogue record for this book
is available from the British Library.

ISBNs 9780857524874 (cased)
9780857525307 (tpb)

Typeset in 13/15pt Fournier MT Std by Jouve (UK), Milton Keynes
Printed and bound in Great Britain by Clays Ltd, Bungay, Suffolk

Penguin Random House is committed to a sustainable
future for our business, our readers and our planet. This book
is made from Forest Stewardship Council® certified paper.

1 3 5 7 9 10 8 6 4 2

We should not be defined by the smallness of our islands, but by the greatness of our oceans.
Epeli Hau'ofa

There are so many islands!
As many islands as the stars at night
on that branched tree from which meteors are shaken
like falling fruit around the schooner Flight.
But things must fall, and so it always was,
on one hand Venus, on the other Mars;
fall, and are one, just as this earth is one
island in archipelagoes of stars.
Derek Walcott

Prologue

An Invitation and a Challenge

Korototoka, Fiji, 25 July 2012

My dear friend,

Can I still call you that?

The stamps on the letter made you curious, I'm sure, but you've probably already realized who it is. Stamps with pictures of iguanas and parrotfish could only come from Kat. A voice from a time long ago, a fellowship we once had. Do you think we could ever find it again?

Thank you for the hugs and the kind words when I needed them the most – I know it wasn't possible to drop everything and travel across the world for the funeral. From where you are, it must be hard to imagine someone being sung into eternity with a four-part Fijian harmony while the mourners come carrying woven mats, of all things. How many straw mats does a departed one need, you might ask. And I would have to answer, as Ateca explained to me, 'As many as it takes to honour Mister Niklas's life.' So I've spread the mats out across the porch. Dried palm fronds in a checkered pattern, an anchor for the body and a firm foundation for the thoughts, which often plunge

1

into the fiery sunsets, alongside the bats, here in Korototoka.

At night the longing comes, the sharp and aching longing for Niklas and the life we lived before. A marathon of global misery, you might say. A long-distance race with a global pandemic or an environmental crisis at every water station? Yes, that too. But I wouldn't change a thing. The bouts of malaria, the lack of water, the nights of itching flea bites — they taught me to make do. Whether it's making do without money, toilet paper, shampoo or a blue-chip pension. And so here I am, sitting on a tiny speck in the middle of the Pacific Ocean, mateless, but not helpless.

And not friendless, I hope. I have twenty-two acres of cocoa trees and a house with plenty of room. I have a body full of minor aches and pains, but I've planted my feet on Fijian earth and I intend to stay here until the last sunset. Why don't you join me? Leave behind everything that didn't work out! Bring with you everything that still matters and move into a room in Vale nei Kat, Kat's House! This can be the place where we find each other again, and if there's nothing to find, we'll create something new!

I haven't been the best at keeping in touch; I know there weren't many updates from me from Nepal, Afghanistan or Mauritius. But I've missed you; I've missed everyone in our old gang. I've read your letters and emails, admired your pictures of children and grandchildren. And now I wonder, would it be possible to bring us together again, after a gap of over forty years? Do you want to join me, and walk the last leg together? To try to help each other if one of us trips and the other one limps? To dip our aching knees in the warm salty waves and bury our toes in white sand?

I'm not looking for free labour; the plantation is in good hands. Korototoka is a cocoa village and Mosese, the manager, takes care of harvesting, fermenting and drying the beans. But maybe we could start something new here, take a chance together? Perhaps make chocolate, or a delicious-smelling cocoa body lotion – what do you think?

I'm sure you understand why I couldn't send this via email. A letter can take days and weeks on its journey from one world to another, and the words find the right depth and gravity along the way. As they fall into your hands right now, they've had time to mature and soften and be cradled by the paper's curve, ready to entice you here. Can you taste the flavour of papaya and coconut? Can you hear the wind whistling through the palm trees on the beach? Can you see the arc of the horizon, where the Pacific Ocean meets the sky?

Of course, if the ice-scraper, the engine heater and the electricity bill are more tempting, please put this in a drawer, never to be opened again. A letter can easily disappear on its way across the seas, and the postal service from the Pacific is more unreliable than a tropical cyclone or a Fijian ministry post. In which case, you never received it, and no questions will be asked.

So I'm going to send this now, stroking my fingers across the stamps for luck, hoping the wind will send you to me. Maybe Vale nei Kat can be a home for all of us, a Women's House where we can dream, hope, drink, laugh, fight and cry together. Until the wind sweeps us out over the waves and it's our mats that are carried up the stairs and spread wide across the porch.

Lolomas,
Kat

1

Sina

'I'm broke! I'm so sorry.'

They haven't seen each other in decades, and the first thing Sina finds herself blurting out to Kat is the depressing state of her finances – for goodness' sake! She bites down on her lip hard, fighting the quiver, and opens her arms to the tall, smiling woman with the sunglasses on her head.

'I . . . Oh, Kat! It's so good to see you. You look amazing!'

In the arrivals hall at Nadi Airport, strumming a cheerful welcome melody, a ukulele band greets the shorts-clad tourists. The singer in a brightly patterned shirt and a flower tucked behind his ear winks at Sina, who quickly shuffles closer to Kat.

'*Bula!*'

Sina's worried frown gets lost in her friend's welcome hug. '*Bula vinaka!* You're here now, that's what matters. One thing at a time, it will all work out. Let me look at you.' Kat pushes Sina away, flashing her a big, sparkling smile, and it's just like old times. She pulls her close again for another hug. 'I can't believe you're actually here!'

'Me neither!'

Sina chokes back a few tears. She's trembling with exhaustion after a journey that took her nearly forty-eight hours, and another loud opening chord from the ukulele trio startles her. A pair of wide hips draped in an orange floral pattern comes swaying towards her: 'Bula, madam. Welcome to Fiji!' The woman, smile aglow with a hundred luminous white teeth, places a flower garland around Sina's neck. Sina grips her luggage trolley tightly and stumbles after Kat as she heads out into the dark, hot, humid October night. Korototoka is a two-hour drive away.

The darkness is thicker than it is back home. As soon as they put the bright lights of the airport behind them, it's like being in a tunnel without walls, so close and yet so open it makes Sina dizzy.

'Look at the stars,' Kat encourages her, and Sina glances up and out of the open window. The night sky is a maze of shining dots, a frozen explosion of fireworks. Her head tips back; she has to pull her gaze back into the car. Kat looks at her and smiles. 'Pretty amazing, huh?' Suddenly she slams on the brakes. Sina lurches forward and the seat belt catches her; she gets a glimpse of a scrawny horse careering towards the side of the road. Kat shakes her head and drives on, a little slower now.

'It can be dangerous driving through the villages at night. The animals roam free – you never know when a cow will just appear in the middle of the road.'

The ocean on one side, trees on the other; sand dunes; fields with plants she doesn't recognize. 'Sugar cane,' Kat nods. 'Sugar and corn are the two most important crops here.'

The darkness is occasionally punctuated by clusters of houses; a light bulb flickers here and there. Sina squints to make out the shapes of the buildings, sees that some of those alongside the road are just small sheds made of corrugated metal. Is this how they're going to live? She's the first to arrive in Fiji; Ingrid and Lisbeth will be arriving over the next few weeks. And eventually Maya, too – apparently there were some health problems she had to discuss with her doctor first. An unsettled feeling surges through Sina: Is there room for all of them? She hopes they won't be crammed in on top of each other.

But Vale nei Kat is no corrugated metal shed. As they approach Korototoka, they drive along a narrow path with houses on both sides. 'This is the main road,' Kat explains. It winds down towards the beach, and at the end of the street Kat turns right into a courtyard: 'And we're here!'

She parks outside a large one-storey house with a roof that juts out like a pointy hat in the middle. A wide porch with an overhang wraps around the entire front side. The roof above the porch is supported by three columns with coarse ropes wound around them. A couple of small sheds line the perimeter of the courtyard, and a path edged with round stones disappears around the back of the house. There are wicker chairs and a hammock on the porch, illuminated by the glow of torches at the foot of the stairs.

As Sina tumbles out of the car, a mosquito-netted screen door creaks open and a short, stocky figure appears, with a frizzy mane of hair like a halo in the lamplight.

'Bula vinaka, Madam. Welcome!'

Kat had warned her that the housekeeper would probably be waiting for them, even though it's late. 'Come and say hello to Ateca,' she says now, as she drags Sina's suitcase up the stairs. 'She's so excited that you've arrived.'

Sina stretches out her hand. 'Nice to meet you.' But

instead of reaching out her chubby hand in return, Ateca claps it over her mouth, which doesn't stop the laughter from bubbling out between her fingers. Her whole body writhes in cheerful spasms as she hurries to take the suitcase from Kat: 'I'll bring it inside for Madam.'

Sina doesn't know what surprises her more: the unexpected laughter, or being called 'madam' for the first time in her life. But she forgets it as soon as Kat waves her over to the porch railing.

'You can't see the view now, in the dark, but you can hear it, right?'

Sina can hear it. With her face turned towards the sea, she can hear Fiji welcoming her. A rush of sand against sand, a rhythm of water and moonlight and promises she can't decode. The breeze is warm against her clammy skin, a gust of something sweet and satisfied, a drop of honey on her tongue.

Between the house and the beach is a belt of tall, thin tree trunks, standing dark against the pale moon. 'Are those the cocoa trees you were talking about?' Sina asks, but Kat shakes her head.

'No, no. The plantation is a little further away, on the other side of the village. These are coconut palms; they grow everywhere here.'

She grabs Sina by the shoulders and gives her a hug. 'You're going to love it here, Sina,' she says. 'Everything is going to work out just fine.'

Sina nods. Repeats it to herself, like an echo she wants to summon into being. Everything is going to work out just fine.

But that doesn't change the fact that she's broke. Not a penny to her name. Sina can't believe she actually went through with it. Closed the door and left it all behind: the house, the leak around the chimney and the car that needs new snow tyres. Here she is in a strange bed in a foreign land, penniless. And so is Armand. Sina tosses and turns and heaves a deep sigh. But when isn't Armand broke? Broke could be his middle name, she thinks, and pictures her son's face in his passport photo with 'Armand B. Guttormsen' printed below.

His passport is filled with stamps. From Argentina, where he stayed behind when the oil tanker sailed on. 'I didn't mean to, Mum,' he had said. 'They gave the wrong information about when it was supposed to leave!' In Russia, it was the casinos that drew him. 'It's a dead cert. There's a flood of cash over there – they don't know what to do with it all!' Real estate in the Caribbean: 'They showed me the properties, picture-perfect views, right on the beach. How could I have known the deeds were fake?' Secret, exciting oil riches in Canada, a luxury resort on the east coast of Malaysia: 'A once-in-a-lifetime opportunity, you have no idea! Just add some tourists with fat wallets and it'll be a gold mine!'

But there's been very little gold and she's always been the mine, Sina thinks, and pulls the thin sheet tighter around her. A mine that's been emptied, no, vacuumed out for all that glittered and then some. She turns over on her side as the wind fills the darkness beyond the mosquito-screened windows with foreign sounds: the rustle of dry palm leaves, the rolling thunder that lies beneath every-thing and is the ocean.

She can't believe she's here. Sina Guttormsen, sixty-six years old, retired, new resident of a house, no, a *bure* is what they call it, in Fiji. *Fiji!* She hadn't even known where it was – she had pulled out a map of the South Pacific and pored over the tiny dots north of New Zealand, like crumbs torn off the east coast of Australia and scattered carelessly across the ocean between Vanuatu and Tonga. The Pacific Ocean! Her heart beats dry and hard in her chest. Her heart, over the eternal, patient rumble out there.

*

The kitchen in 19C Rugdeveien, three months earlier. Another lousy summer day was coming to an end, another afternoon with cups of coffee that stood lukewarm, waiting. She had tried the TV, tried a magazine, tried her luck – on the lotto card, the usual five correct numbers out of seven; on the *Find Love Over 60* website, no new faces. Six cigarette butts in the ashtray and the silence in the kitchen like dust in her mouth. The wall clock with the red plastic frame gobbled up the time in quick chomps: What-now? Will-you-do-it? Why-not? The letter from Kat on the table in front of her.

> *Sina, you've probably torn open the envelope with a worried knot in your stomach: What is it now? Who is it on the other side of the world that wants something from me?*
> *There's nothing to worry about. No one who wants to trick or scam you. It's an invitation. To warm winds and gentle nights, a wicker chair on a porch with a view of the Pacific Ocean. Do you want it? Will you dare to come?*

10

She had jumped in her chair when the phone rang. The house phone in the hallway, a long, high-pitched whine, a relic from the past in grey plastic. A shout from someone who still has her landline number in their address book.

'Hello?'

A small hesitation, and she was about to repeat herself, her voice slightly more impatient. Just impatient, not scared – Armand never calls the home number. He always wants to catch her when she's most unprepared.

'Sina?'

'Yes?'

'Hi . . . It's Lisbeth.'

Lisbeth. Her voice was exactly the same, hoarse and slow. The last paragraph of Kat's letter seemed to glow in Sina's mind: *In which case, you never received it, and no questions will be asked.*

She could just play dumb, deny everything when her old high-school friend asked if she, too, had received a letter from the South Pacific. A silly letter with a ridiculous proposition, an arrogant assumption that they, the poor idiots at home, had nothing better to do in their little lives than drop everything instantly and jump on a plane for a reunion with Katrine Vale.

'Hi.'

Sina knew she had already betrayed herself. By neither acting surprised nor making her tone dismissive, she had sold herself out. Revealed that an identical letter with stamps bearing iguanas and tropical birds lay on her kitchen table, too, this Thursday in July. Removed the option of ducking out.

'Did you . . . Did you get a letter too?'

11

'Yes. Today.'

'You too. From Kat.'

Sina could picture Lisbeth's mouth with the matte pink lips as she stated this with a sigh.

'She . . .'

What was she going to say? What had she thought after the single handwritten sheet of paper had been read, crumpled up, smoothed out again, and reread?

'She hasn't changed a bit.'

'Nope . . .'

A chuckle of surprise from Lisbeth, like a tiny animal ducking out of a trap.

More hesitation. Sina had let the seconds tick on and on between them until she couldn't stand it any longer.

'Well, a trip to the South Pacific, damn, wouldn't that be nice! If you can afford it, that is.'

It was as easy as ever. Just as easy to throw Lisbeth off as it had always been. Sina knew it as soon as she uttered the words: the tiniest jibe at her fortune acquired by marriage would put a crack in Lisbeth's confidence, make her insecurity and self-doubt seep through the layers of make-up. Make her run her long fingers nervously through her hair. Sina hadn't seen that quick hand motion in years, but she suspected the dark brown locks were as voluminous as ever, stiff with hairspray.

When the poison arrow darted out of her mouth, she'd regretted it immediately – oh, be quiet, Sina, stop it! Let her be. Even Lisbeth has grown old. Did she say that out loud? Even Lisbeth must have grown old, and vulnerable in a whole new way. The way that starts to claw around your eyes just after thirty, grabs the corners of your mouth and yanks them down around forty, drains the colour from your hair and sends the bills from the dentist soaring.

'Yes.'

Lisbeth's voice was still non-committal, as limp as a handshake between two people whose paths will never cross again. But the pause after that one small word was too long, too probing. Searching for someone to lead the way, or maybe just someone to spend time with.

And now here Sina is, jet-lagged, her sinuses itching from an aeroplane cold, awed that it has taken an island in the South Pacific to bring them together again. Not just for some extreme high-school reunion, but to actually live together. In a bure with straw mats on the porch and only Kat to keep them together. A home for old ladies! The thought looms like a monster behind her eyelids. What has she done? What has she ended up with here? Four walls – so thin! She can hear the sound of the flushing toilet trickle like a springtime stream through the house – around a simple single bed and promises of moonlight over a sandy beach. Has she sold herself out? Sina, the cautious, guarded one? She tries to calm herself down. Pull yourself together, you've only rented out the apartment; it isn't sold. You can go home whenever you want.

But of course she can't. She can't accept the money Kat has said she'll gladly lend her for the airfare if she changes her mind. How would she ever pay it back? With all of Armand's need for money, plus rent and groceries? She never buys expensive food, and her little car uses barely any fuel. She almost never drives it, preferring to cycle. But still, it's always about money, has always been about money. The day before Armand's twelfth birthday – was it really thirty-four years ago? – when she had only thirty kroner in her wallet. She had tried to explain to him that they couldn't have a party on the actual day, but maybe later, after her pay packet arrived . . . He had looked at her without a word, turned on his heel and walked out, his back an exclamation mark of spite. She had made spaghetti and meatballs, with a candle stuck in the middle of his plate, and had sung 'Happy Birthday' as she carried it over to the table. He hadn't even smiled.

She doesn't quite know what she was thinking when she decided to leave. *She*, Sina, go live in a crazy little commune in Fiji? Sina Guttormsen, retail cashier, library patron, cautious and vigilant cyclist. With traces of early arthritis in her hands and a muffin top that protrudes further over the waistband of her trousers than she can bring herself to address. Single-mother Sina Guttormsen, whose timid existence was contained within an apartment in one of the oldest buildings in Reitvik, one eye on her boy, the other on her purse. Still, she knew that life well, she could manage it and live with it. But this? She turns over on her back and inhales through an open mouth, sucking the warm, humid air into her lungs, as if swallowing steam in the sauna. The narrow line of tiny ants running across the table. The almost overwhelming smell of frangipani. Kat's hands, so happy around hers. 'I can't believe you're actually here!'

The handbag on the chair by the window holds her passport, a coffee-stained boarding-pass stub, and the keys to 19C Rugdeveien. A see-through plastic bag with her lipstick, a small bottle of hand sanitizer and a mini tube of hand cream. A mobile phone without a functioning SIM card.

Sina sits up straight and uses the sheet to wipe the sweat from the nape of her neck. She locates the plastic bottle on the floor by the bed, takes a sip of the lukewarm water. Vale nei Kat. Kat's house. But food costs money in Kat's house, too. Splitting the bills means everyone has to contribute; electricity, soap and toilet paper have their price wherever you live. She briefly wonders, 'They do use toilet paper here, right?' before remembering that yes, she'd seen a roll hanging from a loop of braided rope on the bathroom wall.

How can Kat have become so rich? Sina's mind jumps directly from the toilet paper question to the subject of Kat's wealth. How can she be the owner of a *cocoa farm*? A house and twenty-two acres of land, with a manager to take care of the day-to-day running of the place, and additional hired hands for the harvest – isn't that what she said in the car? Kat, with no more education than the rest of them, who just took off the summer after graduation and got on a plane with a Swede with long curls. And ended up with a life for the adventure storybooks. Three years here, four years there, six years there: building a girls' school in Afghanistan, bringing solar panels to rural India, establishing a fair-trade coffee farm in Guatemala. Typhoid fever after a meditation retreat in Nepal, blood poisoning from a deep-water coral cut after diving with whales in Tonga. Her passport must look a lot like Armand's: a flurry of stamps and visas and special permits. But unlike Armand, she really did it all, Sina thinks as she lies back down, trying to avoid the sweaty damp patch on her pillow. Kat had achieved things. She had moved forward, bearing the typhoid and the malaria like battle scars, gold stars, proof of what she and Niklas had accomplished. The aid they had given the local people, the wells they had dug, the sanitation course they had brought for village midwives that had lowered infant mortality rates by twenty per cent.

Armand's stomach parasites are less of a badge of honour than Kat's typhoid or malaria. The stamps in his passport are drab and faded, reminders of fiascos that make him look smaller and more pathetic each time he appears on her doorstep with a new excuse. The investment schemes that fell through, the broken promises and unreliable partners, the local idiots who couldn't see an opportunity when it fell into their laps. That's when she opens her door and empties her bank account of the meagre savings she's managed to scrape together since the last time he stood there. He's her child – what else can she do?

She had managed to stop herself from asking Lisbeth how much she was ready to pay for her trip. How much more expensive is it to travel first class? Business? Sina has never done either. She wonders what it would feel like never to have to ask how much something costs. She doesn't know much about Maya's or Ingrid's finances, but at least they've spent their lives working. In good jobs, as far as she knows. Ingrid as bookkeeper for the County Bus Service, or Chief Accountant as she's heard they call it now. Good grades in every subject opened up plenty of opportunities for smart girls like her. Those who didn't spend beyond their means and kept a close eye on their reputations. Surely Ingrid has a good chunk of money saved up, more than enough for a ticket to Fiji.

Maya went to teacher training college and ended up teaching in high school. She married Steinar, no surprise that he became an administrator eventually – there was something about his nose, the flaring nostrils, or the glasses perched on it, something hawkish. A teacher couple may never be rich, Sina thinks, but Maya must have enough savings to get her to Fiji. She and Steinar only had one child: a daughter, married to a foreigner. An artist type who paints landscapes, Sina's seen him in the paper several times. She wouldn't have minded if Armand had married a foreigner. Even if he'd moved abroad. No problem. If only he'd settled down with *someone*, found something – anything – to give him some stability. Images flicker through her groggy mind: Armand with a dark-haired woman, maybe Asian, like the downstairs neighbours in the apartment building back home. The eternal wish, the prayer that hangs suspended like a thin thread between her lips and a god with whom she has no relationship: if only Armand could *do* something, anything! I'm sixty-six, Sina thinks and rubs her fists into her eyes. Sixty-six years old and on the run from my son.

On the threshold of her first uneasy dream under the Southern Cross, Sina meets Kat again.

'I'm broke,' she says. 'I can't afford to be here.'

'There are fish in the sea,' Kat says. 'There's no need to go hungry.'

'I can bake,' Sina replies.

'Five loaves of bread,' Kat says. 'There's enough to go around.'

2

Ateca

Dear God, I know what Madam Kat and Mister Niklas have done for me. I've often thanked you for them giving me this job. You know how hard it was for me after the bus crash that made me a widow; how afraid I was that Vilivo and I weren't going to make it. I worked hard, and you helped me, Lord. You made the maize and the beans grow in the garden so I could sell them on the side of the road, and you made my chickens lay eggs every day. And one afternoon, when the doi tree blossomed, you brought the wheels of Mister Niklas's car to a stop in front of my house. You put the words on his tongue when he asked if I knew anybody who could help him and his wife in the house, and when he mentioned the salary, I knew it was you who brought him into my life. When I understood that Vilivo's tuition would be paid, that he would graduate from Form Six with certificate in hand, I knew it was you that made blessings rain over me.

You sent Mister Niklas to help me when I was alone. And now it's Madam Kat who is alone, and she's filling the house with her sisters. I can see that she needs them, Lord, and they need her too. None of them seems to have a man in their lives, and their children don't live with them. So it seems better for them to have come here. Sisters aren't necessarily born from the same mother.

18

Madam Kat has told me stories about her friends from her country that lies many oceans away. About how people from the same village don't live with their own kin. It sounds sad, and unsafe. Madam Kat has been here a long time – she knows Korototoka – but the other madams who have come, Lord? They're going to live here, grow old here, and I'm the one who will have to watch over them. Be merciful and show me how I can do this.

Madam Lisbeth, for one. Most of the time she doesn't look so happy. I saw it the very first day she was here: how she hesitates when someone speaks to her. As if she never quite knows the right answer. And why does she stand in front of the mirror, looking over her shoulder? Why does she change her clothes all the time, even though they're not dirty?

Madam Sina has eyes as sharp as the swamp harrier. She smokes cigarettes on the porch with Madam Lisbeth. But she doesn't look happy either. Her worries have drawn thick lines around her mouth, and her voice is hard and sour. Is there something she fears, Lord?

Madam Ingrid is the largest of the madams. She has long, strong arms and wants to help out everywhere. The very first day she came, she wanted to go out into the plantation with Mosese and find out everything about the cocoa. How can I tell her that sometimes it's better to stay quiet and just watch and learn?

And soon there will be yet another madam arriving, one I know nothing about. I hope she's healthy and strong with a happy heart.

Madam Kat trusts me, Lord. She says it often: 'Ateca, what would I do without you?' I have to protect her, just as she protects me. Help me keep her and her sisters safe, so no evil casts its shadow over them.

And Vilivo, Lord. Keep the shadows away from my son, too. Help him and let him find work, so he can support himself, become an adult and start a family.

In Jesus' holy name. Emeni.

3
Ingrid

She peers at herself in the little mirror over the sink, and the woman staring back at her looks surprised. The gaze of a newborn, rimmed with crow's feet; white cracks in brown icing. It's only taken Ingrid a few weeks to establish her tan, as if the pigment had been lying in wait all these years, reluctant to make itself known. Kat has warned them against the sun. She's still oddly pale-skinned herself, even after years spent under tropical skies.

'Make sure you cover up and don't be stingy with the sunscreen. I promise you, after a while you're not going to care much about having a tan.'

Ingrid isn't quite there yet. Every day since she came to Korototoka, she's thought about how far too much of her life has been spent inside. Work, home, home, work. Inside the apartment, inside the office, inside the car. For years her brother Kjell had tried to convince her to get a dog. 'It'll be a way for you to get exercise every day, and it'll keep you company!' His wife had echoed this suggestion: 'Yes, wouldn't it be *nice* for you to have some company!' But Ingrid had suspected that Gro's enthusiasm for the family Irish setter was mostly rooted in the dog's ability to get her husband out of the house for the week-long hunting trip each autumn. Ingrid has never had any desire for a dog, or any other pet for that matter.

Nor had she ever been part of the group of women from work who went hiking in Jotunheimen every summer, with their lightweight sleeping pads and their thermos mugs that could quickly be repurposed as ear warmers. She would go for the occasional nature walk on a Sunday morning, but nothing too far and nothing too tiring.

She found greater joy in Simon and Petter, Kjell and Gro's grandchildren. They are closer to her than to their own grandparents, she's fairly confident of that. When Simon couldn't quite get the hang of reading right away, it was Aunt Ingrid who had the patience to sit with him and practise with letter and word flashcards. At her house, Petter was allowed to eat his snack on the couch, or bring in a shabby stray cat. Of course she understood that parenting young children while working full-time was exhausting, of course she didn't mind having the boys sleep over when their mother had to travel for work and their dad was on the night shift. They get along, the boys and her, that's just the way it is. She doesn't make a big fuss of them when they come over, but she enjoys cooking for them – tacos, pizza, chicken wings, nothing fancy. Is it because they're so young that it's so easy to be around them? No expectations that they should have something in common. The two dark-haired heads on the couch, bent over their mobile phones or card games. Simon and Petter. The best thing in her life.

When Kat's letter arrived, Ingrid had made herself a cup of coffee before sitting down to study it. Strangely, she didn't find herself surprised by the invitation – could she call it that? The challenge? The summons? Maybe she'd always known that, behind the prim blouse with the turned-down collar and the glasses on a string around her neck, one day it would be Wildrid's turn. Wildrid, her secret inner twin. The one who had stayed home when Kat took off all those years ago, but who had silently nodded and understood. Whose eager fingers trembled as she read down the lines of Kat's handwriting.

Ingrid, I bet you've been standing there a while with the letter in your hand before opening it. Maybe you set it aside for a minute while you made yourself a cup of coffee. Be honest, haven't you been waiting for this? You've visited us in several of the places we've lived; you know it's not all about cocktails by the pool and fun in the sun. You know there are power cuts and water shortages, mosquitoes and malaria. But I think you'll still be brave enough. Brave enough to go for presenting a united front against loneliness and TV dinners, against arthritis and empty nights. Wearing a floral bula dress and sipping from a bilo filled with kava.

Ingrid had put down her coffee cup as she felt a ripple that started in her chest and spread through her body, a feeling she at last managed to identify: she was homesick, for a place she'd never been to. From her hands holding the sheet of paper, all the way up to her lips parting in a flustered smile, she yearned for Fiji. For Kat, the bird whose wings she'd only ever seen from below as she spread them out, soaring high up above.

She knows precisely the moment the bird took flight. From a table in the shade outside Nilsens Café in Reitvik, one August day in 1965. The silence lay thick and perplexing across the table but, as usual, Kat didn't seem to notice the tense mood around her. Her dark, shiny hair cascaded over her shoulders and beckoned them closer, into a hushed circle of admiring moons orbiting the sun. What had she just said? Leaving tomorrow? India? Goa? Maybe Nepal or Sri Lanka?

Ingrid had looked around for help – did anyone else understand what was going on?

But Sina had sat quietly, hunched over, her gaze empty and disinterested, in a world of her own – Kat might as well have said Mars or Jupiter as far as she was concerned! Lisbeth scrunched up her nose, as if she could already smell the unfamiliar spices and foreign-tasting food. Maya's expression of disbelief had been combined with something else – was it the hint of a smirk? Something self-righteous and complacent she had taken out of the pocket of her sturdy brown skirt. The butterflies in Ingrid's own stomach, which had been fluttering since Kat had called earlier that afternoon and asked them all to meet at the coffee shop, turned into hissing, flailing bats. Where did Maya, who had been accepted only into a silly teacher training college, get off looking so smug? Ingrid could easily have got a place there too, and Kat as well, if she'd wanted!

'Niklas has been to India before.'

Kat's voice echoed from somewhere far away.

'The cost of living is low there, and it won't be hard to find a job for a few days or weeks. He knows somebody in an ashram in Madhya Pradesh, who . . .'

24

As Kat kept talking, the words rolled around in Ingrid's head, forming meaningless patterns: ashram, meditation, yogi. She stared at the table's surface, one finger slowly tracing the rim of her coffee cup. The bookkeeping course she was about to start would guarantee her a job, no doubt. Enough money to live on her own eventually, security to take out a loan for a mortgage on an apartment in a few years' time. Close to the park, she imagined. Near the town centre, so she wouldn't need a car.

'A one-way ticket,' Kat was saying. 'Interrail through Europe, and after that we'll hitch-hike if need be.'

The silence around the table had continued. Lisbeth dangled a cigarette between pink fingernails. Sina wrapped her arms around herself, rocking back and forth inside her coat, which was far too large and heavy for the warm summer afternoon.

'Oh, come on! Be a little bit happy for me!' Kat's smile was warm, broad, all-embracing. As always, it had won them over before they could even realize they'd had doubts. 'The world is so much bigger than Reitvik! I want to see more of it!'

Something in Ingrid had held back. A knot had been tied in the enthusiasm that wanted to bubble up in her throat and fly out of her mouth like a sparkling balloon: 'Of course! How wonderful!' Instead, she hadn't been able to get the image of Niklas out of her head. His hair, longer than Kat's; the laughter lines around his eyes that revealed he'd long since graduated into adulthood. He had travelled penniless around South America and seen more than they'd ever read about in all their books combined. While they'd been making their little plans, this Swedish boy – no, *man*, he was nearly ten years older than them! – had worked as a fruit-picker in New Zealand and a ski instructor in Canada.

So this was what Kat wanted. She'd talked about 'working for a year before I decide on university' but had never come up with any concrete plan as far as Ingrid knew. Not until Niklas had shown up earlier that summer, offering his services as a house painter and handyman. 'He's planning to go to Nordkapp,' Kat had explained, and sure enough, Niklas had vanished for a few weeks but had come right back. And here was Kat describing his next disappearing act, in which she herself would be taking part. 'Mum and Dad are going to ask you,' she said, staring each one of them down in turn. 'So you might as well tell them the truth: I really don't know where we're going.'

Her laugh had skittered like pearls over their empty coffee cups and crumpled napkins and made their ice-cream melt and drip from their cones. 'Don't look so sad, Ingrid,' she had said, putting her hand over her friend's. 'Just think of all the stories I'll have when I come back!'

They had all nodded; Maya even choked out a 'How exciting!' But Ingrid had only one thought: this, right here, is where it happens. This is where we go our separate ways. Teacher training college in Hamar for Maya. Lisbeth getting married here in Reitvik. Sina – God knows what's going on behind her sullen face. If she gets a job, she'll probably stay here too. But Kat is leaving. The wind dies down. Our sails hang limp and aimless. The centre dissolves into a million little dust particles and becomes an

26

endless, dreary void. This, right here, is where we go our separate ways.

*

'Foolish,' was Kjell's reaction when she told him about Fiji. 'What are you talking about; have you lost your mind? You're way too—'

He stopped himself in time, but Ingrid heard the word as it butted up against the inside of his lips. Old. You're way too old. Her brother, only four years her junior, apparently felt qualified to decide what kinds of opportunities had expired for her. Moving to the South Pacific was obviously one of them.

She finished his sentence. 'Too old, Kjell? Too old to do anything but sit at home and wait for my pension to come in? Catch *Jeopardy!* and *Wheel of Fortune*, and maybe go on a cruise to Denmark every once in a while?'

'What do you mean? There are plenty of other things . . .'

'Like what? A bus trip to Tallinn? Going to Sweden once or twice a year with you to buy cheap meat? Perhaps be crazy enough to accept a tandem skydive as a seventieth birthday present?'

'OK, but . . . the South Pacific, Ingrid! What do you know about that? And you haven't seen Kat in . . . I don't know how many years?'

What do *you* know about the South Pacific? she wanted to ask, but didn't. Kjell knew very little about anything at all, truth be told. Except hunting dogs. And car tyres. As the purchasing manager for a tyre company, there was hardly a detail about vulcanization, tread depth and balancing he didn't know by heart.

And she really did know a lot more about Fiji than he did. The very same night the letter arrived, she'd searched the internet. She found out the country's population (under a million), the number of islands (one hundred or so inhabited, more than three hundred total), the ethnic background of the population (around forty per cent of Indian heritage, the rest of Melanesian descent), their religion (Christian, largely Methodist; Hindu; and some Muslim), the major industries (tourism, sugar production, copra). 'Quite a bit,' she could have replied to her brother. But he didn't wait for a response.

'This isn't like you at all, Ingrid! To just throw your whole life out the window, it's totally . . . irresponsible!'

Couldn't he hear himself talking? Who on earth did he think she was responsible for, besides herself? Kat's words danced in front of her eyes. *Leave behind everything that didn't work out! Bring with you everything that still matters!*

'I've always taken care of myself, Kjell, and I intend to keep doing that. I've paid off my mortgage, and I have enough in the bank to buy a ticket back whenever I want. What are you getting so upset about – can't you be happy for me? Don't you think I deserve a little dark chocolate and coconut? Haven't I eaten enough boiled potatoes and herring in my life?'

Her brother's glazed-over look showed her that he understood nothing – boiled potatoes and herring, what was she talking about? He ran his fingers through his thinning hair and tried another approach. 'Well, what about us? The boys – Simon and Petter are going to miss you so much! And Arve too,' he added hastily, as an afterthought. 'He'll think you've gone insane!'

Ingrid had trouble imagining her absent-minded youngest brother having an opinion on her sanity either way. Arve had plenty of experience of being judged himself. A fond image of him flashed through her mind: the shapeless baseball cap, the blue jeans and zippered brown jacket. The apartment near the university, with the empty fridge and full bookshelves, where one might find a pair of glasses in the freezer or a two-week-old sandwich next to the computer screen.

'Arve has enough to worry about with himself,' she said, watching the vein bulge through the thin, freckled skin of Kjell's forehead.

'But what kind of *security* will you have for the future, have you thought about that? What if you get sick? What if you—'

'Die over there?'

She gazed at him calmly, not letting herself get upset, keeping her voice soft. 'Then they'll sing for me and bring straw mats to my house.'

*

It's not hard to build a routine when you're starting from scratch. Ingrid has never lived on a cocoa farm, but neither have any of the others, which means all roles are technically available. Kat and Niklas bought the property only six years ago, and they had just started to get the hang of running it before Niklas's terrible accident. Kat says very little about what happened; Ingrid doesn't know any details. Maybe the wound is just too fresh and raw? The only thing Ingrid knows is that Kat wasn't there at the time.

Mosese, who manages the plantation, oversees its daily operations, as he did under the previous owner. 'Niklas always followed close on his heels. Everything he knew about cocoa, he learned from Mosese,' Kat has explained.

But she doesn't seem to share Niklas's keen interest in the farm, Ingrid thinks to herself. Wasn't it she who wrote so enthusiastically in the letter about daring to try something new? To start producing chocolate?

When Mosese comes by once or twice a week to report on the progress of the crop, Kat rarely goes out to greet him of her own accord. And the ageing manager never walks up the four steps to the front door uninvited; he waits at the bottom of the porch until someone appears. Sometimes Ateca comes outside; other times she spots Mosese through the window and shouts loudly, 'Madam Kat! Mosese is here!' This is followed by the sudden peal of laughter Ingrid still hasn't got used to: a laugh that seemingly bursts out without cause and that can last for several minutes. She's heard it on other occasions, too: among the women selling the pointy brown tavioka roots by the side of the road, among Mosese's daughters when they sit outside the house at night. A group of children walking by – the laughter can strike them suddenly and explode into loud roars that leave them gasping. Hands slap against thighs and tiny bodies are brought to their knees in glee.

Ateca's laugh is not meant for an audience, as far as Ingrid can tell, and it erupts spontaneously without her being tickled or hearing a joke. Maybe Ateca simply has a certain amount of laughter stored in her body that must be released every day, like some people have an unwanted excess of stomach gas? Or is it a kind of tic over which she has no control? Ingrid adds 'Find out why Ateca laughs so much' to the list of things she doesn't know about Fiji.

Since Kat shows only a minimal interest in Mosese's stories about fungal diseases, rodents and fertilizer costs, Ingrid quickly becomes the one who often chats with him on the porch when he stops by. Sometimes she accompanies the sinewy, bow-legged man to the plantation to inspect an especially promising cluster of yellowish cocoa pods, or to sigh with worry when he shows her a larvae attack. Not that she can contribute in any way beyond mere interest, but each afternoon walk in the green, humid cocoa forest infuses her with sweet drops of happiness that flow through her veins, washing away the nauseating office coffee that sloshed around inside her for so many years.

Another thing Ingrid gains from her early days in Fiji is a new appreciation for her feet. Large and solid, they've always fulfilled their primary duty: to keep her steady and upright in size eight shoes through autumn storms and other inclement weather. They've always been dependable but she's never quite liked their veiny, hairy appearance. The size of Ingrid's feet always makes pedicurists consider raising their prices, and she's never been able to persuade R. Lundes Shoes & Sons to stock a pair with a pretty gold buckle or an elegant ankle strap in her size.

By the front door of Vale nei Kat is a pile of rubber flip flops. Indoor and outdoor pairs, with and without thongs between the toes. Ingrid has acquired three pairs: the first modest, black and simple; the second orange with a hibiscus pattern on the soles. The third is a glamorous pair purchased last time they were in Rakiraki: broad silver stripes down either side, and on top, between the toes, a cluster of plastic jewels.

And Ingrid's feet have grown determined to live a happier life, that much is clear. Her naked toes fan out joyfully, her soles snugly nestled into their rubber surface, oblivious to mocking stares based on their size. Each foot spreads out in all directions, taking up its rightful space without shame. And it gets compliments!

'You have nice feet, Madam Ingrid,' Ateca says one afternoon on the porch. Her smile always invites a smile in return; Ateca is missing a canine tooth in the corner of her mouth, the small black hole like a winking glance amid the row of white. She sits straddling the coconut grater, a useful little tool with four legs. It has a half-moon-shaped blade at the front, which she uses to grate the coconut flesh once the nut is cracked open. The strips of moist white meat fall into a bowl cradled between the soles of her feet.

Ingrid is taken aback. 'Nice feet?'

Ateca nods. 'Wide. You could easily hold on to this bowl with them. Just try it.'

The sight of her feet gripping the metal bowl full of milky white coconut shreds makes Ingrid overflow with forgiveness. She forgives her feet for their inability to tiptoe down a flight of stairs, for having landed her the nickname 'Goofy' in primary school, and for never having learned to dance. Suddenly she sees her two robust anchors in a more generous light, showered in coconut milk and fully capable of learning new tricks. She smiles at Ateca, and is both prepared and surprised when the wave of laughter comes rolling in. For over a minute – closer to two, Ingrid later thinks to herself – Ateca laughs about Ingrid's nice feet. And just like that, the retired Chief Accountant at the County Bus Service has become the regular coconut grater in Vale nei Kat.

In addition to helping Kat with the bookkeeping, of course. Putting her financial skills to good use is the least she can do, and *Kat's Cocoa* is not a particularly complicated venture. The money generally moves in one direction: out. But the harvest is still several months away, and both Kat and Mosese assure her that the bitter cocoa beans will be worth their weight in gold when they're fully dried. How much would they have to invest, she wonders, to expand to produce chocolate here, rather than just shipping the beans out?

As she sits at the desk in the office nook of the living room, ring binders spread out in front of her, Ingrid sees herself for a moment as a mixture of Karen Blixen and Ellen O'Hara. How silly, she thinks, shaking her head, she's not in charge of a major plantation and she's yet to see any sign of Denys Finch Hatton. Still, there's something vaguely romantic about it: the power that goes out for hours, sometimes days; the kerosene lamps always at the ready. The feeling that the wind and the rain hold the crops and thus the women's fates in their hands. And Ingrid can tell that it's not in the account ring binders, but in the green shadows under the trees, with the trunks swarming with ants and spiders, that reality resides.

Don't be dramatic, she scolds herself in these moments, you're not the owner of the farm. This is Kat's operation, and if anyone should be worried about fungus or cocoa beetles, it's her. Or maybe Sina — Ingrid knows she was active in the gardening club in Reitvik for many years. Surely she knows much more about rot and parasites than Ingrid does. But there seems to be something holding Sina back. She greets

Mosese politely enough, but doesn't engage any further with him, and as far as Ingrid knows she hasn't taken a single walk into the plantation itself. There's something about Sina that still seems unpacked, weeks after her arrival. A hesitation on the doorstep, a decision she can't quite make. I don't know her, Ingrid thinks, and the insanity of it all washes over her: How could I possibly have thought this would work? Neither Sina nor Lisbeth, or Maya when she arrives, are the same people they were in sixth-form English class forty-seven years ago. Nor is she, or Kat.

'And that's why we're here,' Ingrid tells herself out loud.

To find what we need. Which might well be something entirely different from what we think we want.

'I wasn't sure you'd do it, Ingrid.'

Kat's voice comes from the darkest corner of the porch. The rumblings of the surf being dragged back and forth across the ridges of sand are echoed by the rocking of the cotton hammock from side to side. The tiki torches – simple bamboo holders topped with oil-filled containers – flicker, the black smoke leaving a trace of firewood and girl-scout memories on the tongue.

'Do what?' Ingrid keeps her tone light; this evening on the porch invites small talk, not deep reflection.

In the hammock Kat props herself up on one elbow. 'Let go.'

'What do you mean?'

Ingrid doesn't know if she's more hurt or embarrassed. Why would it be so surprising for her to do something on a whim? Why should she be thought of as the sturdy, conventional one? Is it really so hard for Kat – for *Kat* of all people –

to recognize Wildrid? To acknowledge that there is more to her best friend than common sense and practicality?

'Oh, you know what I mean,' Kat says. 'It's not so easy to cut ties. Routines, habits, everything you're used to. Family.'

Suddenly Ingrid's eyes are stinging. And what would you know about that? she wants to say. You cut your ties nearly fifty years ago, before anything had fully grown and rooted under your skin. For you, cutting ties means packing a suitcase, learning a new dish to cook. Not putting a whole life in storage before you jump overboard, clenching the key in your fist.

She doesn't say it. Ingrid Hagen does what she does best: she keeps it to herself. But Kat is awaiting a response, her eyes shimmering playfully from the depths of the hammock, and Ingrid wants to distract her, make her laugh.

'Maybe I'm not as much of a creature of habit as you think,' she says. 'Perhaps I've left two lovers behind, and gone bankrupt? Maybe I just barely escaped the Russian mafia who were after the money I borrowed for speculating extravagantly on diamonds?'

But Kat doesn't laugh. She looks straight at her with a smile Ingrid knows well, though it's grown slightly crooked, more patient.

'Don't be upset, Ingrid. I didn't mean it that way. You know how happy I am that you came. I just mean there's always a price to pay.'

Kat tries to shuffle over to the side of the hammock to make room for Ingrid. It's a challenging exercise in balance and the hammock nearly tips over; she finally gives up and stretches out her hand instead. 'Listen . . .'

Ingrid takes it and squeezes her friend's firm, warm fingers. 'I'm not upset,' she says.

35

4

Ateca

Dear God, what should I do about Madam Ingrid and Mosese? Madam Ingrid is Madam Kat's sister, and it's my job to help her. But Litia is my friend, and she doesn't feel good about this. Who could feel good when a kaivalagi woman disappears into the plantation with your husband for hours on end? You see all they do, God. They talk. But they're gone so long, and then they come out of there empty-handed. You give us food to fill our stomachs with, not to talk about!

It's hard for Mosese, too. He knows well what makes the cocoa turn golden at the right time; he reads the colours of the leaves and the aroma of the pods as he rubs them between his fingers. But he's never heard of the books Madam Ingrid is recommending, and he doesn't know how to use a computer. Did you see how hard it was for him this afternoon, Lord, when Madam Ingrid insisted he come in the house so she could show him something on her computer? My heart wept as he stood there while she pointed at the pictures and words that flashed across the screen. His toes curled towards the ground; I could see how badly he wanted to run away. And, God, what was I supposed to say when she asked me afterwards if she'd done something wrong? 'Why did he laugh, Ateca? Did I say something rude?' Her hands were so afraid, gripping the glasses on the string around her neck tightly. 'Oh, no, Madam Ingrid,' I said. 'It's just that Mosese can't read very well. Especially on the computer screen. The letters are so small.'

They don't understand, God. When we laugh, it's so they don't have to feel embarrassed.

Show me what to do, Lord. How I can help both Mosese and Madam Ingrid. And Litia, too.

In Jesus' holy name. Emeni.

5

Maya

From: kat@connect.com.fj
To: evyforgad@gmail.com
Subject: Maya's health

Dear Evy,

Thanks for your email, and thanks for being so honest
about your mother's health. Maya and I haven't really
been in touch these past few years, and I didn't know
anything about this. So I very much appreciate the trust
you've placed in me. I imagine this situation can't be easy
for you; it's quite a drive from Reitvik to Trondheim, and
between your job and your own family, you must have
your hands full. I remember the last time I saw you, when
you were a blonde little elf of eight or nine – hard to
believe you have a daughter of your own now! I'm sure
Maya treasures her grandchild, and I know you all must
be more important to her than ever now that your father
is gone.

When it comes to what you've shared with me, I see
that the idea of your mother travelling to Fiji makes you
nervous, and I don't think you've betrayed her in any way
by writing to me. I had to be made aware of the situation.

But let me tell you right away that the invitation still stands, and as far as I'm concerned, what you've told me makes no difference. The group of Maya's old girlfriends is a pretty robust and resourceful team, and the fundamental notion behind our arrangement is that we all take care of each other and look out for one another.

I hear what you're saying about her own 'denial' of what's going on; I would think that's a pretty common reaction among those who get this kind of difficult news. If Maya herself doesn't see it as a real problem or doesn't want to talk about it, I don't feel it's my place to push her. I'll do my best to ensure that her check-up appointments are kept, but the way I see it, the most important thing I can do is to be her friend, and support and help her, within the parameters she herself wishes to set.

Unfortunately, I can confirm your assumption that there isn't much specialist expertise in this field in Fiji. Also, we live in a small village and the nearest clinic is over half an hour away. The doctors there treat most ailments with antibiotics, blood-pressure medication and an encouraging smile. But as you say, there is no way to cure Maya or slow the progress of the disease in Norway either.

We'll have a chance to talk more when you accompany your mother down here. You'll get to meet her other friends here, too; I'm sure you'll remember them from growing up in Reitvik. I think it would be best not to focus on her illness when you're here; it's important that Maya gets to meet the others on equal ground, so to speak, as we all enter this phase of our lives together. And if I understand you correctly, her condition won't be immediately obvious to anyone who meets her.

I can tell you want Maya to have this experience in the South Pacific, as I do, and I think we should do our best to make it happen if that's what she wants.

Welcome to Korototoka to both of you!

Lolomas,
Kat

6
Lisbeth

She turns her head, looks over her shoulder and tries to assess how bad the situation is. The white trousers aren't the worst part – they hug the cheeks a little and prevent them from looking like flattened lumps of dough. Still, it's a depressing sight. Plain and simple.

Lisbeth doesn't mind the saggy boobs as much as the saggy bum. The tight, perky butt Harald once couldn't keep his hands off, the one she's always shown off with careful choices of fabric and cut, isn't what it once was. Far from it. As if sixty-six weren't bad enough already, with the turkey neck, flabby arms and boobs like pockets turned inside out. But now that her bum has started to droop mercilessly down towards the back of her knees, inch by cruel inch, it's almost unbearable.

Harald had joked about it just before her fiftieth birthday. 'I guess I'll have to buy you a new butt as a present. Ass job, heh-heh.'

That satisfied grin, she was sure he meant it seriously. And she'd be lying if she said she hadn't considered it herself from time to time.

Lisbeth turns her head so far she hears her neck crack. She squeezes whatever she can find of half-forgotten gluteal muscles and sees a little ripple in the dough. Diet and exercise can only get you so far. In the home stretch, the scalpel is all that matters. But she's waited too long, it's a mad dash to the finish line and she no longer has someone to pay her entry fee into the race.

Lisbeth is still in shock. She can't believe she did it! She sold the car – to a dealer, she hadn't been brave enough to advertise it herself – bought a ticket and dropped off the BMW at the last minute, literally on her way to the airport. Told Harald that she was going to visit Linda for a few days, she's not sure whether he even registered her words. She knew there was minimal risk that her secret would come out in a conversation between father and daughter – the most Harald and Linda ever do is send each other a text message once in a while.

And then, of course, there had been a big fuss in the end. Phone calls back and forth, she's actually not quite sure how Harald found out where she was. Is. Was, is, will be. Will remain. Will she? Linda had cried on the phone, 'Mum, you're not *serious*? Have you gone completely insane? Who are these people you're living with? What am I supposed to tell Fredrik?'

To her amazement, it occurs to Lisbeth that she doesn't really care what they think. Norway, Harald, their fake-tanned daughter who works at a fitness centre – they're all beyond the scope of the soft cushion of mist that's been wrapped around her head since she got here. Her son Joachim and his family too, his wife and twin daughters. Lisbeth doesn't know her grandchildren, and not just because of the distance to Gothenburg. She is aware the twins are into horse riding; she sends money so their parents can buy them gifts and accessories, she knows so little about these things herself.

When Joachim refused to get involved in the family business and instead chose nursing – nursing! – Harald had nothing but disdain left for his son: 'Well, if that's all he wants to do with his life!' And when Birgitta, the Swedish girl he met at school and married, decided to continue on to medical school, it was all said and done: Joachim, who chose to stay at home with their babies, was a fool and a loser, according to Harald, and it was humiliating for him, not impressive, to have a specialist in internal medicine for a daughter-in-law. They rarely see each other. Lisbeth doesn't know the twins at all; she's totally unfamiliar with their lives.

With Linda, at least Lisbeth understands how she thinks. What's important to her. Linda is still on the right side of thirty-five, and her body and face look ten years younger. She's had a few modelling jobs here and there; got a certificate in Marketing a few years ago. She's had a number of boyfriends; has lived with a couple of them.

'I don't know,' she'd replied to her daughter's agitated question. 'I'm sure you'll think of something.'

Lisbeth turns back towards the bed, looking at the clothes spread across the cotton blanket. Dresses with slim shoulder straps, belts to accentuate her still-narrow waist. Two rows of shoes on the wardrobe floor: pumps in neutral colours, open-toed sandals with ankle straps. She may have run away to the South Pacific, but she has no intention of becoming frumpy. Nothing good ever comes from letting yourself go. She doesn't know what life here will be like, but she definitely won't be seen with baggy-kneed jeans or – God forbid – in one of those voluminous flowery tents that every woman here above shorts-wearing age seems to walk around in. And speaking of shorts-wearing age, Kat is in her denim cut-offs all the time. She is something else. Lisbeth doesn't know whether to laugh or cry. Hasn't Kat rubbed shoulders with diplomats and ambassadors for years? And she still doesn't know how to dress? She didn't wear make-up in sixth form and she doesn't wear make-up now. Has she ever worn it in the years in between?

Lisbeth selects a pink tank top to go with the white trousers. Turns this way and that to catch herself from different angles, climbs up on a stool – oh dear me, how hard can it be to get hold of a full-length mirror here?

'Well, *you* look stylish!'

Kat's compliment sounds genuine, and Lisbeth feels a little rush of joy, a moment of recognition. 'Oh, it's just some old stuff I threw on.'

'You look fabulous. As always. Hold on a second!'

Kat walks the four steps down from the porch into the garden, and disappears into the darkness. Comes back with a red flower and tucks it behind Lisbeth's ear. 'There!'

She leans forward and adds knowingly, 'Make sure you wear it on the left side. That means you're single and ready for new adventures. *Left is for looking, right is for cooking.*'

Lisbeth giggles, almost blushes, and lifts her hand to her head reflexively. She's seen women on the street with flowers behind their ears, along the road, in shops, on their way home from the fields carrying baskets of cassava, the yellowish-white root that's used in every meal. She's seen the red hibiscus, the bulging ginger blossom, the bewitchingly aromatic frangipani behind the ears of men too, but she wasn't aware of this secret code for courting.

'Is that true?' She blurts out the question without thinking. 'Sure it is.'

Kat laughs. Lisbeth recognizes her laughter, loudly rolling around her mouth as if to gather volume before her lips part and it emanates in short, powerful bursts. 'You'll have to put yours on the right side when you leave the house, or you'll never be left alone.'

'Oh, I'm sure.' Lisbeth laughs along with the others and knows she's being silly, but she recalls the feeling and begins to turn red. The glances accompanied by quiet whistles. The eyes scanning her behind, taking all of her in. Jealous, nervous scowls from other women in the corner of her eye, nothing to worry about. Confident that her shoes match her outfit. Protected by the knowledge that her hair and make-up are perfectly done.

'No,' she says lightly and takes a seat on a mirrored floor cushion, one of Kat's many bizarre decor choices. 'Those times are long gone, that's for sure.'

'Are they?'

Sina is the one who asks, not Kat. Lisbeth is just as surprised by the blunt question as by the person asking it. She lights a cigarette to avoid the confrontational stare, feels a vague satisfaction when she glimpses her own well-manicured fingernails.

'What do you mean?' She can hear her own question sounding flat and uninterested; it doesn't require an answer. Her eyes don't meet Sina's. Instead they trace the smoke curling into the dark.

45

This seems to be enough for Sina, who doesn't belabour the point. She shrugs and turns away, fixing her gaze on the ocean that no one can see but everyone can hear.

Ateca pulls the screen door aside and sticks her head out. 'I'm leaving now, Madam Kat. See you tomorrow morning.'

'Goodnight, Ateca.'

She's going home to her son; Lisbeth's seen him a few times. A giant seventeen- or eighteen-year old, with coarse sideburns and muscular calves covered in tattoos. Ateca has a Tupperware container tucked under her arm; it seems to be a house rule that she takes home leftovers from dinner. I'm sure the kid devours it, Lisbeth thinks, he probably has an insatiable appetite. According to Kat, he dreams of being a professional rugby player, like most of the young boys here do. Her thoughts float over to Joachim: her son's narrow, delicate face; his hair already beginning to thin. When was the last time she spoke to him?

Lisbeth remains seated, scrutinizing her feet. Pale, a little bony, but the toenails sport the same perfect coat of red she's worn all these years, no reason to change that. Her heels have benefited from decades of regular pedicures, round and callous-free. She crosses her legs out of habit, to hide the sizeable bunion on her right foot. Hallux valgus, the hideous swollen knuckle that's grown to the size of a plum over the years. It aches, and she rubs it carefully. A small price to pay for years of wearing pointy-toed shoes, she knows that, but bloody hell, it hurts. She shuts her eyes and breathes in deep.

'Say it!' Kat blurts out.

'What?' Lisbeth peers at the face framed by dark hair on the wicker sofa.

'Say what you were thinking about just now.' Kat laughs her trumpet laugh.

'Tell us what you were swearing at under your breath. I saw you. Foot pain is hell. I'll start: Foot pain is hell!'

Sina, standing by the top of the stairs, fixes her gaze on Lisbeth, who hesitates for a second before opening her mouth and taking aim. 'I was thinking . . . goddammit!'

Sina's laughter is mocking but not unsympathetic. Then she joins in. 'Stinking varicose veins!'

'Bloody spider veins!' Ingrid chimes in.

'Cursed ingrown toenails!' Kat, again.

The laughter rolls around between red torch flames, the shadows that flicker and hide.

'Blasted creaky knees!'

'Damned flabby thighs!'

Lisbeth stretches out her right foot; the bump below her big toe glows white. Repulsive, ridiculous. She smooths down her creased trouser leg with both hands and swallows the lump in her throat so the laughter can get out.

She can't remember Harald ever commenting on the misshapen joint on her foot, but he's certainly made sure to point out everything else that has faded, drooped or become wobbly over the years. He has gleefully cheered her on when she's been in front of the mirror applying her make-up: 'No use trying to spackle now – you'd better get the iron out.' She does know it, her wrinkles are growing deeper and deeper, the age-defying creams more and more expensive. The hairdresser appointments more and more frequent. Like a long-distance race with the finish line removed, it's all about holding out, lap after lap, her legs growing ever heavier. But she keeps on shaving them, hiding the spider veins with specialty lotion and forcing tender toes into pointy shoes. The dresses aren't as short as they once were, but at least her knees are still presentable. She can still show off her cleavage with the right bra, but concealing the muffin top has become a greater challenge. The loss of her once-perky bum is just another item added to the list.

When was it he stopped pulling the zip down instead of up? It had been a game of theirs, her calling him into the bedroom to help out with the zip on the back of her dress when they were going out somewhere. Him pulling it down instead of up, peeling the dress off her shoulders, cupping her breasts, mumbling 'We have time for a quickie' into the nape of her neck. His fiery breath against her ear. So long ago. She stopped calling. He stopped coming.

Of course he looks for it elsewhere, he always has. Shopping trips, conferences, the girls with summer jobs at the store. Lisbeth can't remember when she stopped caring, although it was a whole new level of humiliation that day this past summer when he took a phone call beside her in the car, without even bothering to hide it. When he sat there and agreed to meet her – whoever it was this time – in Denmark the following week. 'Procurement meeting,' he'd said as he hung up. 'I have to go down to Copenhagen for a few days.' He'd turned towards her and smiled, and she'd waited for the black pangs of nausea and despair, but nothing came. Nothing except a flat feeling of shame and indifference. A pond frozen over inside her, frost covering the surface. A white sheet waiting for her to pull her skates on and leave deep scars in the ice behind her, from gleaming steel blades: I was here. I was somebody. But she's never learned to ice skate. She's only run, long distance, year after year, lap after lap, in front of the mirror.

Without getting any closer to her goal.

And when she came home, Kat's letter in the mailbox. That very day.

I wonder, Lisbeth, if it all turned out the way you wanted. The prince and half the kingdom. Happily ever after. Or is that my letter I hear, rustling in your shaking hands? Ingrid keeps me updated on the old gang from time to time. You and I both know she's no blabbermouth, but I've gathered that the roses that grow at the top of Toppåsen have thorns too. Princes don't always turn into the kings they promised to be.

So here's an offer, if it's time for a change. Could you swap your three reception rooms with panorama windows for one small room under a thatched roof? Or do you have too much to lose?

Lisbeth looks around and sees Ingrid wiping tears of laughter off her cheek. Her thick, grey hair is cut short; a simple look that matches the glasses on a string around her neck. Solid, dull Ingrid – but something in her is new: a lively toss of her head, a glitter deep inside her brown eyes. Ingrid, who appears to have watched her life from afar. Who has known all about Harald's dalliances and heard the gossip around town, to which she herself closed her eyes and ears for so many years. Who has told Kat, and is thus the reason Lisbeth is sitting here right now, with a flower in her hair and the red sun calmly burning its way down into the Pacific. A warm lump throbs in her throat and she reaches for her cigarette case. Happily ever after? Does that exist anywhere?

The wicker chair next to the hammock creaks as Kat tucks her legs underneath her. Joyful, lively Kat, with the open face that knows nothing about playing games. If Lisbeth could be said to have had a competitor at Reitvik High, it would have been her. Kat with her strange laugh, her wide mouth – she had somehow mesmerized them all, captured them. Without ever taking advantage of it. Kat had just laughed, longed and desired without shame, dreamed of things Lisbeth knew were never going to be for her. She had always felt out of breath after spending time with Kat, thrilled and dejected all at once. But she herself had had other goals, zeroing in on them, never letting them out of sight. She knew which weapons she could trust and which prize she was going to bring home. Still, it had been a relief when Kat ran off with Niklas, an unexpected turn of events that left behind only those still dancing to the same old tune. And Lisbeth was unbeatable at that dance, elegantly advancing to the top of the podium, where the trophy's name was Harald Høie. Followed by 'Jr' and then, eventually, preceded by 'Director'. Third generation in his family's building materials business, solid, prosperous and safe. First prize.

Lisbeth shifts her gaze over to Sina and when their eyes meet, she's startled for a moment. Sina doesn't break eye contact, it's Lisbeth who turns away, struck by a feeling she knows well: the sense of being challenged from an unfamiliar, unnameable angle. A relationship where the tightrope is always quivering. Then and now. Were they best friends? Yes, she supposes they were. As different as sugar and salt but we needed each other, Lisbeth thinks. She is just as unable to explain why now as she was back then. Sina, who always had a cold sore on her upper lip. Her coat hanging open – no wonder she had always looked frozen. Round-shouldered and flat-chested, she couldn't even manage the simplest trick of stuffing her bra with cotton wool. Lisbeth still gets frustrated thinking about it; why couldn't she at least *try*? To sit up straight, smile a little more, fix her hair. Sina wasn't stupid, just so . . . weak-willed!

And the other thing – which is still unnamed, which Lisbeth hasn't felt or thought about for many years – wasn't something Sina said. Or did. But it had always been there, in the hint of a smirk on her face when Lisbeth laughed out loud at the guys' dumbest jokes. In the slow gaze that followed her in the ladies' room mirror, while Sina stood there wordlessly, clutching Lisbeth's coat and scarf as Lisbeth struggled with her brush and complained about her impossible hair. Something disapproving. No, spurning. No, disparaging.

Lisbeth lets the smoke stream out of her nostrils as she returns to her old quest for the right word. Judgemental? Mocking? She can't find it this time either. She only knows that it's still there. A kind of power, behind stooping shoulders and sullen replies.

Quiet and passive, that was all the others saw in Sina.

That's why the shock was even greater that autumn after graduation, when it became obvious that Sina couldn't button up her coat any more. It never became clear who the father was; Lisbeth doesn't think anyone knows. But Kat had left; Ingrid was working and living her quiet, little life; Maya and Steinar had left town to go to teacher training college; and Lisbeth herself had a shining ring on her finger and was planning her wedding. It seemed impossible not to care, not to do something, anything, for Sina who had sat at the desk next to her for three years. Sina, who had vaguely mentioned something about going into nursing, maybe, but hadn't started anything – until this. Oh, Lisbeth had been dismayed, even irritated. Yet she'd pitied her as well, and had felt some kind of responsibility. She had ended up talking to Harald about her: a part-time job, even just a few hours a week? In the stock room, so she wouldn't have to listen to the comments (and so that people wouldn't have to see her either – yes, she'd said that too). Sina's mother, a widow in poor health, didn't have much to contribute – couldn't they try to help out? When Harald finally agreed to talk to Harald Senior about it and she could tell Sina, Lisbeth could taste her new life on the tip of her tongue. All of a sudden, she had something to offer. A new gaze to meet Sina's.

She'll never forget it. Nilsens Café, a table against the wall, next to the pastry counter.

'Harald Senior said so himself! You can help out in the stock room, pricing items and doing other jobs. I don't know what it will pay exactly, but at least you'll *have* something, right?'

Lisbeth had felt warm under the collar of her coat,

breathless at the thought of her excess wealth. A sweet and sinister sensation of power.

The black clouds that gathered in Sina's eyes. The throat stubbornly cleared, the jaw suddenly thrust forward.

'*Have* something? You don't think I *have* anything?'

The face that leaned over the table – hot, furious breath.

'I have a lot more than you, Lisbeth, so don't think you and Harald Høie are doing me any favours!'

She'd been paralysed. Felt her fingers start to tremble around the cigarette, her smile start to wither. 'What do you mean? I only wanted . . .'

'You know exactly what I mean. You think I don't know how your mind works? *Poor Sina!*'

Her scowl, crooked and ugly and hard.

'*Poor Sina who ended up this way.* I'll tell you something, dammit: you're the one who needs pity, Lisbeth. You're the one who can't turn sideways without worrying how your arse looks. You're the one who practises your laugh in front of the mirror. Do you really think I want to be like you? Someone who has nothing to show except her appearance? I'm the one who *has* something, Lisbeth. Not you.'

Sina had leaned back in her chair and drained her coffee cup before continuing in a completely new, indifferent tone.

'I'll take the job, of course. I do have to make a living somehow. Give Harald my best and tell him thank you so much.'

In hindsight, Lisbeth doesn't know how she managed to push it away. How she went back to Harald and told him Sina was so happy and grateful, she says thank you so much! Looking back, she could almost convince herself

53

that she'd misunderstood. Of course Sina was upset, she was in a horribly difficult situation. Of course she was distraught, she didn't know what she was saying! And at least her gratitude for the job was genuine; she'd stayed at the store all these years.

It was only natural that they had grown apart. Sina had the boy, and the job. Her little life in her tiny two-bedroom apartment. Lisbeth had so much more. Had it all. The house in Toppåsen, the children. Joachim first, heir to the throne of Høie Building Supplies. Then Linda, the princess. And it had all been good, hadn't it? Busy, but good? And she had kept in shape, stayed thin, held on to Harald to the best of her ability. 'A good fit', that's what they call it nowadays. Have she and Harald ever been a good fit? She's not quite sure what that means. Isn't it simply the days passing by without too much conflict, too many problems? Looking away when the view gets unpleasant? The empty rooms in the house, all those hours spent alone, was it really so bad?

Life could have been much worse, Lisbeth decides as she rests her eyes on each of the women around her in turn. Sina: short of money her whole life, a useless fool of a son. Ingrid: sturdy, safe, but how much fun has she ever had? Have a man's hands ever warmed her up, made her excited? And Kat . . . who can make sense of Kat? Kat, who could have had whomever she wanted but instead chose denim cut-offs and no permanent address. Kat, who lost her husband, but never talks about it – a bit strange, no? And Maya. Maya who isn't here yet, but who will soon move into the last and smallest room in Vale nei Kat – what a name, come to think of it. Kat's House. Lisbeth wishes they could find another name. She can't sit here as a guest in Kat's house for the rest of her life. The rooms she shared with Harald flicker before her eyes – silent reception rooms, empty bedrooms. The thought hits her: I'm just as much a guest there. Everything is tasteful and complete. But there's no one home. No one's been home there for years.

7

Ateca

Dear God, you have to help me protect them. Madam Kat's sisters; they're so helpless! They have plenty of money and more food than they can eat, but there's so much they don't understand.

I know everything is in your hands, Lord. But I have to teach them things. Madam Sina needs to put coconut oil in her thin hair. Madam Lisbeth has to stop covering her face with creams so it can breathe better. And Madam Ingrid, who wants to learn all kinds of things. But she wants to make decisions too, wants to be a little bosso. She's decided that the wet kitchen rubbish should be kept in a pile in the back yard. She mixes it with rotten leaves and fruit peelings, and tosses it all together with a shovel. 'It'll make the pumpkins grow better,' she says. I just nod and smile. She'll find out in due time that the fish skin will make the sweet potatoes taste bad. And did you hear what she asked me today? Why the women don't meet over the grog bowl in the evenings like the men do?

And soon yet another madam will arrive. I watch over them as well as I can, Lord, although it's not easy to understand them. Their choppy language and their pale clothes. The strange questions they ask. They're good people, but they're kaivalagi; they think in different ways.

You say we should give our worries over to you, so I'm leaving the madams in your care. Thank you for holding your hand over them and protecting them.

In Jesus' holy name. Emeni.

8
Kat

I hope they don't see this as an experiment. Something they can figure out whether they like, and pull out of as soon as it gets challenging. I'm not naive – God knows I've seen dreams and good intentions crushed by the sledge-hammer of reality too many times. But I want this to work so badly, and they have to be prepared for some sweat and some tears, each and every one of them!

Can we make it work? Recreate the sisterhood we once had, without putting a name to it? The question churns and spins in my head. We did have that once, a sort of fellow-ship? Or am I completely off base? Maybe it's just wishful thinking and history rewritten, in which case I've surely set us up for mutual destruction.

I never thought I'd need any of it; Niklas was always enough for me. His enthusiasm, the hungry optimism that pulled me towards him and into him, and let me stay there. And I haven't regretted the journey, not for a second! Places I'd never heard of, places I didn't know I longed for. People, smiles, voices. Tears, terror, bottomless despair. Sometimes we could help, but not always. Sometimes the pain was greater when we left than when we arrived. But it was always the two of us, always Niklas and

58

me. I didn't need anything else. It was so easy to keep moving forward, always forward.

The few trips back home over the years were mainly for funerals. A glimmer of grey rain and black clothes, beef patties on toast in a cold community centre. No reason to hang around in Reitvik, not when the district nurse training program in Pakistan was almost ready to launch. As soon as the formalities and thank-yous were taken care of, I was on the next plane to the Congo, or Malawi, or Bhutan. After Father passed away, my brother's suggestion that we sell our childhood home seemed sensible. It was a relief to leave the whole business to him, I'll admit it. If nothing else, there's a kind of security in knowing there's a sum of money sitting in an account in my name in Reitvik Savings Bank.

Children were the only thing we disagreed on, Niklas and me. Well, disagreed . . . it was more like a discussion we never really had. A classic example of the time never being right. There was always somewhere we were more urgently needed, always a new project more critical, more crucial than the previous. The flood that had poisoned the drinking water of a village. A whole population desperately in need of camps with tents and food, having been driven out of their country by rebels. The union of our cells followed by a nine-month gestation was never the right project. The timing just didn't work out. Niklas was and remained the sun in my solar system, the centre of my universe. It was his moral compass that steered us, his intuition for need that showed the way. It was Niklas's straight backbone that made mine straighten out as well, his infallible ability to find new scenes of suffering and crowds of fellow human beings who needed our help. A baby couldn't compete in this arena, so I never brought it up. I couldn't be the one changing the course of his benevolent journey. An egotistical, self-absorbed wish I had no right to speak out loud. We were responsible for so many children who had already been born. So many children, so many places.

Neither one of us had much education to speak of. Niklas carried around a half-finished degree in Anthropology, and all I had to show for myself was a mere high-school diploma. But forty years on the road brought us experience in fields, in jungles, on boats, and even up in the trees: in south China, we carried out a pilot project with elevated house construction in a flood-stricken area. But although our intentions were good, the initiative was shelved. As it turned out, the new tree houses scared away the crested myna that kept the potato crop pest-free, and the people would rather have potatoes than flood-proof houses.

So we didn't shy away from the challenge of a cocoa farm. As a matter of fact, we sought it out: the farm outside of Rakiraki that Niklas first heard of around the *tanoa* one night in a village on Fiji's Coral Coast fit perfectly into the retirement dream we didn't realize we had. After the tenth, or perhaps fifteenth, *bilo* of *kava*, one of the men gathered around the large wooden bowl began telling a long story about his brother-in-law's uncle, who many years ago had made the mistake of leaving a piece of his property to a *kaivalagi*, a foreigner, a 'stranger from the clear blue sky'. The land had been put to proper use while the brother-in-law's uncle owned it: row upon solid row of *dalo*, the dense root vegetable that is the staple of all Fijian cooking. The oversized cousin of the swede isn't my favourite; it's served boiled, tasteless and with the texture of hard butter. The kaivalagi – an Australian, as Niklas understood it – had insisted on growing cocoa beans instead, and look what had happened: not only had a furious neighbour cut him down with a machete after a dispute over a loan of a few dollars, but his wife and son had ended up driven off the road after taking a taxi to Rakiraki to reach safety. 'Cursed,' the man said and drained another coconut half-shell in one gulp before muttering the obligatory 'bula', solemnly clapping his hands three times.

'And the farm?' Niklas asked. 'Was it ruined as well?'

The Fijian glared at him with bloodshot eyes and shook his head. 'The plants grow large and the beans are as golden as sacks of money. But what good is that when you're dead?'

The very next week, we managed to track down the owner's relatives through Mosese, the manager of the farm. 'He'll keep running it until the sale is finalized,' Niklas said, the enthusiasm glowing in his eyes, 'and beyond that, too, if we want. Can you imagine, a cocoa farm! We'll name it after you: *Kat's Cocoa!*'

He loved me. Sometimes it hurts so badly I can't breathe. I have to shut my eyes, grab hold of something and slowly inhale through the nose, exhale through the mouth. He loved me; he wanted beautiful things for me! The joy in his voice: 'We can learn, Kat, it won't be hard!' The fervour that always lit a fire in me. 'Our own project, and if we make it work, we can help even more people. Local vocational training! Microfinancing! Seasonal jobs!'

The enthusiasm in his words, but most of all, this is what I saw: this is for me. He loves me. The sweet, heavy pleasure it takes months to cultivate, a long and laborious process: the love in the glistening, fat, brown cocoa bean. It's all for me.

Now the future has become the past. Ahead has become behind. It's the time after Niklas now. But he maintained the principle, he kept the promise: sustainable development. That was the gold standard in all we did: give a man a fish and he'll have enough to eat today. Teach him to fish and he'll have enough to eat for the rest of his life. Sustainability was always the mantra: long-term, durable aid. Niklas set everything up so it would last. He took care of it all, readied everything. Only now it won't be for us both, just for me.

That's why I'm not hopeless. Not helpless, even though I'm here without him. Without my mate, my true mate, I'm here all alone.

Have I thought it through fully? Probably not. Planning and anticipating consequences has never been my strong suit. I've always gone by my gut instinct, let my heart follow, and brought my head along as well only if there was room in the suitcase. When the mats were folded and put away after his funeral, and the rooms were as empty as the echoes of hymns, I saw the worry draped like a frayed prayer shawl around Ateca's shoulders.

'You need your family, Madam Kat.'

I tried to smile. 'I don't have any family, Ateca. You're my family.'

'*Isa!*' Shock and compassion united in her face as she continued. 'Yes, Madam Kat, you're my sister. But you need family from your own country. You need your sisters from there.'

My sisters from there. I shook my head; what could I say? I need my sisters. What does it mean to need? Niklas and I were always busy figuring out what others needed: identification of need is always the first step. And although it was Ateca saying the words, I knew in the same moment that demand met supply right there and then, like a bird finally landing in the right tree.

'Maybe your sisters need you too, Madam Kat.'

So it was clear what I had to do. Just a letter, an invitation, with no strings attached. If they changed their minds later on, it would just have been a holiday in paradise for them, all expenses paid. I've even promised to pay their way home if everything goes wrong. I'm not filthy rich but the money goes far here, where Mosese brings breadfruit to the front porch in the afternoon, and the chickens lay eggs out of pure joy and fertilize the melons with equal glee.

Of course I'm nervous; this is completely nuts in so many ways. Will I be able to handle all the baggage they bring with them? It's been more than half a life since I saw most of them, what do I know of the problems they carry around?

I'm least worried about Ingrid. If I ever had a best friend, it was her. Perhaps it's not unlike a lover: you're attracted to what you lack in yourself. What you weren't born with but have to accumulate. The ability to persist, the even-tempered conviction that all good things come to those who wait, that those who work hard are rewarded in the end. She's held on to life with sensibly trimmed fingernails – with

Ingrid, you can count on things going according to plan. No need for improvisation, no restless pushing of the on-and-off button. The patience in her gaze, like a loyal Labrador, eyes spilling over with devotion. The selflessness that can become a burden, an unmet expectation. No, no, I'm being unfair, she's not like that! Ingrid is the only one I've managed to more or less stay in touch with – she even visited us several times. She spent Christmas with us when we were living in Mauritius planning a solar-energy project. Came with us to drive around the province of Khorasan in Iran to assess the conditions for Afghan refugee camps. No, Ingrid is no Labrador. If she were a dog, she'd be a watchful German Shepherd. Self-reliant but appreciative of good company.

The others are more closely intertwined. A three-leaf clover from which you can't remove one leaflet without inflicting lethal damage on the rest of the plant. What was it that had bound us all together, really? Silent, inscrutable Sina, her hands fiddling with the tassels on her scarf, a drab contrast to Lisbeth's freshly coiffed hair and tight-fitting blouses. And Maya, so robust in her approach to everything from German verb tenses to winter clothes – I can still picture her sturdy boots that looked just like the ones Mum would affix cleats to in the winter. Clear and direct, simple and straightforward.

How is it possible she is sick? Her daughter's email was very clear: 'This can and will get worse, the doctor was frank about that.' Am I ready to become a carer for the long haul? Are the others ready? I hadn't pictured anything like this, although I should have realized that the years beyond sixty can bring troubles over and above high blood pressure and a slow metabolism. But it can't be that extreme, I'm sure the daughter is just making it sound more serious now to avoid confrontation later. And I certainly don't want to scare the others and risk the whole project falling apart before we've even started. When Evy accompanies her mother down here, it'll at least be a smooth transition for Maya. No reason to cry wolf before it's needed.

To be there for each other, that's the bottom line here! To share the grey years with friends who remember the same green ones. To buy five-packs of reading glasses and argue over who looks better in which set of frames. To joke about heartburn and compression socks. To see the ripples of cellulite as an exciting lunar landscape full of possibility. To be each other's support, without bureaucracy and time-limited appointments, based on familiarity and trust. To find what once was; to build the end around the beginning we once had.

But it was all so long ago. Maybe all my memories are fantasies, nothing but smoke and mirrors. An owl hoots out in the plantation tonight, a melancholy screech that echoes against the walls. If Ateca were here, she'd say it's bad luck, and she'd pray to God to protect us all. The wild, lonely call ripples through the darkness, as if the ocean had stopped whispering and started speaking in a black silver tongue.

9

Ateca

I lay all my worries before you, Lord, and the greatest one is Vilivo. It's been six months since he finished school, and he still hasn't found a job! He's tried and tried, and made the rounds in all the offices and shops. He's asked the people who are building the new bridge over the Waimakare River; he's asked at the electricity company. And they say no everywhere, Lord. The villages along King's Highway, no, all over the island, are full of young people who can't find work. Boys who have much better credentials than Vilivo, but who give up in the end and jump in the stream headed for Suva. Please don't let my son end up there! As a wheelbarrow boy in the bazaar – or worse, in one of the night clubs along Victoria Parade. There are so many stories people tell, Lord, about boys getting on the bus to the capital. Their parents don't hear anything from them until the day they get the message that their son has been charged with stealing a wallet, or getting into a bar fight, or stealing scrap metal from a building site.

Vilivo thinks he's going to be a rugby star; all the boys dream of being the next Waisale Serevi. But his dreams are young and underripe, like the bananas hanging from the tree in the back yard, immature and tangled up in each other. Of course I'd be proud of him, Lord! If I could see my boy run into the stadium in Suva, a Flying Fijian in black and white! But almost nobody makes it that far, and especially not without money. He needs muscles and strength for the training; he needs a lot of food. The cassava grows well behind my house, but it's not enough. The ladies at Madam Kat's house eat meat and fish every day; they eat imported yellow peppers and asparagus for fifteen dollars a bundle. I'm grateful to be able to take home the leftovers.

Lord, you can see that Vilivo is a good boy. Help him to find his way. Let him find work, so he can support himself, become an adult and start a family.

In Jesus' holy name. Emeni.

10

Maya

She knows exactly when it first happened. One of Maya's greatest pleasures since she retired has been reading. Leisurely browsing the titles on the library shelves, her own shelves too, for which she could only spare a quick longing glance back when she was still working. These days, she always has at least three or four books stacked on her bedside table: novels and biographies, travelogues, and even collections of poetry she's attempted. A former colleague had invited her to join a book club, and she always looked forward to the last Thursday of each month. An eager curiosity about what the others thought of this month's book, mixed with the satisfaction that there was still someone who wanted to know what she, Mrs Aakre, who was now just Maya Aakre, had to say.

They had read a fantastic book, a doorstop novel from India with colours and spices and music and poetry spilling out into the margins, a seven-course literary feast. After reading a brief biographical note about the author, they always went around the table. When it was Maya's turn, she was ready with yellow Post-its stuck between the pages that held the paragraphs she wanted to read aloud. 'I thought this book was like a tapestry,' she'd begun, hearing her own voice sounding excited, but focused. 'Poetic and romantic descriptions of nature and art combined with a social message that's both brutal and—'

The word was gone. A blank white space in the middle of her sentence, her tongue empty and helpless. All that remained was a vague sensation of what she'd wanted to say, a slippery shadow. She raced after it, ransacked the innermost corners of her brain for the letters and syllables she knew were in there. A numb panic grew inside her mouth while the eyes around the table stared at her intently; she could see on their faces that her pause was lasting too long. So she let it go, let the elusive word vanish, and cut herself off, mumbling, 'Yes, and . . .' She took a deep breath, pushed the horror away and moved on to character descriptions. Only much later, in the car on her way home, had the word wormed its way out of the crack it was stuck in and reappeared on her tongue. 'Provocative!' Maya had said out loud, surprising herself as she turned in to the driveway.

Everyone forgets things, she'd told herself. Keys and mobile phones and glasses. Finds them again with an irritated shrug: 'Was *that* where I put it?' The first few times she sat in the car and suddenly found herself without a destination, she pushed it aside as well. The empty space that suddenly was her mind: I'm holding the wheel, I'm driving up Stadionveien – where am I going? The cold jolt in her stomach that made her slam on the brakes, swerve to the side of the road and stop the car: *Where am I going?* Just for a few seconds, before a shade was lifted and she remembered she was on her way to the dry cleaners or the petrol station. Too much to think about, that's all, just a little absent-minded. She'd shrugged off the anxiety and put the car in gear.

She and Evy have argued more these past few months than ever before. It's strange, really. You'd think that now that her only daughter was all grown up, with her own family, they'd have more in common, understand each other better. But of course, what Evy would call the *dynamic* between them, the *dynamic* has changed now that Steinar is gone. Now she's all alone in the walnut-brown double bed, her checkered bath robe hanging alone on the back of the bathroom door. Evy feels sorry for her; even in the middle of grieving for her father she feels compassion for her mother, Maya knows that. She'd been glad to have Evy there the first few weeks. But the unannounced visits to Reitvik she's started making over the past six months, always full of suggestions that would 'make things easier for you, Mum', they're downright annoying. Home health visitor every week – Maya isn't sick! It was news to her that the National Health Service had resources to waste on people who could stand on their own two feet, were as sharp as a pin, and could still keep themselves clean and presentable! Appointments for one thing after another, neurologists and specialists, she couldn't believe it! Maya's memory was just as good as Evy's, if not better – wasn't she the one who'd remembered to send flowers for Branko's mother's birthday in May? And thirty years after she knitted Evy's first Marius sweater, she still knew the pattern by heart. Just quiz me on the line of succession to the English throne, or the first twenty elements in the periodic table, Maya thought – then we'll see who's forgetful!

Here in Fiji, there are other explanations. She can't be expected to know where she is at all times when she goes out walking; she hasn't been here that long yet, and the names of all the roads and places are unfamiliar. The others mix them up as well – even Sina's admitted that she's got lost several times.

Maya is grateful, in a way, for the unexpected compassion she gets from Sina. It may take a slightly grouchy, abrupt form – 'For goodness' sake, Maya, get in the shade, you're bright red!' – but she can recognize it as compassion. She doesn't know where it comes from; she's always seen the others as two pairs: Sina and Lisbeth, Ingrid and Kat. She was the fifth wheel. Not that it bothered her that much: she had Steinar, they were together as early as high school. But now she's the one Sina stays closest to. They don't talk much, mostly about everyday things: the weather, food, heat rashes, their swollen feet. But she's the one Sina sits next to on the porch, and Maya wonders about the glances she shoots periodically at Lisbeth.

She sits on the edge of the bed with her eyes closed as the floor fan wheezes lukewarm air towards her face. There's something odd about Lisbeth and Sina. A friendship that already looked lopsided in sixth-form English: the swan with the ugly duckling waddling after her. Where perky, stylish Lisbeth glided through the room, bulky, frumpy Sina followed. Still, Lisbeth's eyes always darted over to Sina's face before she said anything, her mouth turned down in a moment of uncertainty before her carefully painted lips curled up into a smile.

Maya doesn't know much about what's happened between them over the years. Everything got so busy. First school, then work, then Evy, then more school, more work. She'd run into them from time to time, of course. Lisbeth Høie, one of the first women in Reitvik with her own car, a dark

71

blue Volvo. And Sina Guttormsen, always dragging her little boy around. She's not really sure to what extent the two kept their friendship up. Still, a half-century does something to people, Maya thinks to herself. Look at Kat and Ingrid, they're not exactly joined at the hip any more. Everything that happened to Kat, no, everything Kat made happen, none of it had happened to Ingrid. Still, the way they talk to one another, the way their heads turn towards each other, the instinctive intimacy – Maya recognizes that. That was something they had way back then, something she envied, but always shrugged off: she had a boyfriend. She was fine. But Sina and Lisbeth? Maya opens her eyes, places a hand on her clammy throat. There's something strange between them, a dissonance. A high-pitched clanging noise, almost out of earshot. A clashing of swords.

Is that why Sina sticks to Maya now? Is she building new alliances? Or does she see it? Does Sina know what's going on in the moments when reality crumbles around Maya? Can she read her eyes when everything around her – the roads, the houses, the people – are shaken loose and become unfamiliar pieces in a puzzle she can't solve? She hasn't talked about it, not to Sina or anyone else. They're all well into their sixties, surely they all forget and mix things up once in a while? The mind is an unexplored universe filled with vast, secret nebulae.

She hadn't wanted Evy to travel with her to Fiji. Changing planes in London and Los Angeles, it couldn't be that hard? As far as Maya knew, no one had ever gone missing on an aeroplane journey. She knew enough English to ask for directions, and as long as she had enough time to make her connecting flights, she'd be able to manage navigating both Security and Customs, baggage recheck and, not least, United States Immigration, which was the toughest part, according to Branko. But Evy had insisted on going with her. She'd almost had a big fight with her daughter over it – did a fully capable sixty-six-year-old woman really need a babysitter for such a perfectly ordinary trip?

I remember you as someone who doesn't shy away from a challenge, Kat's surprising letter had read. *I know you've closed the classroom door once and for all, and I know Steinar is gone. Would you consider embarking on a whole new chapter?*

She'd absolutely consider it. To carve out some distance between her and Evy's ever-growing concern, and get away from the health service's unwanted helping hand. So if a mandatory travel companion across the globe was the price she had to pay, she might just have to accept it. Anyway, Evy would have to get back to her job – she couldn't stay in Fiji for long.

Maya stands in the centre of the room, slowly taking stock of everything around her. There are no flowers on the table – she would have made sure of flowers if she had guests from so far away. But Kat's never been one for convention, she thinks, and feels a wistful pang when she remembers: Kat who just disappeared one summer, went out into the world in a shower of sparks from a magic wand, while she and Steinar were celebrating their acceptance into teacher training college with coffee and pastries and pats on the back from both sets of parents.

Maya sinks back on to her bed. She looks up sideways, into her mother's smile of approval. The familiar face bends over her and Maya's cheeks flush when she hears the voice, soft, but clear: 'Dad and I are so proud of you.' She smiles back, leans her head against her mother's chest. 'Thanks, Mum. This is what I wanted.' She holds the acceptance letter in her hand as the sweet smell of the bird-cherry tree wafts in through the open kitchen window. Her mother's apron is covered in black and purple flowers. Maya shuts her eyes, breathes in the spicy aroma of bird-cherry blossom.

A light knock on the door as it creaks open.

'Are you awake, Maya? We have time for a cup of coffee before we drive Evy to the airport.' Kat smiles at her and leaves the door open as she turns away.

Maya stays seated at the edge of the bed. Is Evy going somewhere?

11
Ateca

Dear God, Madam Maya is yalowai; her head is full of shadows. Just like my sister's father-in-law. Everyone in the village knows that when he walks into other people's fields with his cane, they must gently guide him home with an arm around his shoulder.

Why doesn't her daughter look out for her? Or Madam Kat? Why do they let her go out alone when she doesn't know where she's going? She could get lost, or end up by the side of the road with a broken leg. Or she could get so scared that her heart stops and she dies. I've seen the fear in her face, Lord. Madam Maya isn't afraid of sea snakes or owls screeching. The fear in her eyes is the one that can summon death.

Madam Maya sometimes goes walking after dark, Lord. Please watch over her. I don't think the other madams understand that they need to gently guide her home with an arm around her shoulder.

In Jesus' holy name. Emeni.

12

Kat

What have I done? I can't sleep, the sheets are sweaty and bundled up around me, as twisted as my thoughts. What have I got myself into? Evy's plane hasn't even landed in Norway yet, and all I want to do is shout for her to come back. What was I thinking, not telling the others? Why have I smiled and hidden and covered up Maya's condition these past two weeks, and interrupted Evy every time she wanted to bring up the subject? And now that she's left her mother here and I've assured her everything will be fine, I've sent away the only ally I had. Why didn't I bring the others into this from day one? Did I imagine that Maya's problems would disappear as soon as she got to the South Pacific? That they'd melt away in the sun, dissolve like ice cubes in a glass?

She dozed in the passenger seat for most of the way back from the airport. When we saw Evy disappear through Security, Maya seemed calm and carefree, smiling wide as she waved goodbye to her daughter. She was tired when we got in the truck, but before she fell asleep, leaning her head against the window, she turned towards me and exclaimed, 'The women's commune was such a great suggestion! What a wonderful idea you had!'

She woke up as I stopped the truck in front of the house, and I saw it then right away. The fumbling hands, the hesitation as she slowly climbed out. The way she paused and stared down at her legs, trousers, sandals – bewildered, as if she'd never seen them before. How she raised her head and listened for the waves before following the sound with uncertain steps between the bare trunks of the palm trees, down the soft slope to where wiry tufts of grass border the sand. I followed her and spoke gently, keeping my voice soft and low: 'Where are you going, Maya? Isn't it a little late for a walk on the beach?'

A blank stare, her face twitching in horror. Her tongue working slowly, struggling to form words. I waited, even though my arms were crying out to pull her back to safety, to tear her away from the abyss on which she was teetering. At last, she found my name. The shadows drained from her eyes, pulling back in a long tidal wave and bringing her on to solid ground again. 'Kat,' she said. Her voice was frail, the words muddled. 'What are you doing here?'

I managed to lead her up to the house without too much trouble, avoiding her frightened eyes by focusing on getting her ready for bed. Luckily the others were occupied elsewhere, so I could help her get undressed and put her to bed. I swallowed my own nauseous fear, turned a deaf ear to her confused babbling, her questions about where Evy was. She's asleep now; I just peeked in her room and heard the faint snoring. But I might as well get up. The sheet will have to serve as a bath robe; I can wrap myself up in it in the hammock eventually. Maybe rocking to the rhythm of the waves will make sleep finally come.

Everything gets turned upside down. When we're old and we don't think we can handle any more, we're left with no goddamn choice. What was up goes down; the oldest becomes the youngest. And people like Lisbeth, who have gambled everything on being watched, have to take their final strut down the catwalk in front of an audience who can't find their glasses.

A black stream of ants marches with determination from a crack in the wall that branches out towards the overhang of the porch. I can't take my eyes off them: so sure of where they're going, although the goal is out of sight. What was my goal, what did I want to achieve with all this? Did I just want a group to assemble with me around the campfire, afraid of sitting there alone at night? Because no one from my own bloodline is beside me, ready to take over?

I've planned and pondered. Considered the responsibility if someone gets sick: there's a hospital, or at least an outpatient clinic, in Rakiraki. I've thought of the inevitable stomach bugs: Ateca knows all about boiling the water and washing the vegetables. I've thought of security. Niklas never wanted to have a security guard, as other kaivalagi do. 'If having local neighbours isn't protection enough, we don't belong here,' he always said. Still, with only women in the house, I hired Akuila to patrol outside at night. I may have caught him dozing off in the hammock once or twice, but I bet his thick strong neck, his military background and his reputation as a sturdy, decisive guy is enough to keep people with dubious intentions away. And he doesn't bother the ladies with unnecessary small talk. 'Yes, ma'am' is his standard response to most questions.

Sickness, food, security – is there more I could have

done to prepare? I'd pictured the sun, the friendly bula smiles, the calm shuffle of daily life on 'Fiji time' – how all this would softly envelop my friends like a warm, tropical blanket. How it would get them away from winter and arthritis and electricity bills and the dreary evening news, free them from telemarketers and frozen vegetables. I had pictured togetherness, laughter and mutual benefits. Was it irresponsible to invite them to form this fellowship with me?

Still, Maya's eyes. Their gaping terror when she had no idea where she was. The flailing hands before they held on to mine for dear life. Can I do this? Maya, who's taken care of children her whole adult life, now becomes the child we have to care for. Niklas would have known what we should do. But there's no 'we' any more. There's only me, me alone. Kat alone. Who doesn't dare reveal her secret to the others, even though they could be valuable supporting players in the enormous game I've taken on.

I know Akuila makes the rounds at night; still, I'm startled when he suddenly appears before me in the darkness on the steps of the porch.

'Everything all right, ma'am?'

'Yes, everything's all right, Akuila. I just couldn't sleep.'

His gaze is concerned but curious. 'Nothing to worry about, ma'am. I'm watching out; you can sleep safely.'

I feel bad that I'm momentarily annoyed, and hide my irritation behind a smile.

'I know, Akuila.'

He stays standing for a few more seconds at the foot of the steps, looking as if he might say something more. Then he reconsiders, nods 'Yes, ma'am', and continues his patrol around the house. I follow his fleshy neck under the cap with my gaze, until he vanishes around the corner.

Maybe I should go and check on Maya again. Is this what it's like to have a child? Always having a small part of your brain occupied with worry? Trying to stay one step ahead by anticipating problems and looking for solutions?

It's impossible to get out of the dangling hammock without producing a thud that sends a shooting pain up into my bad knee. While I rub it, trying to regain my balance, the screen door slides open and there's Sina. We cry out in unison, 'Are you awake?' When she responds that she couldn't sleep, I can't decide whether she sounds drowsy or embarrassed.

I pat the sun-bleached cushion on the wicker chair next to my hammock, and ask her to come and sit down. She takes out a cigarette and lights up. I recognize Lisbeth's leather cigarette case and don't know whether to laugh or cry – is Sina stealing cigarettes from Lisbeth? I suddenly see them in front of me, in the smoker's corner in the high school car park: Lisbeth elegantly flicking her cigarette between pink fingernails, Sina standing beside her, waiting, until she was handed the butt and took a last few drags.

She leans back in her chair and blows a white cloud out into the darkness. 'I should quit,' she says. 'It's bad for my health, and I can't afford it either.'

There's nothing to say to that.

She starts talking about her son.

'I was disappointed when Armand started but I thought, if that's the worst of it . . .'

Her face hardens, she leans forward and taps the ash

over the edge of the porch. 'If his smoking was the only thing I paid for, I wouldn't complain.'

Wow. I give her a minute but nothing happens. The moon pokes its crooked crescent face out from between the clouds, illuminates the gently swaying palm fronds. Sina hasn't mentioned money since her outburst at the airport that first night, and I've left the subject alone. Both Ingrid and Lisbeth have asked me how we're going to manage the division of costs, but so far I've brushed it off and said we'll work it out eventually. I'm sure Sina won't be able to pay as much as the rest of them, and I have to figure it out somehow. It can't be that hard – the food expenses are negligible here and I'd have to pay the electricity bill regardless.

When Sina is done smoking she gets up and walks into the yard, towards a hibiscus bush with blood-red blossoms. Fiddles with a long, curious, pollen-laden pistil and addresses me with her back turned.

'Aren't you supposed to be *finished* with your offspring at some point? You support them, help them, pay for them, encourage them – but it's supposed to be over at some point. They're supposed to make it on their own . . . I guess I'd imagined that *he* would be the one to help *me* one day.'

Her voice fades as she speaks, but now she collects herself and turns up the volume. 'But it never ends, dammit!'

'Sina.'

I don't know what to say. I hurry down the stairs and put my arm around her, feeling clumsy. Sina shrugs my arm off.

'You wouldn't understand. You don't have children.'

I jump back, but only slightly. I've heard this before. The smug disqualification. Still, it prickles in my throat and I want to hit back.

81

'No,' I respond. 'I don't. But I know a thing or two about responsibility.'

Maya's frightened face appears in my mind's eye.

'And responsibility goes both ways.'

Hypocrite, the voice in my head echoes as I walk back up the four steps to the porch. Unless I decide to call Evy right away when she lands and ask her to come back and get her mother, I'll have to let the others know. Let them decide whether they want to share the burden.

I turn towards Sina and the thought crumbles in my mind. Her bare legs are grey in the dim moonlight; her scalp shows through her wisps of hair. A roll of resignation and disappointment bunched up around her waist; her fingers curl, soon they'll turn into claws. Sina is sixty-six years old, broke and worried. I can't say anything about Maya.

13

Sina

From: armandg@noria.no
To: sina.guttormsen@hotmail.com
Subject: Problem

Hi Mum,

I hope you can check email so you see this. Things have become complicated since you left, especially with my finances. As you know, my back has been acting up, and all the lifting and carrying at work made it worse. But my idiot doctor won't clear me for medical leave, so I had to ask my boss to give me easier work. That moron just didn't get it, so I had to show him I wouldn't put up with just anything. I'm sure there are plenty of other places who will appreciate my skills.

I don't want you to worry. I can get a new job whenever I want. I'm looking around at several projects right now. I have a mate who's working on a major deal of imports from Lithuania. He says there's an opening for me, but I have to go in with fifty thousand kroner cash. Since you don't need the car any more, I figure I might as well put it up for sale. It's in pretty good condition, so I'm sure I can get a decent price. I just need you to sign over the title.

You have to remember that it wasn't my idea for you to leave. I'm here all alone with all this stuff and I'm doing the best I can.

I hope you're doing great down there with the other ladies. Let me know if the car stuff is OK with you. I'll get you a good price.

Armand

14

Ingrid

She's heard from both of her brothers. Kjell writes his emails from work; Ingrid can picture him in his office, with the door open on to a large warehouse where thousands of new tyres are stacked against the wall. Short emails in the pompous style that suits him, enquiring about her health, her security, poorly disguised warnings to keep a close eye on her money. Ingrid has written back, promptly and dutifully. She's in good health, all is well and peaceful in Korototoka. No crime, nothing to fear. Give my best to Gro.

She's only heard from Arve once since she came down here, but then again, he's never been one to fill her inbox. In fact, she's not even sure he remembers where she is – his email was mostly about a conference paper he's writing for a trip to Bratislava next month.

Ingrid takes a slow morning stroll around the house. It rained last night, as it does most nights, and the soil in the roughly dug rows in the back garden is muddy and moist. Her bare feet tread heavily between the beanstalks, pressing the soft, warm earth up between her toes. A fresh morning breeze lifts her thick hair from the back of her neck. As she comes back to the front, the sun gleams across the surface of the ocean, making it impossible for her to fix her eyes on the horizon. Ingrid smiles, her mouth widens gradually into a gleeful grin. She gathers her *sulu* around her legs; the floor-length floral piece of fabric flutters in the wind. Wildrid gives her a quick wink before she bends down to pull a dark green pumpkin out of the shade and into the sun.

Wildrid has always been ready for this. She's been there, waiting, hiding under the white blouses and navy blue trousers, biding her time in the pocket of her winter coat. Wildrid has walked barefoot on the beach before; she knows how to navigate the shallows and gather mussels in a bucket. She's emptied the bilo of kava, said 'bula' and clapped three times; she's stomped her feet in a passionate *meke*. Wildrid was there with Kat when she planted mangroves on the shore in Kiribati, stood beside her and heaved bricks to build a children's hospital in Kashmir. She knows Ingrid, and Ingrid knows Wildrid.

'Good morning! Are you checking on breakfast?'

Lisbeth smiles faintly behind her sunglasses. She's doing her best, Ingrid thinks amicably, shutting her ears to Wildrid's irritated outburst, 'Why don't you get a bucket and make yourself useful, too!'

'Just checking how the beans are doing,' Ingrid replies. 'I think we'll have some nice pumpkins here soon as well.'

'Mm-hmm.' Lisbeth flashes a distant smile. She's probably never had anything but coffee and cigarettes for breakfast, Ingrid thinks, feeling a smirk form at the corner of her mouth. At least she's stopped asking Ateca for low-fat milk and yogurt.

Kat comes down from the porch, heading for the small

truck. 'I have errands to do in Rakiraki today, so I might as well get going,' she says and waves as she climbs in behind the wheel.

'Where are you going?'

Ingrid is embarrassed by her own cry, the clingy voice. Kat hears it too, she stops in the middle of closing the car door.

'We need some more pots for the seedlings,' she says. 'And I have to see if I can find some linoleum. The floor in Ateca's house is falling apart.'

Ingrid nods and quickly looks away. Wildrid would never have asked her like that, would never have sounded needy or whiny.

When Kat has turned the truck around and is ready to go, she stops and waits, letting the engine idle. The front door opens; Maya hurries out and plops herself down in the passenger seat. She fixes her straw hat and fastens her seat belt before Kat puts the truck in gear and they roll away.

Ateca greets Ingrid with a smile of approval when she places a bunch of long green beans by the sink.

'Very nice,' she nods, satisfied. 'How do the pumpkins look, Madam Ingrid? Vilivo could help you pick some today if you'd like?'

Ateca has begun offering her son's services here and there – climbing the ladder when something gets stuck in the drainpipe, carrying the heavy storm shutters that have to be fixed to the windows when the meteorologists forecast a hurricane. Ingrid sees Kat slipping him a few dollars for his help; that makes her sad. The boy is big and strong and neither dumb nor lazy; it's a shame, she thinks,

87

that he can't get a proper job. To hang around here like a dutiful house boy for five old ladies in between running around barefoot on a field, throwing his dreams around with an egg-shaped ball. Ingrid thinks of her great-nephews, cheerful, scruffy Simon and solemn Petter; unemployment is not something she sees in their future.

'Maybe,' she says and looks over at Lisbeth and Sina. They're standing there with coffee cups in their hands, only half listening. 'What do you think – roasted pumpkin for dinner?'

She barely succeeds in keeping the smugness out of her voice; she knows Lisbeth prefers to eat only grilled chicken and salad. She always examines the labels on jars and boxes, and won't take a single bite of something before she knows exactly how much butter or oil or – God forbid – sugar is in it. Lisbeth wrinkles her forehead uncertainly before Sina chimes in, 'That sounds good. I can try to make it if you'll help me, Ateca?'

Ingrid looks at her, surprised – Sina's not usually one to embark on a culinary adventure – but new things are happening in Vale nei Kat every day.

'Great! I'll check if we can get some fresh fish as well.'

Mosese's younger brother Jone owns a boat, and is one of the regular suppliers of fish to Korototoka. The bright-red boat isn't difficult to spot on the beach, with the proud name *Vessel of Honour* painted in sturdy, straight white letters under the gunwale. Ingrid walks slowly down towards the boats and lets it all sink in, giving her eyes the time they need: men lugging boxes of today's catch, women in *sulu jabas*, the floral-patterned two-piece outfit. They squeeze the fish to evaluate it before haggling to get it down to an acceptable price. The old man in the shade has a rainbow of fish hanging from a curved metal hook – a few golden yellow, one orange-red, one shiny black and blue. His T-shirt has a big tear on the shoulder and his face wrinkles as he smiles at her, holding up his bouquet.

'Fish, ma'am?'

At the water's edge, with the net gathered around his shoulders, ready to fly out over the glittering turquoise surface, she spots Jone. He's wading out and the water comes up to his waist, his wavy hair sticking out from under a worn baseball cap. A few young boys aboard *Vessel of Honour* are sorting tools. Ingrid can tell the morning catch was sparse; that's why Jone is trying a few rounds with the net. She stands still, soaking in the sight: his strong arms flinging the net in an arc through the air, the net sailing out, opened by the wind, before landing on the water's surface, settling into a silent grid.

Ingrid has never known the sea. She's never experienced how it claims and commands, and gives back unconditionally. But now something in the movement of Jone's shoulder makes her take a deep breath. The muscles tensing, casting out the net, a constant challenge: see if you dare to deny me!

Inside Ingrid, Wildrid kicks off her flip flops. She feels the sulu billowing around her legs as decisive footsteps take her to the water's edge. Hasn't she always had a sailor in her, narrowing her eyes into the wind and trimming the sails with stiff fingers, her hair flapping in the breeze? Wildrid has stood there with kelp around her ankles, gripping the knife in salty, sore hands, gutting fish after silvery fish, scraping out innards with deft motions. She walks out to

Jone, grabs the net dancing like a spider's web on the waves, and pulls it in alongside him in a rhythm they both know.

Ingrid quickly dries her sweaty palms on her sulu and smiles at Jone as he wades in towards her, his net bunched up on his shoulder.

'No luck today?'

The fisherman shakes his head and suddenly it's there, the laughter with no purpose or meaning. It rumbles out from somewhere in his powerful belly, rolls up his chest and into his face, his meaty cheeks scrunching up his eyes. The laughter rolls back and forth under his skin, billows out of his broad nostrils. The boys on the boat join in, guffawing with their pink mouths wide open; one of them places his foot on the bow and throws his arms wide so suddenly Ingrid thinks he's going to fall in.

'No,' Jone finally manages to get out. 'Nothing today, ma'am.'

She turns around and heads back; the man with the fish rainbow in his hand is still under the tree. She buys the orange-red one, a gaping coral trout that gets a stump of nylon rope threaded through its gills before it's handed to her, and she thanks him.

'Vinaka!'

Ingrid takes the long way home. She walks along the beach to the outskirts of the village, where the last houses stand uncomfortably close to the rubbish dump. Plastic bags grow out of the sand, rusty oil barrels, buckets of paint, a washing-machine drum, cracked plastic watering cans, rotted pieces of rope covered in slippery seaweed, and bottles, hundreds of bottles. Fiji Water is one of the country's proudest exports, but this is the other side of the coin: tons of empty plastic bottles with no system for recycling them. Ingrid keeps walking, leaving the beach and cutting across an unkempt field of cassava, on to the road. Two little girls stand guard over a simple shed filled with pyramids of yellow papayas. The smaller one, with lighter skin than her older sister and golden streaks in her brown curly hair, speaks up.

'Pawpaw, ma'am? Two dollar bunch.'

Ingrid pulls out a green note bearing the portrait of Queen Elizabeth II and gets a plastic bag containing four papayas in return. There are several papaya trees in Kat's back yard, but Ingrid can't resist the little home fruit stand, the first of many she passes along the village's main road on her way home. Papaya and long beans are in season now, so papaya and long beans are what everyone tries to sell to each other. And to kaivalagi like her, thinks Ingrid, who's sentimental enough to let a purple dress, a pair of dirty legs and big eyes under a golden-brown fringe win her over. She smiles at the girls, but only the younger one smiles back. The eldest is already busy refilling the empty plastic dish with four new pieces of fruit from the pile on the road beside her.

Cling! Clang! Cling! A harsh sound of metal on metal thuds a rhythmic accompaniment to her steps as she walks the last stretch back to the farm. She's passed the church and the chief's bure with the horizontal beam atop the thatched roof; she can glimpse the cocoa plantation on the

91

ridge behind the school. The young boy outside the corrugated metal shed crushing kava in the large mortar is barely taller than the iron rod he pulses up and down. Over the constant motion of his arms, his face has no expression; it takes patience to mash up the stringy kava root to a fine paste.

After a few months in Korototoka, Ingrid has learned to recognize the village's sounds. The birds' hysterical welcome to the new day when darkness loosens its grip. The flurrying stampede of the schoolchildren's feet when they take the shortcut in front of the house and down along the beach in the morning. The secretive rustle in the tops of the coconut palms. The chirping of the geckos from the ceiling above the porch. The sound of hymns in three-part harmony pouring out through the open church doors on Sunday. But to Ingrid, it's this heavy, rhythmic thud from the coarse metal bowls outside every other house that is the heartbeat of Korototoka. *Piper methysticum*, the intoxicating pepper, is hammered into submission before it's mixed into the brew that's devoured, seeps into the blood and becomes part of the stories and songs at the tip of everyone's tongues. The bitter brown drink that bears holy truths and keeps honourable myths alive. The thud of the pestle in the kava mortar is the echo of the waves, Ingrid thinks. The rhythm of the dance underneath it all.

Ingrid's feet haven't done much dancing. But here she can feel new possibilities opening up. With a glistening coral trout in her hand and four papayas slapping against her thigh, she can hear herself giggling out loud. She pictures Kjell's worries spelled out in black typeface on a grey screen: 'Precautions . . . secure your possessions . . .' She dangles the bag of papayas from her wrist and nods to the man stacking a pyramid of watermelons outside his shop. You should come here and check out the security for yourself, Kjell, she thinks with a smile on her face. Take a trip to Fiji, put on a bula shirt and learn to laugh from the innermost part of your belly!

*

Ingrid has thought about it for weeks, and waited for Kat to bring it up, but one night on the porch, she blurts it out herself.

'Chocolate.' She lets the word glide around in the air on a test flight. It's not really a question, more of a contented sigh after a good dinner. 'Have you thought any more about it, Kat – what you mentioned in your letter?'

Kat looks up from her book. 'Hmm?'

'Chocolate,' Ingrid says again. 'You said something about that in your letter. That maybe we could extend the cocoa production into making chocolate. Was that something you and Niklas were planning to do?'

Kat removes her glasses and slowly shakes her head. 'Planning . . . Well, I don't know. We might have fantasized about it. Niklas wanted to. He used to talk about learning how to make it – taking a class or something. Getting someone here who could advise us on training and investing. It's quite a big step, after all.'

'So what is it that's required?'

It's Wildrid who pipes up. A dense, pleasant aroma dances in her nose; a sweet golden taste fills her throat. Her

93

tongue runs along her teeth; her mouth is filled with saliva and she gulps it down.

Kat takes a second to think. 'I'm not really sure of the details. I think the beans have to be fermented and dried, then roasted and crushed to separate the kernels from the shells. Then they're ground up, and . . . No, you know what, I just don't know enough about it. Is it that the cocoa butter has to be separated from the cocoa mass? And then there's something about cooling. It's supposed to be pretty painstaking work, full of sensitive processes.'

'Don't you want to try it? Oh, Kat, can't we try it!'

Wildrid gets out of her chair, her face lit up with enthusiasm. 'Making our own chocolate, just think how amazing that would be!'

An astonished silence, full of possibilities. Lisbeth sits on the bottom step with her gaze fixed on Kat; the cigarette between Sina's fingers has burnt out. Maya twirls her bulky hat between her fingers as she softly nods her head.

'Healthy chocolate!'

Lisbeth has suddenly got to her feet too, gesticulating with her skinny hands. 'Dark, low-fat chocolate. Healthy food is trendy!'

'Yes!' Wildrid's excitement grows. '*Kat's Cocoa, Kat's Chocolate* – it makes sense, right? We could make something totally unique. Nothing complicated or super-exotic. Just clean, pure, simple. Good for your happiness, good for you!'

'Good for your happiness?' Sina's laughter is scornful, but there's something different in her eyes. A desire to jump in, to partake in the enthusiasm spreading across the porch at Vale nei Kat.

Lisbeth's voice is animated. 'Yes, happiness! With the image of Fiji that people have back home – pure raw materials, crystal-clear water – we can market the chocolate as . . . pieces of happiness!'

Ingrid looks at her in surprise. Pieces of happiness? Is this really Lisbeth talking?

Kat has the same reaction. 'Wow, Lisbeth! Have you been taking night classes in sales and marketing or something?'

Lisbeth turns red, but stays standing. 'No, I . . . Linda's done a few things like this, so . . .'

The mockery is gone from Sina's voice; it's replaced with something tentative, an offer. 'I know nothing about marketing and I'm clueless about chocolate. But I do know something about working hard and never giving up.'

'Good! We all do. So then the question is whether Kat wants to give it a try.'

The sulu billows around Ingrid's legs, her hands planted firmly on her hips. In just a few minutes a new business concept has been launched in the Women's House, and the director's chair looks to be empty. If Kat will be the main investor, Ingrid would be happy to act as manager.

'You mean, whether I have the money.'

Kat's voice is full of laughter. Does she think the idea is stupid? Ingrid looks around quickly: are they all just kidding her? But no, Lisbeth's cheeks are still flushed, Sina looks determined, almost stubborn, and Maya . . . she hasn't said anything?

'We'll need beautiful packaging,' Maya says, and places the hat back on her head. 'I'm actually not so bad at drawing.'

Ingrid turns back towards Kat – is this all just a wild fantasy? She pushes Wildrid aside. If this is going to be more than babble and daydreaming, she has to talk seriously to Kat. Here we are again, she realizes. The circle around Kat. Our ideas, our plans, they all have to be filtered through her: Is this important? Is it worth something? But it's different this time. Our reliance on her is concrete and quantifiable. Without Kat's ability to invest, it won't go beyond airy dreams on the porch steps.

'Why not?' Kat says. 'Why in the world not? Didn't I say we were going to take chances together? Let's start by finding someone who can give us some advice, and we'll take it from there.'

Her laughter starts in the pit of her stomach, rolls around in her mouth and showers them in wild bursts. Throws them on to a carousel that spins around so fast Ingrid has to hold on to the railing with both hands.

Ateca

Something's happening to Madam Lisbeth, Lord – have you seen it? Her face looks happier and it's been a while since I've seen her in front of the mirror craning her neck over her shoulder like an ibis. I think she was talking to her daughter on the computer yesterday; there was a young lady on the screen who looked like her. There are good things in store for Madam Lisbeth, Lord. Like the little papaya tree at the bottom of my yard. It hasn't borne fruit yet, but I can see the flowers. Something is on its way.

Mosese isn't happy, Lord. The ladies want to make chocolate, they say, and I know what Mosese is thinking. When something new comes in, the kaivalagi often throw away the old. Dear God, don't let the ladies get rid of Mosese. Comfort his old heart so he won't have to be afraid.

I don't know what all this chocolate business means, but you can see I have hopes for Vilivo, too, Lord. Maybe he can learn what's needed, so he can help out? Let him find work, so he can support himself, become an adult and start a family.

In Jesus' holy name. Emeni.

Lisbeth

Lisbeth bends forward to get a better look at her earrings in the mirror. The miniature seashells, pink as the inside of a baby's mouth, dangle from her ears on thin silver hooks. Paired with her white blouse and dark purple slim-fit trousers, they add a perfect dash of tropical flair to the outfit. She'd planned to wear the lilac-coloured top with skinny straps, but had to reconsider when she found the nasty tear from the side seam to the fabric in the front. She'd never noticed it before; how could it have happened? The top is completely ruined. She'll have to wear the white one instead. Lisbeth pulls her shoulders back and surveys herself one last time, satisfied. Even Linda would approve.

She'd been nervous to talk to her daughter on Skype yesterday. She was relieved that Linda seemed to want to talk, but anxious about her sharp tongue. Her emails have been full of recriminations – 'Mum, what are you actually doing down there?' – and her own responses have been vague and evasive. But the wave of chocolate that washed over the porch the other night has awoken something in Lisbeth. Hadn't she been head of publicity at their student newspaper back in the day? Hasn't she often thought that Harald should have been more aggressive with marketing and presentation, even in his dreary building materials business? She never pushed her ideas on him, and he was never interested. From the start Harald made it clear that her duties were at home, with the house and the children. She didn't give it much thought when Joachim and Linda were little; the days were busy and she was living the prize she'd won. When the children were grown up, the days grew longer and she offered to pitch in at the store, but Harald didn't want to hear it. 'You at the check-out? That'd give them something to talk about!' When she explained that wasn't what she had in mind – she had ideas for modernizing the product selection, maybe freshening up the store decor a bit – all he did was laugh. 'You don't know the first thing about this, Lisbeth.'

She'd bitten her tongue and instead filled her days with the Women's Institute, the bridge club and as a Red Cross volunteer. But when Linda came to visit one day and showed her the syllabus for the marketing class she'd just signed up for, Lisbeth felt herself growing interested. Consumer behaviour, product planning – she knew what these things meant! Why couldn't Harald see that this would be great for the store? She'd ached to take it further, but as soon as Linda had shut the door behind her, Harald had shrugged and turned back to the TV, and market orientation and sales channels retreated into a dusty corner with all the other things that would never come to pass. But chocolate! Lisbeth has butterflies in her stomach. The sweet delight in her mouth, the smell, the rustle of the paper. *Kat's Chocolate*, oh dear me, this could be so fabulous!

The conversation with Linda had exceeded all expectations. Her daughter had been surly at first because Lisbeth hadn't quite understood what her job entailed: 'I don't work at a fitness centre, Mum. I'm in charge of product development and campaign strategy for the whole brand. For all the B FIT studios nationwide!' But when Lisbeth explained the chocolate idea to her, something in her demeanour changed. 'That's great, Mum! This actually sounds really cool! Let me think about it and talk to some of the people in charge here.' A tone in her daughter's voice that Lisbeth hadn't heard before. A tone she reserved for people she took seriously.

Lisbeth presses her hands to her face and feels her cheeks burning. I want to be part of this, she thinks. If this is actually happening, there's going to be a place for me in it, too.

*

Vilivo carries, organizes, delegates; he's been tasked with driving Lisbeth and Sina in to Rakiraki so they can go shopping. It's December, and Vale nei Kat is hosting a Christmas party. It was Lisbeth's casual question that set the whole thing in motion. 'What do you eat for Christmas here, anyway? What's the traditional dish?'

'*Lovo*,' Ateca replied. 'We make a huge lovo with all kinds of good things: pork and chicken and fish. And dalo, of course. And *palusami*,' she added, her tongue darting across her lips. 'Spinach cooked in coconut milk. That's the best of all.'

Lisbeth hadn't been tempted right away, but there was something enticing about it: pork and chicken, whole grilled fish. A rich bounty, setting the table for a feast. That's something she knows well! If there's one thing Lisbeth Høie is good at, it's throwing a big bash! Kat wasn't hard to convince, and so it was settled: a Christmas party at Vale nei Kat. With a lovo.

'Buy more of everything,' was Kat's only piece of advice. 'Everyone will come.'

Sacks of onions and coconuts are dragged on to the truck. Bundles of roro leaves and tavioka, bunches of big brown heads of dalo on their stems; the root vegetables look like dirty, oversized lollipops. Pork chops in greasy wax paper, whole chickens, large colourful fish she can't identify. Lisbeth lets Vilivo handle the negotiating with the stall holders while noting that the selection of dinner napkins in Rakiraki is rather scarce. She's looking for purple ones – for advent – but has to settle for green, and matches them to paper tablecloths in pink, which is the closest she can find to yuletide red. She complains to Sina, who doesn't seem that interested in the problem; her eyes are fixed on the small mountain of vegetables piled on the back of the truck.

'For goodness' sake, how many people are coming after all? Are we really supposed to cook all this food?'

But Lisbeth isn't worried about the cooking.

'Ateca will help us,' she says. 'Kat says she's rallying a bunch of women from her church to lend a hand. But what do you think we should we do for centrepieces?'

'We need stones,' Vilivo explains as he turns up the road towards a house that consists of a few aluminium sheets on a rickety frame. A shadow appears from between the trees behind the house; the man is so skinny, Lisbeth is tempted to climb out of the truck and help him carry the large round rocks he retrieves from a pit behind some bushes. But he and Vilivo manage to lug them on to the truck bed, along-side bundles of dry yellowish-brown firewood. Lisbeth counts about twenty-five stones.

'What are they for, Vilivo?'

He looks at her, surprised, and the laughter begins to bubble at the back of his throat. 'You want to make a lovo without stones, ma'am?'

She's not quite sure what this means – is he making fun of her? Is it some kind of stone soup they're making?

It's not until Mosese and his brother arrive with shovels on Friday afternoon, and dig a hole behind the pumpkin patch that grows enormous, that Lisbeth realizes what it is she's playing hostess to. They're going to bury the food! They will light a fire on the smooth, round stones and place the food on top, then bury the whole thing in soil and sand. She shudders. The food isn't going to be cooked in pots and pans in the kitchen. It's going to be wrapped in leaves and twigs from the trees, packed down with bird shit and aphids and roasted on an underground fire! The party she has planned, with tablecloths and Christmas napkins, withers before her eyes; what is this really going to be like? Ateca tells her they don't need to worry about chairs and tables; there are plenty of *ibe*. More than enough mats? Does she mean they're supposed to serve dinner on the *ground*?

On Saturday afternoon, Ateca and six other women sit cross-legged on the porch. Nestled between them are big plastic bowls of bluish-white milk squeezed from the coco-nut meat Jone's sons have been scraping for hours, with Ingrid's good help. She wanders around barefoot in a faded sulu she's borrowed from Ateca, with printed letters reading 'Golden Treasure Resort' running down one side.

Ateca sits next to Litia, Mosese's wife. They make little packets of roro, leaves of the dalo plant, and fill them with coconut milk and a fatty brown mush scooped out of cans labelled 'corned mutton'. Based on Ateca's delighted expression, Lisbeth realizes this must be the long-awaited palusami. Roro and soupy, fatty sheep's meat from a can, cooked in coconut milk?

Ingrid comes towards them; her glasses are splattered with coconut spray, and she flits nimbly past a pile of banana leaves next to the wall. 'Can I see, Ateca? How do you do it?' Litia's face grows darker, she hunches her shoulders over her work and inches herself further behind Ateca, away from Ingrid. Lisbeth furrows her eyebrows in surprise, but doesn't have time to wonder why. She turns around, her eyes scanning for Kat. She spots her friend on her way around the house and runs after her.

'How are we going to set the table? Silverware and, I don't know . . . How many are we expecting?'

Something in Kat's quiet eyes makes her stop; she feels her cheeks flush without knowing why.

'How many are we expecting?' Kat repeats slowly.

'Yes, I have to . . .'

Decorate, she wants to say. Make sure there are enough serving spoons and flower vases and folded napkins for every guest.

But the words won't come out. They don't fit in here; they're meaningless to Jone, who has walked all the steps of his life on this beach. Tea lights in matching holders won't make the lovo taste better to Ateca's church ladies.

Hot and flustered, Lisbeth forces herself to look Kat right in the face. So what's left for her to do?

She's looked forward to this party so much. This is something she knows – arranging, planning, decorating, displaying. What else does she have to contribute, besides napkin-folding? She lacks Ingrid's fearless appetite for mud crabs and other challenges, and Sina seems content to play a cameo role without too many lines. Maya is the passenger who's brought along her own little world of books and enlightened conversation. Kat is the captain, and Lisbeth's not even sure whether she qualifies as the ship's cat – something for everyone to kick once in a while.

'I just wanted to . . .'

Just wanted to do something, she wants to say. To be somebody.

Suddenly she hears her own voice on the porch on the chocolate evening, when she'd got to her feet. 'Pieces of happiness,' she'd said. Her own idea. The silence around her, the approval in Ingrid's eyes. Kat's astonished 'Wow!'

Their eyes meet. 'I know,' Kat says. 'But you don't need to. All these people expect is . . . joy. They don't need to be served or entertained or impressed. It's not your responsibility to make sure they have a good time. We'll make certain there's plenty of good food and good company. The rest they'll handle on their own.'

Good food and good company. By the time the men dig into the smouldering pile of soil with shovels and unearth one banana leaf packet after another, Lisbeth has forgotten the aphids and snails. The steaming-hot packets dripping with meaty juice envelop the yard and the porch in an aromatic haze of anticipation. Deft hands peel away the scorched banana leaves and place glistening cuts of meat and succulent whole roasted chickens on to generous plastic trays.

The palusami is ladled out of a big green basin, the pearls of fat swimming in coconut milk with lumps of thin skin floating on top. Lisbeth looks around at the hands shamelessly heaping more on to their plates, large bodies softly sinking on to straw mats and surrendering to the comfort of satiated bellies. Wide-framed men and heavy-set women, smooth young calf muscles below shorts, children's bare feet tripping in between the adults' crossed legs. Someone's strumming the first few chords on a guitar; the laughter rolls off the porch and invites the fireflies in the yard to dance.

Never again, Lisbeth thinks. I'm not going to fold another napkin for the rest of my life. The absurd thought makes her laugh out loud all of a sudden; a hoarse, unfamiliar sound. She claps her hand over her mouth and her gaze meets a pair of dark, sombre eyes under a golden-brown fringe. The little girl who sells pawpaw by the side of the road is standing right in front of her; her upper lip bears an orange shadow of Fanta. She's saying something; Lisbeth has to lean forward to hear.

'You're pretty, *Nau*,' she says. She extends a skinny hand and strokes Lisbeth's long skirt made of shimmering blue Thai silk, her version of a sulu. She doesn't understand the name the girl is calling her and automatically wants to take a step back, pull her skirt away from the sticky child fingers, but she stays put. The girl has a shell in her other hand, and now she holds it out to Lisbeth. A yellowish-white treasure, a gesture of affection in her palm. Lisbeth takes it wordlessly, runs her fingers over the smooth spiral with wavy edges. The pale-pink mother-of-pearl mouth, a silent entrance to secrets and mysteries.

She bends down on one knee; the Thai silk absorbs the muddy soil at the bottom of the porch stairs. 'Thank you,' she says. 'Vinaka.'

Without thinking she pulls off her gold necklace, the one with the Venetian-style pattern, a gift from Harald. She can feel her hands trembling as she carefully fastens it around the girl's slender brown neck.

'What's your name?' she asks.

'Maraia,' the girl replies. 'It means star of the sea.'

A few hours later, it's hard to tell the hosts apart from the guests. Eight or ten women – Lisbeth recognizes Jone's wife and daughters-in-law among them – clean up food scraps and empty dishes while squealing with laughter. The door from the kitchen out to the back yard stays open; propane tanks are carried in and rubbish bags are thrown out; someone shouts Akuila's name and gives the guard a plate with a piece of fish and a few thick slices of dalo. The music ebbs and flows from the porch. Kat sits on the bottom step, talking softly to a woman whose little girl is half asleep in her lap. It's the girl with the shell; the gold necklace around her neck glints in the light from the torches.

Two young boys sit strumming their guitars; Lisbeth thinks their songs sound familiar and foreign all at once. She doesn't understand the words, but something about the melodies reminds her of choir class at school. A mix of melancholy ballad, country twang and the Salvation Army. Occasionally one of the boys starts singing along, sometimes both of them; sometimes voices from the kitchen and from the darkness under the trees join in, forming sudden, beautiful harmonies.

'Do you know "Amazing Grace"?'

It's Ingrid who asks the question as she stands by the boys in her bright-green sulu jaba. Lisbeth cringes; did she really have to copy their clothing to such an extreme? But there's a glow surrounding Ingrid. The large flowered pattern seems to soften her step, makes her face warmer, more delicate, wide open.

The boys confer, and one of them strikes a few practice chords before hitting the right one, strumming his fingers down the strings.

> 'Amazing grace! How sweet the sound,
> that saved a wretch like me . . .'

The song isn't just a string of words everybody knows. It's a voice in unison, a common breath, a joyful stream of notes, something broad and magnificent. Grace, Lisbeth thinks. *Amazing grace, how sweet the sound*. It means something here.

An older man steps out of the shadow of the bougainvillea that droops heavily over the railing. A white short-sleeved shirt and a grey, knee-length sulu in the style worn by all those who hold official positions. Short and barefoot, he plants his stocky legs wide as the young guitarist continues to play. His voice is mild but clear and deliberate when he opens his mouth. Lisbeth can't comprehend the words but understands that the man is leading them in prayer when she sees heads bow all around her.

Long words full of big, round vowels dance on the wistful melody. A young woman beside her moves her lips silently with her eyes closed; Maraia's mother folds her arms around her daughter. When the man stops and a sighing chorus of *'Emeni'* echoes across the porch, there's a moment of silence. A beat, a breath, a twinkle of the Southern Cross before the guitar changes key.

'Silent night,' the Christmas guests intone in perfect clarity.

'Holy night,' Lisbeth whispers, stroking her thumb across the soft, hopeful mouth of a seashell.

17

Kat

We're jumping right into it! Not wildly and recklessly, but we do have to make a few long-term investments. An oven for roasting the beans, equipment for grinding the nibs and pressing the cocoa mass. A conche and moulds for the chocolate bars. Ingrid and I have done some rough calculations, and my inheritance plus the money from the house in Norway will be enough to get us started.

Am I doing this mostly for Niklas? Because I want to hear him cheering me on in the back of my mind? I'm not sure. It's so hard to know what I owe him.

What I told the others is true: we had briefly toyed with the idea of taking the next step and giving chocolate a try. I just haven't had the energy. Haven't mustered up the strength for anything other than letting things run their daily course under Mosese's watchful eye.

Of course I've been bothered by the thought that Niklas would be disappointed. He thought I was as passionate about the farm as he was, or at least he wanted to think so. He wouldn't have understood my passivity, my withdrawal. Is it because of my guilty conscience that I let Ingrid talk me into it? Sometimes I see it from the other side, and it seems totally ridiculous: a group of bumbling, liver-spotted old ladies in a house far from home, with their whole lives' worth of baggage in tow. What have I set in motion here? Is there any chance this could possibly work?

It might just be the others' enthusiasm that's seducing me. They're happy in Korototoka, that much is obvious. Watching them crane their necks towards the sun and curl their bare toes in the sand brings a smile to my face every day. But the spark in Ingrid's words when she brought up the chocolate was more than that; she sounded like a teenager in love! The smile that enveloped her whole face, her hair bobbing up and down gleefully. And Lisbeth's excitement as she jumped up and started chiming in with ideas. Lisbeth! But isn't this exactly what I've learned from my years with Niklas? How a team project fosters not only unity, but a new kind of happiness? In rediscovering oneself by mastering new things unexpectedly. Yes. I want us to make *Kat's Chocolate* work.

It'll be important to get Mosese on board. *Kat's Cocoa* wouldn't exist without him, and *Kat's Chocolate* won't either. I'll freely admit that our walks in the plantation, in dense, damp, suffocating undergrowth, is a chore I don't take much joy in. If I could get away with it, I'd gladly never go again, just hand him the reins and tell him, 'Do your best, I'm sure it'll be great!' But I do have to make the rounds with him occasionally – they're my trees; it's my responsibility.

The wiry figure ahead of me walks on and on. I swat away the insects and nearly lose sight of him. For practical reasons he keeps the cacao trees trimmed to eye level; the pods are in various stages of maturation. The large, drop-shaped capsules glisten in shades of gold, yellow, orange, traffic-light red, and brown with specks of violet. I'm no seasoned cocoa farmer, but I know enough to say that Theobroma cacao, the food of the gods, is a picky, sensitive lady. The temperature has to be between 24 and 29 degrees Celsius for her to thrive, with a consistent humidity. When the mercury rises above 29, as it often does here on the north coast of Viti Levu, I can read Mosese's worried face like a thermometer.

Niklas, as usual, could only see the positive. 'That's why it's genius to have a farm that already has full-grown trees,' he'd enthused when we were considering the purchase. 'The tall trees – papaya and banana, and all the others that form a canopy of shade – will protect the cacao plants and keep the humidity in check. That way we won't have to irrigate, and it will mostly run itself!'

Run itself was a bit of an overstatement, to put it mildly. Mosese makes his rounds in the plantation every day, cutting and clearing and mostly managing to keep the two biggest threats at bay: the fungus that turns the pods black and destroys them, and the rats that climb up and help themselves if you don't trim the brush around the tree trunks. It's only in the busy harvest season that extra hands must be hired to help with plucking, fermenting and drying.

Out among the trees, behind Mosese, I always feel like the apprentice that I am. But his respect for me, or at least for Niklas, runs too deep for him to ever call me out. He shares his knowledge patiently, again and again. 'Here it is, Madam Kat.' I peer at the tree he's pointing to: the pods growing straight from the trunk are black and shrivelled. Although I know the answer, I ask, 'What can we do about it?'

He shakes his head – the fungus is hard to get rid of. But

then he lights up suddenly when he cups an orange pod from another tree in his giant hand. 'Look at this, Madam Kat! This one must have more than thirty beans!' With a quick flick of his knife he slices the capsule in two and gives me half – a bowl full of glistening fruit pulp, with brown pearls hidden in the greyish-white flesh. The sweet aroma hits me right away as the green flickering light filters its way down through the treetops. A chalice between my fingers.

Mosese waits patiently, his brown eyes lodged in a knotted wreath of wrinkles. When the lump forms in my throat, he just nods.

It's almost a joke that it's Lisbeth's daughter who's going to serve as our liaison back home in Norway. When Lisbeth told me about their conversation, I was sceptical – I certainly hadn't seen Linda as a business maven. But when I spoke to her directly and heard her ideas – and not least her energy and enthusiasm – I knew what it was I'd seen in Lisbeth's face. Something vague and undeveloped that comes into clear view when the lights are switched on. If we make this work, Linda Høie will be the point of contact and distributor for *Kat's Chocolate*, and our head of marketing in Norway! Pretty incredible, but no stranger than everything else that's happening these days. The fact that some friends in Suva put me in touch with Johnny Mattson, for example, and that he's willing to give us some training. The retired chocolate-maker with a past that's here and there, who now does ocean fishing and enjoys life from his boat anchored at Labasa.

'You'll have to put up with me for a few days if I come all

the way over there,' he said when I invited him. 'I'm too old to make the trip one day and come back the next.'

What I want is to get Maya involved as well. Hasn't it been proven that engaging in activities and projects can slow the onset of dementia? I see how she often pulls away from us, is gone somewhere for long periods at a time before suddenly snapping back into sharp focus. I try to capture this fragmented existence in the emails I write to Evy, making them truthful without being alarmist. If we're being honest, can't we say that Maya has a better life here? The pace of daily life is slow, and the people around her have time and patience.

I don't think she's afraid. I wouldn't be able to watch fear tearing her to pieces in front of me. Some days she reacts to everything around her with mild surprise; as if spending hours behind a soft veil, that's how it looks to me. Of course I've read that confusion and anxiety often go hand in hand, and that disorientation is inevitable. But it looks like Ateca has a sixth sense for this. As if just by taking Maya's hand, she passes on some of her own imperturbable calm; as if some of the strength in her sturdy, brown fingers flows over into Maya's slender, bluish-white grip. That's a lesson I've learned down here, which I have to remember to lean on. To trust. To let the boat take its own course.

It's strange what Fiji does to them all. I watch and wonder. Sina gets stronger when Maya gets weaker. She pulls out a new kind of compassion, something affectionate cloaked in something rough. Maya without Steinar and Sina without Lisbeth, a strange new configuration. I sometimes allow

113

myself a discreet pat on my own shoulder. Isn't Sina doing better here as well? Away from her son, with all his whining and complaining about money. And Ingrid, she's practically blossoming! Flowers on her sulu, behind her ear, between her hands – pretty amazing that such a green thumb has been buried in the account books of the County Bus Service all these years. Even Ateca, who regards many of Ingrid's schemes with a sceptical eye, has admitted that the pumpkins and tomatoes look especially good this year. Did I once see Ingrid as a dog? Now she's a jungle plant! Strong and resilient and exploding with colour!

But maybe the pat on the shoulder is mostly for myself. Isn't this just the kind of life I wanted? A living house, complete with joys and worries, conversations and arguments and song? So I could have people around me, and so I could be around people?

'You need your sisters, Madam Kat,' Ateca had said back then. And yes, she was right.

18

Sina

Salusalu. Reguregu. Bolabola. Sina opens her ears wide when Fijian is spoken around her; the words explode like fireworks and the voices trill and boom. This language sounds so strange to her! Supposedly it's not that hard to learn – the grammar is simple and there are only a few tricky things to remember about the pronunciation.

'A "d" in the middle of a word is pronounced *nd*,' Kat explains. 'The city's name is *Nandi*. Only tourists say Nadi, remember that. And you've heard how Ateca's name is pronounced. Not Atecka, but *Atetha*. The "c" sounds like a *th* in English.'

And the sounds are so weird! Every other letter is a vowel, a round 'o' or a string of 'a's bursting through the air. The words are like nursery rhymes, repeating the same syllable over and over again. Everyone in Fiji does speak English, but a lot of the conversation around her takes place in *vosa vaka-Viti*, this Fijian singsongy vowel-speak which always makes it sound like they're planning something important. It's as if the words gain a whole new level of meaning than when they're spoken in English. It was no coincidence that the pastor in Korototoka Methodist Church prayed in vosa vaka-Viti at their lovo party.

She doesn't often get Ateca all to herself; Ingrid or Kat is usually close by. But one early afternoon, when the house-keeper sits on the living-room floor folding clothes, Sina gets a chance to bring up the subject. Ateca nods and knows what she's asking right away. 'Does it matter whether we talk about things in Fijian or English? Well, yes. It does. In vosa vaka-Viti, it's . . .' She takes a second to think about it. 'Deeper, in a way.'

'More profound?' Sina's not quite sure whether she understands.

'Yes. Well, no . . . deeper. More genuine.'

'Genuine?'

Ateca nods. 'Yes. When you say something in Fijian, it belongs to you. Like the land. *Vanua*. Do you know what I mean?'

'It doesn't directly translate,' Kat has tried to explain. '*Vanua* is the land you and your clan belong to, but it's more than that. It's the people who live there now and those who have lived there before. It's the traditions they've had and the songs they've sung. What they believe in and what they've loved, the togetherness and the memories. The joy over babies who are born and the grief over those who have died.'

Sina thinks she gets it, at least partly. She's seen it on her walks in and around the village, she's seen it in ways big and small: the cane knife resting naturally in the palm, the gaze out over the landscape under the hand shielding eyes from the sun. A wide-open, grateful ownership. The security of being part of something. Vanua.

'Yes,' Sina says. She knows what Ateca's saying. To speak about the things that really belong to you, you need a deeper language.

116

Standing guard is the only thing she knows how to do. Watching out and keeping track, trying to anticipate problems and avoid danger. And when the damage is done, recovering what's left and making the best of it. Bearing the brunt of it to the best of her ability. To comfort when needed, to hold a hand. But these days she's mainly comforting herself. It's been a long time since she's held Armand's hand – oh, how well she remembers those skinny, restless squirrel fingers. Today, thanks to online bank transfers, their hands don't even have to meet when he grabs her money. But his words are the same as always: 'Thanks, Mum. I'll pay you back next week, I promise!' Usually via text message; once in a while in a rushed phone call.

The strange thing is that she can talk about it with Maya. Or *to* Maya. The years have treated us differently, Sina thinks. Fiji-Maya, with a bulky straw hat on her head and a contemplative look out over the waves, is more remote, more quiet than the confident, pragmatic friend she remembers from high school. The pieces have moved around the board; the whole game has changed.

'First we have to break free from our parents,' Sina tells Maya, who nods under the brim of her hat. 'And now we have to break free from our goddamn children, too.'

In sixth form and all the years in Reitvik that followed, Sina was never in the same league as Maya Aakre. Maya and Steinar, they had their jobs, their co-workers, their circle. Sina's never had a 'circle'. A woman who spends her days shelving sealant and raw linseed oil in the stock room and sorting wallpaper samples by price doesn't have such things. They would greet each other in the street and ask how the children were doing; Maya in a polite tone of voice,

Sina with shameful jealousy. Would things have been different if she'd had a daughter?

One time, Maya's son-in-law, an artist, had an exhibition in Reitvik called 'Colours and Landscapes' – Sina remembers the title from the ad in the paper. She'd wanted to go, she knew where the gallery was, on the second floor above the photography studio. But she didn't go – what did she know about art? Admission was free, but what if you were expected to buy something? How much did a painting cost? Sina's walls at home are covered in pictures of Armand: baby pictures on a sheepskin rug and teenage photos in confirmation robes. A woven tapestry of a sunset and a few pieces of embroidery she's done herself. At one point the store had taken in a batch of pre-framed pictures, flowers in vases in a kind of Japanese style. They didn't sell many of them, and after a year she had been allowed to take three of them home, practically for free. No, 'Colours and Landscapes' probably wasn't for her. So she didn't go. And she didn't say anything to Maya the next time she saw her at the supermarket. She just nodded and kept pushing her shopping trolley towards the next aisle.

But she's saying something now. Now that Maya's shoulders are stooping and her words are slower, Sina is there, ready to lend a hand. She and Maya take the same walk every day: down to the beach, past the short pier with the ladder at the end. Back up past the hill by the cemetery, where they sometimes sit down on the side wall and take a rest. Onward to the village chief's bure.

It's located at the highest point in the village and has a thatched roof and walls, but no windows. They've asked the locals about it; Sina finds it easier to talk to people when she's with Maya. Her friend is often silent, standing there with her big, mute sunglasses and her matted curls tucked under her hat. But Sina can speak for both of them; it becomes a duty she fulfils, an act of compassion. And so it's also for Maya, the retired Literature and History teacher, that she finds out no one but the chief is allowed through the front door. No one lives or sleeps in the chief's bure, but important decisions are made here. Sina and Maya get a peek inside through a side door, which confirms what they've been told: that the walls are decorated with strips of *masi*, the thin bark of the mulberry tree, painted with black and brown patterns. That a huge tanoa, the big kava bowl festooned with polished cowry shells, takes centre stage in the room. That the floor is covered in *coco*, the fanciest mats, and the walls are lined with clubs, axes and spears, symbols of war. Sina shudders at what she's heard about the old cannibal weapons: the axe to cleave the skull, the club with a hook on the end to dig into the brain.

They politely say thank you and leave; they don't discuss what they've been told. They're almost back at the shop with the piles of watermelon in front of it before Maya makes a comment.

'Those clubs look way too heavy. When you need something like that, you need it quickly.'

Sina nods. If you want to club someone in the head, there's no time to waste.

When they return to the house in the afternoon, there's a pick-up truck parked in the yard. 'Rakiraki Cooling Services' is painted on the side. 'We make you freeze.'

Maya retreats to her room. Sina is momentarily tempted

to take a nap as well, but Lisbeth is sitting on the porch, and she plops down next to her and points to the truck.

'Why is the cooling company here? Is the freezer broken again? Or is Kat's house getting air-conditioning installed?' She smirks to herself, as if she's made a joke.

Lisbeth shakes her head. 'I don't think so. But if we're going to make chocolate, I'm guessing we'll need to cool down the sweet house,' she says, using the name Ingrid has given to the unused shed they're planning to turn into a production site. 'They're probably here to find out about isolation and refrigeration and things like that. I'm sure it's not cheap to turn an old chicken shack or whatever it was into a chocolate factory.'

Sina nods, and takes a cigarette from Lisbeth's case without asking.

'And the gardener-in-chief, where's she?'

Lisbeth looks around. 'Ingrid? I'm not sure. Maybe in the back yard?'

Sina doesn't respond. She doesn't engage in Ingrid's efforts to make the pumpkins grow larger and the melons sweeter. She doesn't have the energy to compete; her experience from the gardening club in Reitvik pales in comparison with Ingrid's staunch determination to teach herself everything there is to know about tropical produce.

It's as if Lisbeth has read her mind. 'Well, she'll have more things to think about than pumpkins and beans when she's the chocolate director.'

They sit in silence for a while. Sina is tracking a boat on the horizon with her eyes when Lisbeth suddenly asks, 'How's Maya doing?'

120

Sina turns towards her. 'Fine. Why do you ask?'

Lisbeth shrugs. 'No reason. She just seemed so tired.'

'Everyone gets tired sometimes. It was hot on our walk.' Sina feels the irritation bubble up; why does Lisbeth have to butt in? Her annoyance picks up steam and she mimics her friend in a mocking voice: ' "How's Maya doing?" It's not like she's a child! Why don't you ask her yourself?'

Lisbeth looks surprised; her voice grows apologetic. 'I didn't mean anything by it . . . I just thought—'

'You thought what?' Sina bristles. 'Maya's the sharpest of all of us, she always has been. Age doesn't change that. You yourself are not exactly the same person you were when you were twenty either!'

That was a low blow, and Sina regrets it immediately. She should shut up, but it's so irritating, so *ridiculous*, that Lisbeth still worries about her looks – she's an old lady! A memory prickles and seethes inside Sina, a shame she's almost managed to repress: standing in front of the mirror in Lisbeth's room, all alone in the house. Greedily grabbing at her silk blouses and high-heeled shoes, trying to squeeze into her narrow pencil skirts and form-fitting jackets. The lilac top that didn't fit: baggy across the chest, way too tight over the stomach. The sudden tearing of the seam. The hole ripping through the fabric, impossible to repair. The feeling of indifference when she draped it back over the hanger.

Sina's not sure why she jumps so fiercely to Maya's defence. Her friend may be quieter than before, but she has the same air of authority. Her knowledge of the South Pacific islands – about their history, geography, culture and politics – is far superior to the others'. Maybe with the exception of Kat – although Sina has a suspicion that their global nomad's expertise in all the international projects she parades around is actually pretty flimsy. Maya's knowledge isn't tried and tested, but it is cross-referenced and thoroughly documented. In their evening conversations on the porch, she's usually the one to make the interesting connections, Sina thinks. The other night, for example, when they started talking about the constellations, the South and the North Star. 'Ursa Minor,' Maya said, 'or what we call the Little Bear. The North Star is the brightest star in that constellation. *Stella Polaris* in Latin. But did you know it was also called *Stella Maris* in the Middle Ages? Star of the sea? That's actually one of the names they used to call the Virgin Mary.'

Lisbeth looked at her with interest. 'Really? That's exactly what she said. That little girl. She said her name was Star of the Sea.'

Maya nodded. 'Yes, exactly. "Our lady, star of the sea" was one of the holy virgin's names.'

She leaned back in her chair, satisfied with this evening's lecture. The Maya they'd always known, savvy and capable.

Except when she isn't. When Maya's face becomes a blank canvas, when her eyes become a pair of closed doors only slightly ajar to reveal slivers of fear, something in Sina shudders. A discomfort she doesn't want to share with anyone; it coats her vocal cords and propels her to reassure her friend it's all going to be OK, she'll handle it. When Maya loses her words, Sina finds hers.

Is Sina the only one who sees it? She thinks so. She's the only one who has seen right through Lisbeth Karlsen, high-school princess. Seen that it wasn't self-confidence lurking behind that smile and ample cleavage, but rather a tightly wound coil of anxiety. A string that Sina could flick so it trembled whenever she wanted: one harsh glare and the artificial laughter through pink-glossed lips was stifled. Sina's never been jealous of Lisbeth. Of her money, maybe, her life of leisure. But she'll be damned if she's ever felt inadequate. Power lies in knowledge. Especially in deciding whether to use it.

In fact, she feels sorry for Lisbeth. What's the point of this whole charade? She's so tired of it all.

19

Ateca

Dear God, you know that I trust in my dreams, that they always tell me things. But tonight I had a dream that scared me. I dreamed about Drua, the big, holy ship. I was standing in the middle of the deck, in the chief's spot, watching over the hull and the steering oars on both sides. I was afraid because I knew it wasn't my place. I shouldn't be the one in charge of trimming the sails when the sea got rough. But I couldn't move. We were going fast and the waves were strong, and I was all alone on the ship when Dakuwaqa, the shark god, suddenly rose up from the deep. And then I became Tokairahe, son of the gods, with the magical fish hooks. The one who can catch all the fish in the sea – except for Dakuwaqa. I had his necklace around my neck, the chain made of bone hooks glittering in yellow, blue and purple. And then Dakuwaqa came surging up from the sea, coming towards me in a giant leap, and grabbed the necklace in his terrible teeth. But they didn't touch me – I didn't get a single scratch! When the shark vanished back down into the waves, Tokairahe's hook necklace was gone. I was wearing a thin gold necklace instead.

The dream frightened me so much, Lord. Help me have faith that you'll protect me.

In Jesus' holy name. Emeni.

20
Maya

The scary thing isn't not remembering. It's when she remembers that she hasn't remembered, that the dizziness turns into terrified nausea. When she realizes she's been on the outside. All the way over there on the other, unknown side. That she's stood there with a blank stare and trembling lips, mumbling at faces she can't recognize that she doesn't know who they are.

It's later on, when she has no idea why she's standing here, with an unfamiliar umbrella in her hand or groceries she can't remember buying in her bag. It's when the gate has shut behind her and shoved her back among familiar surroundings and faces, that her throat constricts and she feels the panic racing in with deafening hoofbeats: where was I?

Still, Maya gets annoyed. At Evy, who tried to hide her concern behind cheerful comments before she left. 'Remember to stay out of the sun, Mum. Too much of a good thing, you know how it is.' At Ingrid, who bosses everyone around in the garden and warns them that too much papaya can lead to an upset stomach. At Kat? No, not at Kat. Kat knows. The night they drove Evy to the airport, was that really just a few months ago? The terror when she awoke in the truck and suddenly didn't know why she was there. The sound of the ocean, its beckoning song. Kat's face, so familiar, but she couldn't bring herself to associate it with words or thoughts. She'd cried when Kat put her to bed that night. Bitter, exasperated tears over the chaos within her; the desperate feeling of losing your grip. Kat knows. But Maya doesn't think she's told the others.

She glances over at her friend in the hammock, which sways silently in the afternoon heat on the porch. It's still there, what none of them could put into words back then. The attraction they all felt for her, the bubbling excitement that filled your body just by standing in a circle around her. The smile you wanted to have bestowed just on you. It's still there. Kat's hair has as many streaks of silver as her own; thick, blue veins run across her hands holding a book. But where Maya's worn golden ring rests loosely on her ring finger, a blue-green flower garland is wrapped around Kat's. Proving in eternal ink that she belongs with Niklas, but in their own unique way. Kat wears a white linen shirt with nothing underneath; Maya can see the outline of her small breasts against the thin material. The sense of freedom she always seemed to radiate, even in the crowded, overheated classroom at Reitvik High, still glows strong and undisputed around Katrine Vale. A heavy wave of emotion washes over Maya, a bitter taste in her mouth. She has to think for a second before she realizes what it is, a feeling she's long since forgotten. There isn't just one word for it, the tart mixture of jealousy, admiration and inadequacy. And here she is again, in Kat's circle. And just like before, none of them can see that what they've always wanted, is to be her.

Kat props herself up on one elbow and sighs.

'Hot, isn't it? I don't know how you're sitting in that chair in the sun, Maya – aren't you burning up? Poor Johnny who has to come into this sauna tomorrow – he's used to more breezy conditions out on his boat, I'd imagine. But it'll be exciting to hear what he thinks of our plans.'

Johnny, who's that? And is she sitting in the sun? Maya wraps her arms around herself and squeezes her eyes shut. The feeling of losing her grip. A door nearly slamming shut before it halts and glides back open. A lamp flickering. Her thoughts grow sheer and full of holes, like veils. She longs for Steinar so much her whole body aches. He would have understood how afraid she is.

Just an afternoon walk, some fresh air before dinner. The rapid sunset surprises her every day when, at exactly quarter past six, the sun waves goodbye and melts into an orgy of pink and gold in just a few minutes.

'I'm going for a walk on the beach,' Maya shouts to no one in particular as she takes the four steps down from the porch. 'I won't be long.'

No one answers, nor does she want an answer. She glimpses Ateca through the kitchen window and briskly waves at her as she strides across the belt of seaweed and dry palm leaves at the edge of the sand. Her legs lead her to the right; the houses she passes glint gold as the afternoon light hits the broad glass louvres that are never closed. A woman sits with a pile of split pandanus leaves next to her on the ground; she's weaving a mat and sends a friendly 'Bula!' in Maya's direction. Her hair crowns her head in a thick, frizzy halo. Maya can glimpse the *vale ni soqo*, the community hall,

127

through the palm trees; a few boys are throwing a rugby ball back and forth in the square right outside. A dog lopes behind her for a while before losing interest and scurrying over to a torn plastic bag.

She intends to walk around the harbour, through the unploughed field by the rubbish dump, as far as what she considers the back of the village, then home along the main road that branches out into packed dirt paths leading to the small houses and courtyards. Just before she passes the harbour the sun begins to swoop down the sky, piercing holes in the clouds and forming columns of light. 'Our Lord's fingers' – she suddenly recalls her mother's name for the slender rays that punctured the grey skies and re-invigorated the earth after soggy afternoons of rain. The columns melt as they reach the water, dissolving into a quivering glitter. It grows dark around her as the light is sucked into the sea; patches of pink and orange dance a few last, passionate steps across the sky. Maya remains standing as the dance keeps twirling inside her. How lovely just to stand here and let herself be overwhelmed, to let the lyrics fade and surrender to the melody.

'Nau, are you all right?'

The colours are still blooming inside her when a warm hand grabs her fingers. Maya looks down into a pair of wide eyes. The evening breeze nips at the fringe of the little girl who has called her 'Auntie', blows it into a flurry around narrow, nearly translucent ears. The dress billows like a sail behind her, and Maya recognizes the girl from the Christmas party. It is Maraia, to whom Lisbeth gave her necklace – both Sina and Ingrid muttered about that afterwards.

'Yes.' Maya smiles, delighted to see her. 'You're Maraia, right?'

'Yes,' the girl replies. Her voice is as bottomless as her eyes. 'It means star of the sea.'

'I'm Maya,' Maya says. 'That means dream.'

Maraia nods.

They remain where they stand, Maya and Maraia, as an invisible hand squeezes the last colours from the day and drops it empty and used into the sea. In the darkness that begins to shroud them, Maya feels hollow and dizzy, exhausted by the ecstatic play of light. She blinks uncertainly, trying to remember where she was going. But the wonder, the fascination over the godly fingers still teems around her like a mystery; something inside her doesn't want to be switched back on. Maya tightens her grip around the little girl's hand, tries to catch her breath. Where was she going again?

The girl's eyes sparkle as they look up towards her, two lighthouse beams of irrefutable knowing.

'I can walk with you,' she says. 'Come on, Nau. Let's go home.'

It feels safe walking along hand in hand. The ocean's steady assurances on one side; Maraia on the other, showing Maya where she's going without saying a word. Home to Kat's house, no, it's her house now, where she lives, where they all live. When they arrive, she asks if Maraia wants to come in.

'You can have dinner with us if you like,' she says.

But the Star of the Sea shakes her head. One, two, three quick steps and she's gone, into the darkness.

21

Lisbeth

Lisbeth looks around. Her gaze follows Ingrid, who gets up from the table. The piece of fabric she's tied around her waist is faded and has a faint, indistinguishable border at the hem. Kat's silver-streaked hair is flying in all directions; she probably hasn't been near a mirror today. Sina has never had much to show off, Lisbeth thinks and glances at her friend by the window, but at least she always wears a bra. The saggy bounce under Ingrid's T-shirt reveals that she's thrown caution to the wind, and Lisbeth heaves a deep internal sigh: does she really have to let everything go?

Suddenly Maya appears in the doorway and Kat welcomes her loudly in a cheerful voice. '*There* you are! And we're almost done eating!'

Maya just smiles and Lisbeth's critical scowl glides over her stocky frame. She is wearing a shapeless sack dress, bluish-green, its hem falling somewhere mid-calf. The straw hat she always wears is plopped down over her flattened curls. She slips into the empty place at the table, and Lisbeth feels something like compassion softening her irritation.

Still, the fact that Sina has assumed the role of – what should she call it, Maya's personal assistant? – is above and beyond. The way she's never more than two steps away from her, the way she drops everything the second Maya puts on her ridiculous hat and wants to go for a walk. Lisbeth had to say something about that today, when Maya announced that she was going out, and she saw that Sina was ready to run after her.

'You're not going to leave me to prepare dinner all alone?' she had to say. 'It's Tuesday – our turn!'

Sina hadn't replied and just continued chopping onions, but Lisbeth felt the antagonism like a gust of wind around her. Dear me! As if Maya, a grown woman, couldn't take a walk on the beach by herself! And now here she is in the doorway; they're almost done eating, but so what? She just went a bit too far and took her time getting back, right?

'Long walk, Maya?' she asks casually, and pours some more water in her glass. 'Or did you get lost?'

She doesn't mean anything by it, she really doesn't. She herself has got lost here several times, especially at night when it's hard to navigate between the small, identical houses in the dark. So she's completely taken aback when Kat snaps across the table. 'Leave her alone! She just walked in the door!'

Lisbeth blinks in surprise; she hadn't meant to offend! She opens her mouth to explain herself, but Kat shoots her a dirty look and leans forward to create a wall between Maya and the others.

'You must be starving,' she says to Maya. 'I hope the food is still hot.'

Sina looks worried; she lifts her arms as if to do something, but they remain suspended in the air. Only Ingrid seems unperturbed; she's put her glasses on, and takes a seat in the chair under the one reading lamp.

Suddenly Lisbeth can't stand another minute with any of them. 'I'm going out to buy some cigarettes,' she says, and gets up abruptly. 'I'm sure Salote will open up for me.'

Lisbeth appreciates the wonderfully flexible opening hours in Korototoka. The shop is open whenever the customer arrives, and there's no food safety inspector to worry about. When someone stops outside Salote's pink corrugated metal house and calls out '*Kerekere* . . . ? Excuse me . . . ?' the door glides open, whether it's five o'clock or seven or nine thirty, and Salote will emerge, key in hand. The key opens the padlock on the door of the little side extension, which reveals a counter with a few shelves on the back wall. Salote will slip behind the counter and retrieve a box of completely melted margarine, or she will brush the ants off a bag of brown sugar, or pull down a box of matches or a package of powdered milk. Or, for Lisbeth, a pack of Benson & Hedges.

'Vinaka,' she says, and sticks the cigarettes and change back in her bag. She lingers for a while outside Salote's 'canteen', as the small, home-operated shop is known for some strange reason, observing the owner as she gets out the broom and starts sweeping the stairs in the gleam of the light bulb above the door.

Why did she do it? Why take the turning up towards the church when she could have just gone straight home? When she should have turned around and taken the same way back, straight past the dalo field, past Ateca's house and the cobbled-together mess of extensions and porches that form the home of Jone and his numerous family members. But Lisbeth doesn't. She's suddenly determined to end the evening with a breeze in her hair and a cigarette at the end of the pier, and takes the long way there. Along the main road, past the houses that are mostly dark at this hour. There's a grog party underway on a *bolabola*, a wooden deck with a thatched palm roof; a strong, tattooed arm lifts up a bilo. None of the men take notice of Lisbeth. She's startled by a sudden roar of laughter; she hugs her handbag under her arm and sets out up the long, gentle hill.

It happens right after she passes the chief's bure and is on her way back down, in the direction of the beach and the crashing waves. The man who comes walking towards her has a knife in his hand, the large cane knife that's as common in the hands of women as men as they walk to and from their plantations, the grandiose name for the small patches of land that feed their families' stomachs. The most useful of all tools, with a wooden handle and a blade with a blunt tip, she still feels uncomfortable to see it. Wiry old men with muddy rubber boots and rags wrapped around their heads, gently swaying women bearing woven baskets filled with sweet potatoes and tavioka, barefoot young boys carrying frayed burlap sacks on their shoulders – they all carry it, the *sele kava* that looks so fearsome. Lisbeth sees it every day; Mosese has it in his hand when he brings dalo or breadfruit to them in the afternoons. Still, she can't help shuddering. The giant fists, fingers gripping the steel, the pictures she's seen online and in Maya's books: threatening poses, the clubs and axes they clutch in their hands. The war paint and the gruesome whale-tooth necklaces. Kat has explained that miniature cannibal forks are among the tourists' favourite souvenirs here: a carved handle with four long prongs forming a neat square, perfect for scooping brain matter out of crushed skulls. Kat had laughed when she told them about it, but Lisbeth felt a chill run through her. It's only been a hundred and fifty years since the last person was killed and eaten in this country!

There's something about the enormous knife, dangling so carelessly from the man's hand as he comes up the hill towards her. Something that makes the fear surge in her stomach; Lisbeth suddenly realizes it's been there growling all along. Now he's directly in front of her, she can see he's young, his face soft and strong. Smooth muscles tense under the skin; blue-black tattoos wind their way around his powerful biceps. He blocks her path with a wide stance. The hand with the knife lifts as the scream rises in her throat.

22

Ateca

Dear God, it's as if the light changes colour when Maraia and Madam Maya are together. I heard them singing this afternoon. Maraia's high-pitched voice, and Madam Maya's deeper and looser tones. They were sat on the floor with two brown-and-green pieces of fabric between them, which they had folded into the shape of small animals with bodies and heads.

'We sing for the turtles,' Maraia said. She must have told Madam Maya about the princesses Tinaicaboga and Raudalice, who were transformed into turtles when they were kidnapped by fishermen from a village on Kadavu. They found a way to escape, but had to go on living as sea turtles in the bay off the island.

Maraia knew the song as well, the one the women in the princesses' village sing to them from the cliffs on the beach.

The women of Namuana are dressed for grief,
They carry their holy clubs, decorated in strange patterns.
Raudalice, come up and show yourself to us!
Tinaicaboga, come up and show yourself to us!

When the women sing, the giant turtles come up to the surface and listen.

135

Maraia's family isn't from Kadavu. But she has wise eyes and knowledge about many things. And I think it's good for Madam Maya to get to know the sea. Perhaps she's the least kaivalagi of them all, Lord? Madam Maya has let so many things go; that's why she can take in so much more.

Dear God, thank you for bringing together those who need each other. Thank you for letting Maraia sing with Madam Maya.

In Jesus' holy name. Emeni.

23

Lisbeth

Why didn't she say anything? Why didn't she rush up the stairs when she got home and shout that she'd been attacked? Kat would have taken charge. She would have found out who he was, who his family were, and the village's own penal code would have taken care of the rest. Why did she only give a brief nod to Ingrid and Kat on the porch? Said 'hi' to Sina, who stood in the living room with a coffee mug in her hand and questions on the tip of her tongue.

'You were gone a while – did something happen?'

Instead of telling Sina about the young man with the large knife, she'd forced herself to stop and flash her a calm smile.

'Happen? No . . . I took the long way home, that's all. It was so nice to take a little evening stroll.'

She doesn't know why. All she knows is that there is so much about these people she doesn't understand. She doesn't understand their laughter, their voracious appetite or their loud, incomprehensible language. But what happened on the road below the chief's bure wasn't something she needed to understand. When the young man dropped the knife and grabbed for her handbag with both hands, she had yelped, hugged her bag closer and met his eyes at once. What she saw in them startled her. No crazy rage. No thirst for her, no blaze of desire. As he tugged at the bag and tried to yank it off her shoulder, his eyes were just full of regret.

Lisbeth has never been attacked before. She's shuddered when reading about elderly people being mugged and beaten up for fifty kroner, but never imagined that she'd find herself standing here in the middle of a gravel road on the outskirts of a Fijian village, struggling stubbornly and silently against a handsome and well-built young man. Who obviously wanted to mug her, but dropped his knife instead of using it to threaten her, and looked at her with a kind of plea in his eyes: let's do this without fighting, please.

She'd lost her footing and fallen as he snatched the bag from her, turned and began to run in the other direction. Her fingers grabbed hold of something on the ground, his knife. She automatically raised her arm as he tossed the bag aside and came back. He held her money, a meagre clutch of notes, in his hand as he slowly approached, his eyes on the knife she still held high in the air.

'Give me back my money!'

She was the first to speak.

He shook his head. 'I can't. I need it. And I need my knife, you have to give it to me.'

'Not if I don't get my money back!'

He stood right above her and stretched out his hand to help her up, a whiff of sweat coming off his body. She swayed slightly as she got to her feet; his hand was warm, it enveloped hers around the handle of the knife and she let go without a struggle. Suddenly she felt a lump form in her throat; the tears ran warm and bewildering down her cheeks. Clumsily he patted her on the shoulder.

'There, there. It's OK, it's OK.'

I don't want it to be OK! The words rushed through her head. What I want is to feel your arms around me and your hot breath against my face. I want your eyes to glow as they rest on me, your lips to search for mine.

Lisbeth's heart hammered as she swayed towards his chest. She couldn't see his face, but felt him go rigid as he pushed her away.

'Ma'am, are you OK? Do you want me to walk you home?'

'No, no, I'm OK. Just give me my bag.'

She rummaged through it quickly, found a handkerchief and wiped her face. Her cards were still in her wallet, though the young man held her cash in his hand, clearly seeing it as his property no matter how much concern he might have for the woman he'd taken it from.

Lisbeth didn't ask for the money again. She slowly extended one finger, aching to touch his round, strong face. For a moment, he stood completely still and let her do it. Then he took a step back and the darkness swallowed his polite goodbye.

'*Ni sa moce*, ma'am. Goodnight.'

She remained standing, her pulse beating hot and heavy in her throat. *I need the money*, he'd said. The truth, a flash of clarity in her mind: it is about sharing. When those who have so much don't think to share, this is what follows. The regret in his gaze was not about what had happened. Only that it had happened in a way that scared her.

Other pieces of the puzzle hurtled through her brain and

fell into place: the afternoon she'd complimented Mosese's wife Litia on her handbag, a simple shoulder bag made of straw. Litia had responded by emptying out its contents and handing the bag over, and Lisbeth had stared at her in shock. 'No, no, please! I just said I liked it, I didn't mean . . .' But Litia had walked away, and Lisbeth was left sitting with the bag in her lap, red-faced and embarrassed.

She stood motionless in the middle of the road as fragments of Kat's explanation ran through her mind: how custom and courtesy urge you to honour someone's admiration for your possession by gifting them with it. Suddenly it all made sense. You're supposed to share. And we just sit here with our belongings and our money; clinging to it, not sharing. So this is how it has to be.

She had kept going down to the beach, had walked out to the pier as intended, had lit the cigarette as planned. But it had been so long since she bought it from Salote's canteen, half an hour and a whole dream ago.

What would have happened, Lisbeth thinks, what would he have done if I'd said it? *Can I have you? I want you; can I have you?*

24

Ingrid

The chocolate expert is almost bald. His bare scalp is evenly tanned and his shirt is stretched taut across his shoulders. Kat has picked Johnny Mattson up from Rakiraki, and Ingrid thinks she can already smell the aroma of sweet, bubbling cocoa mass. Wildrid smells it too; she's the first one down from the porch to meet him with her flowing sulu and eager smile. 'How nice of you to come and teach us a few things. We have a million questions!'

They dive right into it, starting by inspecting the shed they have named the sweet house. Kat explains how she plans to install a cooling system here, along with a new water tank and pump. Johnny nods, advises them on where to place benches and basins. He attended what he calls a 'chocolate academy' in England, and worked in product development for a large chocolate producer in Belgium for many years. Ingrid sees that Lisbeth is paying close attention. She herself is more focused on his hands, with which he enthusiastically underscores his points as he speaks. Strong and brown, with short, wide fingernails.

'Did you take part in the chocolate production directly?' she asks, without quite knowing why. Maybe because she can't imagine his bulky fists tinkering with soft caramel and finely ground liquorice powder.

'Oh, yes. Every step in the process. White chocolate, milk chocolate, dark chocolate.' A much younger man suddenly smiles through the wrinkles surrounding his brown eyes. 'There isn't a sweet temptation that doesn't lure me in.'

Ingrid has to smile back, feels the optimism like a gust breezing through her. No, like a taste on her tongue! Wildrid can feel the saliva pooling behind her teeth: soft mint spreading out on the back of her tongue, salty caramel sticking to her molars. Chilli chocolate burning the inside of her cheeks, rum cream with ginger melting down her throat.

'Pineapple truffle!' she says. 'Mango nougat! Marzipan-covered kiwi!'

Johnny looks at her and chuckles. 'I thought you said you wanted to start slowly and carefully?'

The others grow quiet and Ingrid stops, embarrassed by her outburst. An erotic poem wrapped in cellophane.

'Well, how about that!' Kat is the first to break the silence; her rollicking laughter fills the tiny shed. 'Let's jump feet first right into the cocoa fat!'

'But that's not what we discussed.'

It's Lisbeth who objects. Sensible from head to toe today, in flat shoes and loose-fitting trousers, she reminds them succinctly of the basic idea they had all agreed on: 'If the idea is to break into the health industry, we have to think "less is more".'

Where on earth has she learned these things? Ingrid thinks, and sees that red patches have flared up on Lisbeth's throat as she continues:

'We have to focus on the clean, the pure. Something that reminds people of an uncomplicated, relaxed lifestyle – the opposite of lavishness. Simple, pure experiences. Linda says that's what people want these days.'

Ingrid knows Lisbeth is right, and shoves away the dejection that replaces the effervescence of chocolate-covered starfruit in her mouth. Wildrid tosses her head and says no more.

She likes him, plain and simple. Johnny neither flirts nor tries to impress; he's solid without being heavy. Sure of himself without bragging. The air is charged with electric excitement as they sit on the porch and he guides them through the production method. Ingrid feels herself sitting up straight, her hair standing ever so slightly on end, and a whiff of something unfamiliar hits her nostrils. Sea and a fresh breeze. A gust of new possibilities. His calm voice describes the process: first the fermenting and drying they already know about.

'Then roasting, where the cocoa beans are tossed under hot air for an hour or so.'

'Could we use a regular oven? A convection oven?' Kat asks.

'I'm sure you could.'

Ingrid has retrieved a notebook and scribbles away as Johnny talks them through the grinding, in which the nibs are ground and heated until they form a liquid cocoa mass.

'It doesn't taste good at this stage, just strong and bitter,' he explains.

Onward through extracting the butter and mixing it with the correct amounts of cocoa mass, fat, sugar, milk . . .

'And whatever else you might want to add.'

Ingrid takes note, and Wildrid holds back about mangosteen, guava or pineapple.

'You'll have to give some thought to preservatives. As I understand it, you plan to export, so it'll take some time before the product reaches the customer. But you also want a healthy image, so you probably don't want too many preservatives on your list of ingredients.'

Lisbeth looks deep in thought, and Ingrid knows she'll be consulting with Linda tomorrow. How great! she thinks and flashes Lisbeth an encouraging smile. We have expertise in this part of it too, just an email away.

'What's really important is the conching,' Johnny continues. 'That's what gives that silky smooth feeling, that delicious melt-in-the-mouth texture. The one that makes you want to fill your mouth with it, over and over again.'

He pauses for a moment, and Ingrid looks away when he catches her eye. She fixes her gaze on her bare feet on the wooden floor and suddenly feels them twitching. 'Dance,' Wildrid whispers.

'That delicious feeling,' Johnny says.

He goes on to talk about tempering and moulding, but Ingrid has stopped taking notes. It's too much to take in all at once. They'll have to pick it up as they go along.

'Mattson?' she asks Johnny over a cup of morning coffee the next day. 'You don't have Norwegian ancestry by any chance? Or Swedish?'

He takes a sip of coffee before answering. 'Well, you can guess,' he says with a smile. 'Where do you think I'm from, anyway?'

Ingrid is suddenly shy and feels put on the spot, as if she should know the answer.

144

'I don't know.' She hesitates. 'I've just assumed that you were . . . Australian?'

He laughs out loud. 'Is that what I look like? With this nose? And this hair?' He strokes the crown of his head, with its sparse, frizzy tufts of grey hair.

She has to laugh as well, her shyness gone. 'Well, there's not much left of it, so it's not easy to tell! But . . .'

'Maybe I'm not as dark as I should be?' He grins and throws his hands up. 'You got me! And I just might have your fine ancestors to blame.'

Ingrid listens with interest to the story of how he was born on Kosrae, one of the islands in the Federated States of Micronesia. She tries to picture the map, the tiny specks of islands to the . . . north? North-west?

'The surname is actually Matson-Itimai,' he says. 'And my first name is Yosiwo. Joseph. But it's easier to go by Johnny Mattson in most of the world.'

She examines his face, takes it in. He's much lighter-skinned than most people here in Korototoka, though he has similar features. The broad nose; the thick, solid neck that folds under the collar of his shirt. He meets her gaze with a wide grin. An easy-going invitation: go ahead and look, I am who I am.

'I don't know how much truth there is to it,' he says, 'but my grandmother always said there was some connection to Norway.'

'Norway? Madsen, you mean?'

He nods. 'It's possible. You've heard of the whale hunting in this part of the world? Apparently, there was once a Norwegian whaling station on Kosrae. Maybe one of the Norwegian whalers fell for a Micronesian beauty and settled down on the island? Maybe there's Viking blood running through my veins as well?'

His eyes land on her face, and she quickly nods. 'Maybe.'

'By the way,' he adds, 'I think Viking blood is just as hot as the Micronesian variety.'

His smile lines tense up at the corners of his mouth again. Ingrid feels herself turning red but she doesn't break eye contact. She moves the conversation in a different direction. 'Do you go back there often? To Kosrae?' She stumbles over the name. 'What's it like there?'

Johnny takes a moment before responding. 'It's been a while since I've been there. I don't have anyone there any more.' His eyes turn away. 'But it's beautiful.'

His smile pops back up again. 'I've mostly been doing my own thing in Labasa for many years. I have a small place on shore, but I more or less live on the boat.'

She waits for him to continue.

'Deep-sea fishing,' he explains. 'I charter both myself and the boat. I sit in the captain's chair and seek out the big guys. Tuna, mackerel – the massive schools still get an old man's heart racing!'

'You're not old!'

Ingrid's face starts burning when she realizes she's said it out loud. She hurries to grab her mug and gulps down a big mouthful of lukewarm coffee.

He doesn't laugh, and looks at her. She can see he knows what she meant.

'Thanks,' he says. 'You'll have to come out on the boat with me sometime. Just let me know when you're ready.'

They have to learn the bulk of it from him in three days. Johnny has 'a couple of crazy old fishing dudes' he's going out with over the weekend; he has to be back in Labasa by Thursday night at the latest. 'We'll have to make the most of our time,' he says, 'and do feel free to ask all the questions you have.'

He gives the top of his head a quick stroke – always with his left hand, Ingrid has noticed – and looks at them encouragingly.

She knows she should ask about the business side. The administration. Licences and regulations. But the words Wildrid pushes on to her tongue are all about flavour. About sweetness and texture and lingering aroma. Ingrid holds them back behind clenched teeth and doesn't ask any questions. She lets Lisbeth enquire about the additives and Maya wonder about the importance of the wrapper. Ingrid and Wildrid sit at the back of the room and let their mouth fill with saliva and anticipation.

Her heart nearly stops when Kat says it, right after dinner. She pulls her aside while the others clear the table; her tone is casual.

'You could just go up to him.'

Ingrid stares at her, feels the blood rush to her cheeks. 'What do you mean?'

Kat keeps her words light, but there's something affectionate in her voice that makes a lump form in Ingrid's throat.

'Johnny. He's leaving tomorrow morning. And in half an hour everyone here will be asleep. Just go up there. He'll be happy.'

Ingrid is paralysed. 'Has he . . . said anything?'

What are you thinking? was what she meant to say. What are you imagining?

But there's nothing judgemental about the look on her friend's face. Nothing disparaging or pitying. Only a wish for her to find happiness.

'You've loved so little, Ingrid,' she says. 'Just go to him.'

She doesn't dress up, doesn't even glance in the mirror before leaving the house. Doesn't take special care when opening the front door, doesn't tiptoe down the stairs. This is madness in any case; it'll just have to be what it is. There are lights in a few of the houses down the road but there is no one outside. Just her own footsteps along the road where the dust has settled for the night, and a solitary bird calling out a short message.

The room Salote rents out is around the back of the house. It has a door facing into the back yard, but Ingrid still has to go down the driveway, past the little shop and around the cassava field by the fence. If Salote comes out and finds her here now, it's all over. 'No, no,' Wildrid whispers. 'Just pretend you're sleepwalking.'

His door is shut. She can do it; she can knock. Can say goodbye to Ingrid Hagen of the County Bus Service once and for all. Become someone she's never been. She lifts her hand, feels the deep taste of dark chocolate spread across her tongue, swallows it. *You've loved so little, Ingrid.*

She knocks twice, hard.

His eyes are happy and bright when he opens the door.

'I've been waiting,' he says. 'I thought you would come.'

The hands that close around her wrists and pull her in are warm and dry.

25

Sina

What in the world does Armand want?

Sina is nervous and embarrassed. Nervous to tell Kat and the others. Embarrassed that he's just planning to show up, unexpected and uninvited. And unwelcome, she thinks. She lets the thought rise to the surface: I don't want him to come.

She's been mulling over the email for two days. Worried and scared one moment, irritated the next. He doesn't ask whether it's a good time or whether there's a reasonable place for him to stay, just takes it for granted that everything will be arranged for him: *'I'm taking a trip down to Fiji. I land in Nadi on the 29th.'*

He doesn't say a word about the great deal with the Lithuanian imports, or about whether he's sold her car.

How is it possible that her son still makes her nervous and embarrassed? Does she really have any face left to lose when it comes to Armand? Hasn't he bled her dry long ago?

You chose this, Sina reminds herself. Repeats her mother's words in her head, the small, piercing arrows she shot out of the corner of her mouth when the boy had cried all night and Sina stood there in the morning, dead tired, with her handbag over her shoulder, on her way to Høie

Building Supplies to sign for paint sample deliveries and take inventory of linoleum flooring rolls. 'You chose this yourself, Sina, dammit.'

And yes, she had chosen it, in a way. She'd heard, not least from Lisbeth, that there were 'ways'. And from her mother, who wrote to a friend in the next town asking if Sina could come and stay there until it was all over. But she didn't want to! Weak-willed, unambitious Sina Guttormsen – she knew how they looked at her, all right – had held her own: she was going to have the baby and she was going to have it in Reitvik.

It hadn't occurred to her that Lisbeth and, by extension, Harald would help her out; at first it was enough to have to wrap her head around her own crazy decision. She wasn't the first person this had happened to in Reitvik, and she wouldn't be the last. But Sina wasn't Kat with the carefree laugh; she wasn't buttoned-up Ingrid or sensible Maya. She wasn't Lisbeth with the hair and the body and all the things Sina would never have.

So this became what she had. The boy. And the secret, dizzying triumph that she was the one they all looked at now. It was Sina who had done what made them shudder, tremble and whisper.

She hadn't thought about money either – not much, anyway. After all, what does a nineteen-year-old know about the cost of living? From paying for salami sandwiches for school lunches, ski boots and bus tickets, to money for football trading cards and pool entrance fees? But she'd learned and she'd managed. She had fought tooth and nail to hold on to the little apartment she found, had gone to work, paid the rent. A sudden sharp pain, a deep pool that Sina rarely dives into: can't he see any of what she's done for him? Why hasn't Armand appreciated any of it? Where did she go wrong so that a forty-seven-year-old man still sees his mother as an open wallet? A middle-aged man with nothing to show for himself but an endless string of disappointments and things that have gone wrong. And it's never his fault.

She'd had high hopes for Astrid. Armand was in his early twenties when he met her, college student and king of the world back then, too. But there had been something about the young girl from the south coast, something sturdy and dependable under her ponytail and her dark eyebrows. Something that had given Sina hope that she saw through Armand, right through his gloating arrogance, and was encouraged by what she glimpsed underneath.

He'd brought her home for a few days over Christmas and Sina had observed the tone between them, thinking she saw something real there, something respectful. But when spring came there was no more mention of Astrid, and by autumn, student life had lost its luster: 'Two more years just for a *piece of paper*, what am I going to do with that?' That time, it was a few of his friends who had started a band; the money and the opportunities were in London, and Armand was the one they needed. 'Manager, right? With a good manager, these guys are a sure thing!'

She'd never seen anything come of it, but that's not what hurts. He'd never needed to be rich, her boy, never needed to be famous. It would have been more than enough if he'd held down a job, bought an apartment, built a life.

When Harald Høie kicked his son Joachim out of the

house, the rumours in Reitvik flew. Sina had been promoted to the front of the store then, and said a brief hello to Lisbeth when she stopped by once in a rare while. Harald's office was upstairs, and all Sina usually saw was the back of Lisbeth's expensive coat on her way up the stairs. The director and his wife had moved away from the town centre long ago, to a custom-built palace high up in Toppåsen. But she'd hear things, of course, there was always talk about the boss. About how the missus never came along on business trips and to conferences. About who had seen and heard and been offered this, that and the other. About how Harald Høie had been furious when his son wanted to become a nurse instead of fourth-generation director of the building supplies company.

If only Armand had done what Joachim Høie did and found a vocation; if only he'd learned to demonstrate knowledge and show compassion, how proud she would have been! Not of a diploma or a title, but of purpose and drive. Armand has neither of those. And that's why Sina is embarrassed.

*

'Why are you so nervous, Sina? Third cigarette in a row – what's wrong?'

Maya hides her rebuke behind a chuckle, but the wrinkle in her nose is real enough. Sina reflexively puts out her cigarette and looks up at Maya guiltily. Had it been anyone else, she would have shrugged and kept smoking, but Maya still has this teacher's air of authority about her. She's judging everything we do, behind those sunglasses, Sina thinks.

'Nothing! I'm just sitting here and . . .'

And what? Dreading Armand's arrival? Because she doesn't know what he wants? But of course she knows. Armand is coming to Fiji because something fell through at home; he's run out of money and now he hopes that something easy and lucrative will fall into his lap here. That he'll manage to charm his way into something – he doesn't yet know what, but he's dying to grab a hold of it. The chocolate, she thinks suddenly. The adventure she's going to be a part of. She, Sina. Not Armand.

'Well, you look terrible,' Maya says. 'Come for a walk with me; you'll feel better.'

Sina sighs. 'It's too hot. I have no energy.'

Maya doesn't give up. 'It was just as hot yesterday. Come on, I'm sure we'll pick up a little breeze at some point.'

But Sina has her excuses ready. 'I can't, really. I'm going to the doctor. Remember I told you I have an appointment today? Vilivo is driving me to Rakiraki.'

Maya removes her sunglasses, and the light blue eyes are clear and strong. 'Do you want me to come?'

Sina shakes her head. 'No, it's fine. It's just a check-up. And a few test results from last time.'

She hasn't been able to face talking to them about it. That part of her life was over long ago. So it's probably nothing, just a couple of episodes, erratic and far between. Dark, slimy bursts from a forgotten place, unwelcome missives from an organ she no longer needs. A nuisance she has chosen to ignore; she doesn't have time to be sick now that things are happening around here, chocolate production and all the rest. She thinks about it as little as possible. It's probably nothing.

But Maya slices through and doesn't sugar-coat anything.

'Get it removed,' she says. 'I had it all cut out years ago.'

Her voice is neutral. 'I was bleeding and bleeding. It was just as easy to have it all gone.'

She shrugs and looks at Sina. 'Don't be afraid; it makes no difference. For one thing or another.'

Sina just nods. It's been a while since that one thing or another had mattered to her in the least. 'It's probably just a little thing,' she says. 'I'm not worried.'

Maya examines her for a moment. 'Yes, you are,' she decides. 'But I'm telling you, there's nothing to be afraid of.'

Vilivo drops Sina off outside the yellowish-grey brick building with a faded red cross painted on the wall. The sign by the door says 'Health Centre'; brown stripes of rust from the screws run down the plaster. They agree that he'll come back to get her in an hour and Sina hurries into the waiting room.

'The woman doctor', as they call him here, is only at the clinic once a week, and the chairs along the walls are filled with pregnant women. Bulging bellies and swollen feet, faces flabby from heat and hormones. They look so young! Some of them have their relatives with them; they sit fingering their mobile phones or fidgeting restlessly on their chairs while mothers and aunts talk to each other and break out into sudden howls of laughter. A white-haired, Chinese-looking woman with the impassive face of a sphinx sits in the middle of all this bubbly, exuberant fertility. She's wearing a pair of trainers and grey trousers, her knees splayed open; a belly bulges forth under the web of strings crisscrossed between toggles on the front of her

154

tunic; she's almost the same size as the pregnant young women.

Sina finds an empty chair. No magazines on the table or a water cooler with cups in the corner, only a large weighing scale on the floor next to the counter and a blood-pressure monitor on a stand.

'Madam, please . . .'

She's weighed and measured in front of everyone, and feels sure that the shameless staring doesn't mean they're judging her weight, only that they're generally interested. Everyone here has something they're forced to share. A thermometer is stuck in her ear and read before the nurse points her back to her chair to wait. It's clear it might be a while before it's her turn.

Sina's mind wanders back to Armand. Goddamn Armand! she thinks and glances around the waiting room, afraid that someone's heard what she's thinking. Where did her son get fifteen thousand kroner to buy a ticket to Fiji? Oh, for goodness' sake, it hits her: he'd better have bought a return ticket! The thought of Armand possibly coming to Fiji without a ticket back home makes Sina feel sick. She can't wait any longer. She has to tell Kat tonight.

'Madam Sina, please!'

She gets up so abruptly that the blood rushes to her head and she has to stand still for a moment before she can walk across the floor and into the doctor's office.

'Surgery,' the doctor says. 'That's the best option. Just to be safe.'

Maybe the conversation with Maya should have prepared her for this but Sina still stares at him blankly. Surgery?

'Have it all removed,' he continues. 'Ovaries too.'

He smiles, but his smile is frayed at the edges. 'The pap smear shows that there may be something that's not quite right.'

May be. She doesn't catch the rest of it. Something about the risk being very low, in all likelihood, and surgery will be all she needs. 'That way you'll be done with it,' he says.

Low risk? Does that mean cancer, or is he unsure? She can't bring herself to ask, just nods in time to the pen he taps on the table as he speaks.

'For women your age, it's usually best to have every-thing removed.'

She opens her mouth, mumbles something in reply.

She has to plan, she has to think, she has to find the money. She says she'll call when she's decided what she wants to do.

26

Kat

The others don't know that Sina doesn't pay as much as they do every month. Her outburst that first night – how could I break her confidence? Reveal to them that her first thought on arrival, palm trees swaying in the soft evening breeze, was whether she could afford it? Evy Forgad punctually transfers Maya's contributions into my account in Norway. Ingrid pays her share in local currency, and Lisbeth transferred what she calls 'the BMW money' to me and asked me to tell her when it's used up. That moment between Sina and me at the airport, the need that gnawed at her, that's nobody else's business.

And she can't say no to Armand, that much is obvious. She looked more dejected than ever when she mumbled that her son 'wants to come and see how I'm doing. He really wants to see with his own eyes that I'm doing well.' Dear God – isn't he ashamed? Almost fifty years old and here he comes, whining to Mum when the money runs out. Why should it be any harder for him than for anyone else to find a job and make it on his own?

It couldn't have come at a worse time, full stop. Now that we're in full swing with the sweet house and I've managed to talk Mosese into joining our new venture. My manager is still sceptical about the chocolate business but I've assured him that his responsibilities will stay the same. The only thing that will change is that we'll take a small part of the cocoa we usually sell off and use it for ourselves. I described the product to him: dark chocolate, a pure taste of Fiji, wrapped in cellophane and packaged into neat boxes. But Mosese is no chocolate lover. The cocoa beans he checks by biting into them are bitter and fresh; that's the only standard he knows and cares about.

Either way, there's nothing we can do about Armand. He's coming to Korototoka, and Ateca and I have arranged for him to stay with Litia and Mosese. I have no plans to offer him a room in Vale nei Kat.

Ingrid tries to be optimistic: 'I'm sure he won't stay that long. He'll get bored here with us old ladies, for sure.' She tries to make me laugh: 'We can put him on the chores rota. When he sees that he has to take his turn cooking dinner, he'll make himself scarce.'

But I'm not in the mood for jokes. 'He'll come down here to be fed, you can be sure of that. Where else would he go? He probably doesn't have a penny to his name.'

Ingrid nods. Her smile fades and she looks around to make sure nobody else is nearby. 'You're right,' she says. 'But I'm even more worried about how he's going to handle the jealousy. Jealousy and dependency are not a good combination.'

Jealousy – what does she mean? I'm about to ask, but hold back when Maya comes round the corner and climbs the stairs to the porch. She removes her sandals slowly and sinks down into a chair. 'Sina?' she says with a question mark, and looks around. 'Isn't Sina here?'

*

For the most part I think it was a dream. Like when you've seen childhood photographs of yourself and you're not sure whether it's the situation you remember, or just the picture. You shake your head and tell yourself it's impossible, you were too young, you've just looked at the album so many times that you think you remember being there. Only the picture is real; the memory's invented.

The images from the last *balolo* night aren't in any album. But I've had them described to me, time and time again, until the details are in high definition, as crystal clear as if I'd been standing on the beach when they pulled him out. As if I'd crouched down in the shadows behind a boat pulled ashore, and seen it all myself in the cold white moonlight. It's only the incomprehensible reality – that he's no longer there in bed beside me in the morning – that tells me it must have happened. But I wasn't there. I couldn't have been there.

It's the same thing every year: the village teems with hectic, electric excitement as everyone gets ready in the days leading up to balolo. November is *Vula i Balolo Levu*, the month for the big balolo night, and there are home-made nets, baskets, buckets and fishing lines ready and waiting in all the houses along the road. The one night a year when millions of balolo, tiny sea worms, come up from the deep and transform the surface of the ocean into a billowing, undulating carpet. The small deep-water serpent that's lifted up by the full moon for one single, magical night to lay its eggs and sperm in a gelatinous soup – it's a gastronomic delicacy the people of Korototoka can't get enough of.

I'll never forget our first year, the descriptions I heard of the balolo's fantastic colours; how they could vary from red to blue and iridescent green, brown and yellow. I was slightly less enthused when Ateca explained that only the torso of the serpent floats up to spawn: 'The heads are left in caves at the bottom of the sea!'

Her eager description of the way one would gorge oneself on the slimy little worms hit me with a wave of nausea. 'We love balolo, Madam Kat! We scoop it up with our hands – like this!' She made scooping motions with her hand and shovelled big handfuls of air into her gaping mouth. 'Or we boil it with herbs, or fry it. Or put it in the lovo.'

I gagged at the thought, picturing the glow-in-the-dark worms in their sticky, swimming millions. Niklas, on the other hand, was rapt as Ateca went on. She explained that it was crucial to be ready at precisely the right minute, in the shallows or in a canoe, when the sea suddenly changed colour under the full moon and became a swaying mass of rainbow-coloured worms. Who only had a few breathless hours to complete their fertilization cycle, chased by nets and buckets from one side, greedy fish from the other. 'We don't have much time,' Ateca went on. 'When the sun comes up, the balolo sinks back to the bottom of the sea and puts its head back on.'

I shuddered, but Niklas asked, 'How do you know exactly when it's going to happen?'

Ateca looked at us patiently, as if she wasn't sure how thoroughly she should bother to explain.

'We know when it's the right *vula*, the right month, Mister Niklas. And when the bananas are ripe on the tree and it's time for the *tivoli* harvest, that's when the balolo comes.'

I nodded. Why would you need more explanation than that?

But I was never tempted to go out with them. If Niklas wanted to sit in a shallow canoe and rock back and forth in a crawling sea of worms, roe and milt, let him.

Was he upset? Disappointed with my lack of enthusiasm? I tried to compensate for it by going down to the beach that first time. When we were woken by the knocking on the door – 'Balolo! Balolo is here!' – I got out of bed and went with him. The undulating, rippling ocean, the smell of raw, headless bottom-feeders. The chaos on shore, the men leaping into their boats. Salote running with a bucket in each hand, Ateca and Vilivo, Litia with her daughters-in-law. Niklas's face aglow with anticipation as he climbed in the boat with Jone. I stood and looked out after them for a while, tracing the shadow moving further and further away, swaying in a living, multicoloured swarm. A journey I chose not to take with him, illuminated by a moon that followed me all the way home.

I was in a deep sleep when he returned, and didn't even notice him lying down next to me. When he woke up, I made coffee and asked how it had been. 'So, did you eat raw balolo with Jone and Vilivo?'

He laughed in response. Tossed his thick, white hair and laughed a rolling belly laugh. 'If you choose not to come on an adventure, you have no right to ask questions afterwards!'

He never asked if I wanted to come along after that. Just slipped out of the bed as soon as the loud knock came on the door; I barely heard him when he tiptoed back in the next morning.

That November night a year and a half ago is now a series of flickering, out-of-focus pictures. Driftwood dancing on the waves. But I know I woke up, know I heard Akuila's deep voice outside: 'Balolo, Mister Niklas! We're going out now!' I know I lay there, quiet in the dark, and saw his silhouette in the doorway as he left.

I watched him go, but didn't say anything. He went out alone.

What remains from that night? Pieces of dreams and lies and hopes. Things I've heard, stories that are no longer told. But I'm sure that I didn't run down to the boats on the beach. That I imagined what it would look like down there, but wasn't there. I know I pictured Litia with her biscuit tin, her sullen scowl softened by the prospect of a delicious meal. I heard Jone's voice as he ordered his sons around, pictured Vilivo hurrying down to the beach to shovel down handfuls of teeming worms. But I didn't go down. I wasn't standing there when Sai came running with the little girl in tow, the girl with caramel-brown curls and light, golden skin. I wasn't there when Niklas passed by them, mother and daughter. When he hurried past them without stopping, sat upright in Akuila's canoe and started to prep his

162

camera equipment. When Sai stood beside Ateca and some of the other women – Litia with her biscuit tin and Jone's daughters holding a fine-mesh fishing net attached to two bamboo poles between them – I was in bed, in my bedroom. And when Akuila's canoe returned, was emptied of buckets and basins, and turned around to head back out, I had no idea that Niklas had stayed at the water's edge: 'You guys go out, I'm going to take a few pictures from here. I think I've had enough raw balolo for now.' The laughter in his voice, I'm just imagining it, I didn't hear it. And when he cast a quick glance at Sai and the little girl before turning his back, I wasn't there.

I've heard the story in various long-winded versions. In poorly written police reports, in Ateca's weeping desperation. 'I've talked to everyone, Madam Kat, and no one saw it. Everyone thought he'd gone home, he'd said to Akuila that he'd had enough balolo. No one heard anything either. He would have shouted if he needed help, right? But no one heard anything. You have to believe it was his heart, Madam Kat. Like it says in the police papers. His heart stopped, and he fell and got caught in the mangrove roots. They're long and tangled, Madam Kat, and Mister Niklas . . . they think he got stuck with his head underwater. And when Jone's son found him . . . Solomone was walking a little further down the beach with his net, and that's when he saw him. There, in the water.'

At this point in Ateca's story, I always have to nod. This is the precise point at which we trade places and it becomes my job to comfort Ateca, to assure her that there's nothing she could have done, there's nothing anyone could have done.

And I wasn't there. It's the pictures in my head, the album I flip through in my sleep, that makes me invent things. Makes me retrace my steps over to the window and see his back with the black camera backpack disappear as he walks towards the boats and the shouting, exhilarated crowd. It's the things I've been told that form pictures in my mind of the boats going out, myself pulling on a pair of jeans and a checked shirt and sitting there in the dark, fully dressed. I have no emotions about these pictures, no thoughts in my head. Like a film, I watch myself sitting still for a long, long time. And then, going outside and down the porch stairs, walking towards the shouting on the shore, but staying in the shadows, behind the strip of stiff grass and coconut palms that divide the beach from the houses further inland. I know it's only my confusion, fragments of wishes and fears, that plays the film reel in my mind's eye at night. I didn't sit there in the dark behind the boat pulled up on the beach, didn't see a tall figure with a backpack walking slowly out among the mangrove trees and bending down towards the surface with his eye pressed against the viewfinder. I wasn't the one who saw him stumble, wave his arms and fall forward. Reach out his hands to catch himself and drop the camera before his body sank headfirst into knee-deep water with a soft, inaudible splash. I wasn't the one who stood there, unmoving, without a sound. It wasn't me. I wasn't there.

27
Ateca

There's something I don't understand, Lord. Madam Sina's son is coming to Korototoka, but why isn't he staying with her? There's plenty of room in Vale nei Kat, but that's not what the madams want. Salote has other guests, so I told Madam Kat that Mosese and Litia have a spare room. But I regretted it later, Lord. Madam Kat has been here in Fiji so long, but she still doesn't understand that for iTaukei, hospitality is a duty. She didn't see that it was impossible for Mosese to say no.

Madam Sina isn't happy that her son is coming. Her face is hard, like the stones around the foundations of the house. Madam Sina is sa qase, old. She gave her son food and money for school and clothes. He's an adult now – shouldn't he be taking responsibility for her? I asked whether he was sick, but she said no. And when I asked if it was hard for young men to get a job in his village, too, there was both laughter and tears in her voice. 'Armand isn't young,' she said. 'He's almost fifty, but he doesn't understand that.' How could her son not know how old he is? Hasn't he gone to school?

Maybe Madam Sina is ashamed, I can understand that. I'm ashamed in front of Madam Kat, Lord, although it's not Vilivo's fault! Mister Niklas paid my son's way through school, but even though he has papers, he can't find a job. I don't understand it. The roads are bad, the bridges are collapsing in the rainy season, the seabed is full of sea cucumbers that the Chinese pay good money for, and there's still no work to be found?

There are so many signs that make me afraid, Lord. I've heard the barn owl hoot many times. That empty, cold sound that warns of danger. And I think it's going to thunder tonight; the snake god is tossing and turning in the mountainside.

Dear God, let Madam Sina's son understand how old he is, and let her be happy that he's coming.

In Jesus' holy name. Emeni.

28

Ingrid

It's not just her feet that are experiencing a new spring in Fiji. Her thoughts, her shoulders, her smile – Ingrid can feel everything becoming looser and smoother. There's a fair balance in the world. Isn't that what she's always known deep inside? That those who work and wait and hold out will finally get to fill their mouths with chocolate?

Some of the equipment they need for the sweet house has already arrived. She and Kat unpacked it yesterday: the new oven, the rolling machine that's going to finely grind the cocoa mass. Ateca has promised that Vilivo can help assemble it all; Ingrid just hopes he can do it without breaking anything. Her thoughts flit to Johnny; it would be best if he could make another trip out here again. Just to help us get started, she tells herself. No ulterior motive. One night doesn't automatically turn into more. Happiness isn't a guest you can just invite back in.

Sometimes it feels as if it couldn't have happened. The narrow bed in the room in Salote's house, the light they didn't switch on. The curtainless window covered by a mosquito net. The smell of sweat; his, her own. And as she walked home, the daylight that came, the same bird that called out to her again, crisp and clear. Her steps lighter than before.

It did happen. Ingrid knows it. Wildrid runs the images through her head every night. And Kat knows. Thank goodness Kat knows.

The thought of Sina makes a shadow fall over her breakfast plate. Sina has only just had a taste of freedom, Ingrid thinks. Her stubborn I-don't-care demeanour has softened, and she's spending more and more time in the kitchen with Ateca to wrest the secrets of roro cooking away from her – how the big rough leaves of the dalo plant must be salted and stirred to exactly the right softness so they don't bring scratchy discomfort to the throat. She has even tried a sentence or two in vosa vaka-Viti, causing Ateca to burst into the occasional howl of laughter – and Sina's not usually the one to inspire glee.

But now this. Armand. And the bleeding. Which has increased, and gone from something Sina played down to something the doctor insists she take seriously. That, too, Ingrid thinks: that she could even sit down last night and tell them straight out what the doctor had said, that's all part of what the Fijian sunshine has done to them. Warmed them, opened them up. And now, is it going to be over for Sina before it's even begun?

She's not going to let worry take over this morning, though. Ingrid stares down at her hands as she brushes crumbs off her lap: wrinkles and knobbly knuckles, the veins like thick, well-fed worms. But her skin is healthy and well-moisturized; the pores plumped with the tropical nectar that is the very air down here, she thinks. An organic collagen injection into every cell, with no side effects and very encouraging long-term effects. Ingrid gets to her feet.

New experiences await her. It's Sunday, and she's going to church. Not because she finds the toll of the bells irresistible, but because this is yet another piece she wants to add to the puzzle that is Fiji.

She noticed it from the start, that Sundays are sacred here, just the way she remembers them from her childhood: softened, dampened days on which even the weather, rain or shine, was toned down. The difference here is their joy, Ingrid thinks. The anticipation shining in the eyes of the people on their way to church, the evident certainty that they're about to take part in something good. Or had it been present in Reitvik Church too, in the faces of the single women scattered like black raindrops in the pews on the few occasions she'd been there? Confirmations and a wedding now and then; the last time she was in church must have been ten years ago, when Petter was baptized. Had the same happy conviction been hidden there too, in the out-of-focus pale faces behind the hymn books? She's rarely given it much thought; church and religion have played minor parts in her life.

But it's a different story here. Church doesn't just play a major role in Fiji; it's the warp and the woof, a cornerstone of society. 'Along with the system of local chiefs, of course,' Maya had elaborated when they'd discussed it a while ago. Although she sometimes goes off track, Maya's mini-lectures on the local culture have often been more helpful in navigating unexpected situations than Kat's half-baked explanations, Ingrid thinks.

'Most *iTaukei*, ethnic Fijians, are Methodist, and a significant portion of the Indo-Fijian population belong to the same church,' Maya had read aloud that night, from one of her innumerable articles and books about Fiji.

Ingrid had lost the thread briefly when Kat took over and started talking about the thorny relationship between the church and the self-proclaimed prime minister Bainimarama after the military coup a few years ago; politics in this country was a complicated landscape, she'd gathered that much. She understood that the coup leader held the real power, that the president was a figurehead, and that the Methodist church had to suffer both censorship and political intervention.

But what really captivates Ingrid, the reason she's sitting here this morning in a newly pressed *jaba*, waiting for Ateca, is the weekly procession down the road. Every Sunday morning, long before the church bells start tolling, the villagers pour out of their homes, headed for the houses of God. Most of them to Father Iosefa's Methodist church, some to the white chapel where the Assemblies of God congregation gathers. A colourful, yet restrained and dignified sight: the men for once out of their loud patterned bula shirts, instead wearing white short-sleeved collared shirts with ties over their dark, knee-length, formal sulus. The women in their finest jabas; many in white, shimmery rayon. Just-washed, damp, curly hair, fresh flowers tucked behind their ears, Bibles in thatched rectangular bags woven especially for this purpose. Neatly groomed children wearing shoes for the occasion, little girls with their hair in tight braids, and boys dressed like miniature versions of their fathers, in dark sulus and clunky sandals. Dishes covered in tinfoil are carried high above heads: scones or cassava cake or boiled dalo to be devoured over a communal lunch after the service. There are smiles and enthusiastic chatter, but the unrestrained belly laughs are missing from the procession of people on their way to church on Sunday morning. A peaceful joy, Ingrid thinks. Not a forced march to church out of fear or coercion. A hushed sense of anticipation at the start of a holy day.

Ateca waves from down the road. '*Ni sa yadra*, Madam Ingrid, good morning! Are you ready?'

The girl they call Star of the Sea stands beside her. Holding a basket, she nods to Ingrid without a smile.

'I brought Maraia today,' Ateca says. 'Her sister is sick, so Sai couldn't get away from home.'

Ingrid smiles. 'How nice that you want to come to church with us, Maraia.'

The girl's eyes are filled with a golden light, her tiny voice is strong and sure. 'When someone calls, we must come.'

Of course the whole thing is in Fijian, Ingrid hadn't thought about that. She's picked up a word of the language here and there, but knows she won't be able to follow a long sermon. She copies Ateca and the others and kicks off her shoes; barefoot seems to be the norm in the church pews. But when the organ, just as excruciatingly sluggish as she remembers it from home, pipes in with the first hymn, she forgets to worry about understanding the language. The members of the little choir, shuffling their sheet music, look pitiful, standing in a corner by the altar, but when they open their mouths and belt out the first note, she is startled. A full vocal orchestra chimes in behind her, in front of her and all around her; deep, resounding voices in soft, perfect harmony. The whole packed church, standing, sings in several parts, verse after sonorous verse, so both organ and

171

choir fade into the background. Ingrid holds on to the pew in front of her with both hands; the singing thunders through the church and up to the ceiling, meets the sunlight pouring through the open side doors. It beats and rumbles through her body, embraces the wooden cross on the wall by the choir. When the last note glides over into a long hold of '*Emeeeni*', she glances at Ateca, astonished.

'You all harmonize like a . . . choir of angels! How did you learn this?'

Ateca shrugs. 'The ear and the voice know what notes belong together. They're friends. One knows what the other needs. You just let the notes come into your mouth and flow out between your lips.'

She smiles and folds her hands in her lap. A slow and heavy man comes up the centre aisle and begins to read from a sheet of paper. Ingrid recognizes a few words as names, names of men and women, and there's nodding and sighing all around her. Ateca leans in towards her. 'He's telling us who needs help, who's grieving, who's sick, and who we should pray for.'

Back in Norway, Ingrid might have looked away and smiled politely. But here, barefoot in a long skirt, her body still filled with sparkling song, the only thing she can do is nod and wonder.

'I'm heading home now,' she says softly to Ateca when the blessing is complete and Father Iosefa leads the procession down the centre aisle to stand in the doorway and greet each congregant on their way out. The silver cross on his chest glitters in the white light.

'But it's time for the lunch!'

'I know, Ateca, but I promised to go home and help Kat with . . .'

She can't quite find the words to complete her white lie, but it doesn't matter. Ateca knows as well as Ingrid that the service and the singing have been enough for her to take in this morning.

Ateca flashes a wide, calm smile. 'See you tomorrow.'

From inside the sanctuary, they can hear cups clinking and a man's voice bursting into a peal of laughter.

She takes the long way home. Instead of walking past the chief's bure and down the main road, Ingrid goes the opposite way, through a cassava field and down to the beach.

She knows she wants to stay in Fiji. There's nothing she misses about the County Bus Service office with its grey cubicles and the humming printer in the corner. Not the lunch breaks when everyone always sits in the same seats, not her co-worker's long-winded stories about his dachshund's kidney stones.

Her apartment is empty for now but she's planning to have Kjell arrange for a tenant starting in the autumn. Not that she's desperate for money – her savings go a long way down here – but she no longer needs the security of an empty apartment waiting for her back home. Kjell will moan and complain, no doubt, but he'll help her. Her brother will see the wisdom in getting a return on the unused capital that's just sitting there gathering dust. As long as she doesn't ask him to sell it. Property, the only truly safe investment; he won't help her rid herself of that. Ingrid will have to settle for renting it out.

Wildrid wants to sell up. Wildrid doesn't look back, doesn't cling to old security blankets. Wildrid wants to sell her place back home and buy into *Kat's Chocolate*. Acquire a share of Jone's boat, plant yellow honeydew in the field behind Kat's house – why wouldn't the Rakiraki market learn to accept something new? Wildrid has no patience for learning the meticulous art of straw-weaving, but she wants to dance on the mat's firm, soft surface, sit cross-legged and pound her fists into the floor in a meke. Unlike Ingrid, Wildrid can dance: since her big feet have always been bare-foot, she can stomp with the right force and intuitive rhythm as she sings and claps along with the drums. Wildrid totally masters the hip-swinging, the rotating pelvic pulse that makes the masi-cloth draped around the sulu crackle when she twirls around in age-old stories that can only be told through movement. What use does Wildrid have for an apartment in Norway? She's on the verge of buying a bra made of coconut half-shells!

Ingrid rounds the corner down by the cassava field that nobody seems to own, and catches her first glimpse of the ocean. The glinting white flashes across her field of vision, sparks behind her eyelids. Wildrid laughs and throws her arms wide open.

Kat is sitting by the sewing machine when Ingrid gets home. The needle works its way across a colourful piece of bula fabric, red and white flowers on an orange back-ground. She stops when she sees Ingrid in the doorway, unplugs the sewing machine and gets to her feet. 'Let's go and sit outside for a while. Do you mind checking if there's any iced tea left in the fridge?'

The afternoon slumps hot and heavy over Vale nei Kat. A pool of condensation forms around the pitcher on the table; Kat shuts her eyes and nearly dozes off. But a heavy, pulsating beat is still rippling through Ingrid's hips, and she tosses the question on the table. 'Can you dance, Kat?'

Something in her stings when she realizes she doesn't know the answer. She and Kat, haven't they been best friends for ever? And yet, a faded memory of their high-school dance in the mid-1960s, that's not what she means. She's wondering if Kat can . . . *dance*?

A long sideways glance under a pair of sunglasses perched high on her forehead. 'You mean Fijian? Meke?'

Ingrid nods. That's what she means.

'No, not really. I've watched a lot of mekes, but it can be complicated. It's a story, kind of, about a historic event or something. The same steps and moves are repeated in many of them, but I don't think it's something you can just' – she lifts her hands and forms air quotes around the word – ' "learn".'

Ingrid waits as Kat tries to explain. 'Meke is more than a dance, it's . . . a way of passing down stories. Ensuring that myths and traditions survive.'

'Like our folk tales,' Maya's voice chimes in. She suddenly appears at the bottom of the steps, peering up at Kat and Ingrid. Her pale forehead is moist with beads of sweat under the frizzy red mop of hair; she fans herself with the straw hat in her hand. 'God, it's hot!'

'Well, you *are* out walking at the worst possible time of day,' Kat says and gets up from the chair in the shade. 'Come and have a drink. I'll get you a glass.'

She sets out towards the screen door, but halts and turns

around. 'It's not quite the same as our folk tales, actually. Meke is more concerned with the spiritual. A connection to the other side, in a way, where the ancestors live.'

Ingrid has stretched out in the hammock; she closes her eyes and sways back and forth. Maya grows quiet in her chair; the thunder of waves crashing in over the deserted beach is the only sound. A heavy rumble rolling in, deep and vibrating, and then lighter, fluttering notes as the waves roll back out. The symphony envelops Ingrid and the hammock floats away in a cascade of song, filling her ears so the blood rushes to her head.

Wildrid is stomping with bare feet. She bows her head behind the woven fan as the dancers enter in procession, clapping their hollow, curved palms to the beat of the thumping dance drum, *lali ni meke*. A garland made of pink frangipani flowers and vibrant green leaves adorns her neck; the scent covers her face like a veil. Her hips start to rotate, gathering up the story to be told. Spears brandished by men with faces painted black; the chief's beautiful daughters, traded for costly whale teeth. Canoes paddled with rhythmic strokes; gods raging and fighting until islands sink into the sea. What was once here and must never be forgotten.

Ingrid's Sunday jaba has a border of purple flowers. In the quiet heat on the porch, they sway back and forth, big and blossoming, like a wish someone has just said out loud.

29

Lisbeth

'It's disgusting,' Lisbeth says with a shudder, and lights a cigarette. 'Just revolting, plain and simple! What kind of swine would do something like this?'

The headlines appear in the local newspaper almost daily, usually hidden at the bottom of a page towards the back: 'Grandfather Sentenced to 18 Months for Raping Grandchild.' 'Sexual Abuse of 10-year-old Daughter.' 'Baby Raped, 39-year-old Arrested.'

'I can't imagine it. But I guess it happens all over the world.' She sighs and blows out a cloud of smoke.

'Mm-hmm.' Kat gives her a long look. 'It does. But the statistics here in the South Pacific are worse than the world average. They say that on a global scale, one in three women will experience rape or abuse over the course of her life. In the South Pacific it's three out of five.'

'Oh dear me, but why?' Lisbeth furrows her eyebrows. 'I thought the culture here emphasized . . . protecting their own, in a way?'

'Yes.' Kat takes a moment to think. 'But "culture" is a word that can cover up a lot of crap. It's part of the "culture" here for men to help themselves to women, even little girls. And the vast majority of rapes and assaults are never reported.'

'Why not?'

'Because the assailant is usually a family member. Children here are surrounded by big brothers and uncles and cousins and grandfathers who come and go as they please; these are people they grow up with. So if a girl is raped by an uncle she's known her whole life, how easy is it to then take it to the police? It'll have consequences for the whole family – the whole village, most likely. So they'd rather keep quiet.'

'Well, this isn't the only place that happens, goddammit!'

Sina's voice is hard and jagged. Lisbeth peers at her inquisitively. For the most part, neither of them gets too involved in what she quietly calls the mini-lectures at Vale nei Kat; it's usually Kat and Ingrid, and sometimes Maya, who do the talking. But right now, all eyes are on Sina.

'It's hardly news that men can't keep it in their pants. It's always been that way.'

Something foreign and wounded lies beneath her terse words. Lisbeth stares at her, but Sina doesn't meet her gaze. A sudden silence sinks over the porch. Sina's chair creaks as she leans forward and grabs Lisbeth's cigarette case. 'And we trust them, too, don't we? That's not exactly unique to Fiji?'

Lisbeth leans back, sees that the hand holding the match is quivering slightly.

'What pisses me off' – Sina's voice is calmer now – 'is when they tell us to watch how we dress. How we behave. Us! As if that has anything to do with whose fault it is. And by the way' – she hesitates a moment – 'it's not just women with short skirts and great tits who are exposed to sex.'

Lisbeth stiffens; is Sina hinting at her? What a strange

178

thing to say, 'exposed to sex'. Like a sudden rainstorm or a car accident. She waits for Sina to continue.

But Sina doesn't, and the surprise over her outburst is tempered by sorrow; it floats out over their heads in the grey cigarette smoke.

'You mean rape?' Lisbeth asks finally.

Sina shrugs, as if she's suddenly lost all interest. 'Call it whatever you want.'

'Well, most of us do like it – being exposed to sex, as you say.' Kat chuckles. 'The consensual kind, that is.'

Sina shrugs again. She obviously has no intention of contributing further to this discussion.

'Well, that's one of the things we're here for, isn't it?' Lisbeth dares to speak up again. 'How else would children be brought into the world?'

'Oh my God, Lisbeth, sex isn't just about making babies!'

Lisbeth squirms and mumbles, 'No, no . . .' But in the next moment, Kat's trumpeting laughter spurts out across the porch and Lisbeth is sure she misunderstood, that her friend didn't mean to rebuke her.

'I don't have children, but I've been exposed to sex, as Sina calls it, and been happy about it. Haven't you all?'

She looks around with challenging Kat eyes, but her laughter rolls down the walls and lands on the floor. Sits there, butting up against the skirting board, like a day-old deflated balloon.

'It's like fårikål.'

Maya's tone is matter-of-fact recalling the traditional, pungent dish of boiled cabbage and mutton on the bone, seasoned with whole black peppercorns.

'There's nothing better when you only get it once in a

while. Seasonally. But if it were on your plate every day, you'd eventually start to lose your appetite for mutton. Sometimes the smell is enough. Or just the thought of it fills you up.'

Lisbeth is not the only one grinning now, she knows Kat and Sina are picturing the same thing she is: a naked Steinar with twisted ram's horns covering his ears. His pointy nose quivering, sniffing boiled cabbage and peppercorns.

'What fills you up?'

Ingrid appears around the corner of the house, flashes an oblivious smile and holds out a large plastic bowl of green beans. 'These will be great for dinner. What were you saying, what fills you up?' She kicks off her flip flops at the bottom of the stairs.

'Nothing,' Kat says, laughter still dancing in her voice. 'At least I hope not quite yet.' She throws the ball right into Ingrid's lap. 'What about you? Are you done with sex?'

Ingrid freezes on the bottom step. She turns in surprise towards Kat's curious, carefree grin. Lisbeth feels the empathy well up inside her. Poor Ingrid! With her lumpy body and her big feet. The sharp eyes, and the clothes that cry out for help. Poor, poor Ingrid! How could Kat be so heartless?

But Ingrid's not offended; she doesn't pick up the bowl of beans and walk stiff and indignant into the house. On the contrary. She takes off the scarf wrapped around her head and dries her face with it.

'No, why?' she tosses the ball back to Kat. 'I think I'm just getting started!'

Her laughter is playful, as if she's sharing a joke with Kat alone. 'Or do you all think the ship has sailed for a pale kaivalagi?'

Lisbeth does a double take, staring at her. Is this really Ingrid talking?

It is and it isn't. The thick, bristling hair is definitely Ingrid's, but it's flicking outwards at the ends, suddenly taking up more space. Her brown eyes are make-up free as always, but there's someone stirring in there, someone with glittery eyeshadow and bright-red lips. Her hips in the faded sulu are wide and heavy, but Lisbeth spies deep, swaying rhythm in them, a fearless claim.

'It's not over until the lights are turned off,' Ingrid says, smiling mysteriously, before grabbing the beans and disappearing into the house. 'And I don't intend for that to happen any time soon!'

The slam of the screen door echoes in the air for a few seconds.

'Well, I'll say!'

It's Sina who breaks the silence. 'Still waters and all that!'

Kat laughs. 'Ingrid knows how to tell it!'

Lisbeth looks around, confused – is she missing something here? But before she can process the thought, Kat's eyes fall on her again.

'And you, Lisbeth? You're not having any more children, so it's over for you, then?'

Lisbeth puts out her cigarette and folds her bony hands in her lap. Pictures her strong, agile, red-nailed fingers in an elaborate dance across Harald's back. He liked to feel the scratching down his shoulderblades; not too hard, not to draw blood, just enough so she wasn't just 'lying there like a lump of dough'. 'That's the absolute worst,' he'd said one of the first times they slept together, 'when the woman just lies there like a sack of potatoes.' She'd nodded and smiled, and made sure to keep moving. To run her nails carefully down the freckled skin of his back, to stop just in time when he flipped her on her stomach and held both of her wrists locked in an iron grip above her head while he finished. The smack on her bum afterwards. 'You know you're a hot piece of ass.' The gratitude she had felt. For being a hot piece of ass.

'Of course it's not just for making babies,' she says, feeling her face flush bright red. 'Of course it's good . . . for us too. It's only . . . natural,' she stutters at last. She could never bring herself to call it hot. Has it ever been that? Hot? *Being* hot, she's enjoyed that thoroughly. But thinking *it's* hot – has she ever?

Suddenly it's in her nose. The smell of the young man's sweat; a dark, pungent prickling. The flex of his arm muscles as he helped her up from the ground. The strong, hard chest she pressed up against. The shame cascades silently through her – he pushed her away! But the heat remains in her body, a throbbing red heat she can't remember the last time she felt. A reverberating wish that makes her hands tense up in her lap as she forces them to stay still. What if I'd said it? *I want you; can I have you?*

*

One week later, she sees him again. Lisbeth and Ingrid have been to Rakiraki with the truck, Vilivo behind the wheel. Ingrid had insisted she could drive but Kat had been sceptical. 'The traffic's horrible right now because of the sugar harvest; the trucks drive like maniacs to get in line at the mill in Ba.' She'd been right: they ended up behind teetering towers of sugar cane and were constantly passed by more trucks with even higher and more precarious loads.

The new gaskets for the water pump, which had been on the blink, were on the truck bed along with a sack of the imported rice Kat loves, and new upholstery material for the cushions on the wicker couch.

Lisbeth is bowled over by the heat and is half dozing, pressed up against the window, when they approach Korototoka. Suddenly Vilivo slams on the brakes and she is hurtled forward before the seat belt stops her.

'Sorry, ma'am, I just have to go talk to my friend Salesi, over there, on the rugby pitch. Just a minute!'

She looks behind her. Ingrid is in a deep sleep on the back seat. She turns back round and follows Vilivo with her eyes as he jogs over to the trampled grass. It looks as if there's a break in the game: most of the guys are sitting in the shade, some are throwing the ball loosely back and forth. Broad shoulders, short black shorts. Big hands around the oval rugby ball. Noise, roughhousing, pushing and shoving. One of them throws himself down on his back and spreads his arms wide. Now Lisbeth sees there are girls there, too, around the edge of the circle. Slender brown arms, their hair in perky buns, shyness behind waves of teasing laughter. In denim cut-offs they sit cross-legged, sipping from plastic bottles of yellow soda. Vilivo approaches the circle, where one guy has just jokingly pushed a girl over on her back. She giggles and kicks in his direction; long calves dance in the shadow play under the tree. The guy bends over and grabs one of her ankles, pretends that he's going to drag her along the ground away from the others. She squeals in protest and whacks her bottle in his direction. As Vilivo steps up to them, the guy releases the flailing girl. He gets up and turns towards Vilivo, greets his friend with a wide grin. Lisbeth feels the redness in her face pour down the rest of her body like a shower. She wants to sink down into her seat, disappear behind her sunglasses. It's him. The smooth upper arms with clumsy blue tattoos. The genuine concern in his eyes: 'Ma'am, are you OK?' The shoes on his feet are shiny and new. Black, with neon green stripes down the sides.

The guys are done talking. Her assailant high-fives Vilivo and turns back towards the girl. Tears up a tuft of grass and throws it at her before nudging her in the arm. She shouts and explodes in a string of vowels that mix glee-fully with his laughter.

30

Kat

He looks exactly the way I pictured him. A combination of shabby cowboy and pathetic business fiasco – am I being cruel? A black leather jacket hanging over his arm, a pastel blue shirt with sweat marks down his back, unbuttoned one button too far. His stomach sagging over the big shiny buckle of his belt.

But when Armand Guttormsen embraces his mother, it's with something resembling happiness. He towers over Sina's plump figure and holds her tight. I keep my distance until the moment of reunion has passed, and his handshake surprises me – it's firm and long. 'So this is the plantation owner,' he says in a hearty, booming voice. 'Thank you for coming to get me.'

Coming to get him – did I have a choice? His smiling courtesy makes it difficult to be as curt as I'd planned, and the words that come out of my mouth are, 'It's the least I could do.' His smile grows wider; he obviously agrees.

He dozes off for most of the car ride. A day and a half of travelling is exhausting, and he has a problem with his back, unfortunately. He's had it for years, he tells us as he wiggles around in the passenger seat. 'And there's not exactly a lot of room to stretch out in those cramped plane seats. If you can afford to fly business, it's another story, but . . .'

Sina turns away in embarrassment, as if it's her fault that poor Armand has to travel in economy class. I feel the irritation prickling. 'Well, there aren't many people who can afford a ticket to Fiji at all. It's expensive enough, right?'

Instead of answering, Armand turns towards his mother in the back seat. 'I didn't get much for your car, by the way. There was more rust on it than I'd realized.'

He lowers his voice now but I can still hear him. 'When my partner gets started on the Lithuania business for real, you'll get your money back. With interest, I promise.'

I can see Sina's blank stare in the mirror; it glides off her son's face and out the side window. He turns towards the front again. 'I think I'll take a quick snooze, if that's OK. You don't have anything to drink, do you? Some water or something? A beer would taste pretty damn good right now, if I'm being honest.'

When we get home, Lisbeth and Ingrid have lunch ready. They smile at Armand's compliments, and Lisbeth keeps heaping more food on to his plate. She's wearing more eyeshadow than usual, and a necklace with large, flashy rhinestones around her neck. She giggles when he gives her a flirty wink; Lisbeth can't help being Lisbeth, after all. But even Ingrid laughs at his lame quips. I find myself needing some air and invent an errand I have to run in the village. 'I'll be back in an hour or so,' I tell Armand. 'Then I can walk you over to Mosese and Litia's house so you can see where you're going to stay.'

'There's no rush,' he replies without looking in my direction. 'I'm perfectly fine here.'

He leans in towards his mother and pats her hand on the

table. In a loud, jovial voice, 'I'm so glad to see you're doing well here, Mum.'

Salote sits on the top step outside her house. She waves to me as I approach. 'Bula, Madam Kat! Do you need something?'

She gets to her feet and pulls out the key to the padlock.

I shake my head and tell her I just felt like going for a walk. 'I've spent too much time sitting in the car today, Salote.'

The shop owner is well-informed as usual. 'Yes. You've been to the airport.'

'That's right. Sina's son got here today.'

'Yes. The big *bosso* from Australia.'

I try to clarify. 'Sina's son isn't from Australia; he's from the same country as me. Norway. In Europe.'

Salote nods, no problem. In Korototoka, foreigner automatically means from Australia, which is plenty far enough away.

'And Armand isn't anybody's boss. As far as I know, anyway.'

Salote looks more sceptical at this. 'But he runs a business? That's what Ateca says, that he runs a business, like me.' She points proudly towards the padlock. 'Madam Sina told her he does a lot of different kinds of business. Internationally.' The last point is accompanied by a proud smile, as if she herself were running a major import and export business from her counter in front of the dusty shelves of biscuit packets and matchboxes.

Oh God. If this is what Ateca's been telling people, there's probably no end to the expectations Mosese and Litia have for their new lodger. Armand Guttormsen has only been here half a day, and he's already given me several

187

headaches. But this isn't something I can discuss with Salote, and I force a smile.

'Sina's proud of her son,' I say quickly. 'I guess all mothers are.'

We sit back down on her front steps.

'Ateca says he's in good health, even though there's white in his hair,' Salote says.

We agree that it's best when people are in good health. She wants to know where his wife is, and how many children he has. I tell her Armand isn't married, has no children.

'Why not?'

Again, I wonder what Ateca's been saying. I tell her there are many kaivalagi who don't get married or have children. That they move out of their parents' house and live alone and work. Salote starts laughing so hard she coughs, and I have to slap her on the back.

'What's the point of that?' she asks when she catches her breath.

That night we celebrate Armand's arrival with a glass of wine. Ingrid plays hostess, with beans and pumpkin from the garden, and even Lisbeth seems to like the chicken, although it's swimming in a thick, fatty sauce. The two bottles I've been keeping in the pantry are gone in the blink of an eye, and I have to shake my head when Armand suggests another round. 'A toast to Mum, I think, who's been lucky enough to find this wonderful coop of hens. And no rooster to bother you either!'

He laughs so hard at his own joke that he barely hears me respond apologetically that no, unfortunately the wine supply in the Women's House has now run dry.

'So,' he says, and leans back in his chair with ease. 'What is it you're up to these days? Cocoa?'

I nod, and can feel my smile growing stiff. It's cocoa we're up to.

'Is there any money in that? I mean, is that the big business down here?'

I'm too tired to be offended. I know I'm never actually going to have a serious conversation about the commercial side of the farm with Armand Guttormsen.

'We manage,' is all I say.

He furrows his pale, almost pink brow. 'I'm just thinking of Mum,' he says. 'I just want to make sure she's secure.'

I have to bite my tongue to hold the swear words back. What the hell is he sitting there and saying? That I'm financially responsible for Sina now? And he wants to make sure I'm up to the task? My eyes dart over to Sina, who is staring at the table and fiddles with a spoon. My sleepiness is gone; I'm gasping for words.

But I don't have to say anything. It's Ingrid, of all people, who shares our business concept with Sina's son.

'We're going to start making chocolate,' she says. 'Our own recipe. The taste of Fiji. Pure and simple. Pieces of happiness.'

Her voice when she says it – suddenly it dawns on me, a bittersweet realization. Ingrid finally knows a thing or two about happiness. The dark, succulent kind; the kind you stake your claim to.

Armand doesn't ask any more questions. He glances back and forth between Ingrid and me. Thinking, scheming, calculating.

Maya has already yawned a few times, and now she gets up and leaves the table. Sina shoves her chair back right away and follows her out. Armand looks at his mother, astonished. 'Are you going to bed already, Mum?'

I'm about to suggest that it might be a good idea for all of us to call it a night, but Lisbeth is one step ahead of me. 'Maya's tired,' she chimes in. 'She doesn't see so well in the dark, and Sina's kind and helps her out if she stumbles along the way. Especially after a little wine.' She smiles at Armand. The look she throws him leaves no doubt that this doesn't apply to her – Lisbeth can handle a glass or two whenever it may be, without letting it throw her off balance. She stands up suddenly. 'I can walk you over to Mosese's,' she offers casually. Pulls her green blouse down over her hips and runs her fingers through her hair. 'That way I can have a smoke on the way home.'

Armand shoves his plate away from him. 'Well, who can resist an offer like that?' he grins back. 'Can I nick one off you?'

He glances over at me. 'Thanks so much for a great meal. Will you tell Mum I said goodnight, and I'll see her tomorrow?'

He vanishes out the door with Lisbeth.

My head is dizzy and pounding. The two glasses of wine are spinning round and round in there, and I know I should go to bed. But Ingrid is still up, and I know she's thinking what I'm thinking. I turn towards her so sharply that my chair scrapes the floor. 'Can you believe that?'

Ingrid rolls her eyes. 'Incredibly rude. But we knew that. Maybe I shouldn't have told him about the chocolate. I don't know why I did that.'

I shrug my shoulders. It makes no difference. It's obvious Sina's son is greedy no matter what.

Ingrid heaves a deep sigh. Places both her elbows on the table.

'I think it might be a blessing not to have children,' she says. 'The fear of everything that could happen. The worrying about their future.'

I know exactly what she means, and complete her thought. 'The disappointment over how they turned out.'

A moment of silence. Maybe it's the wine, maybe it's Armand, I don't quite know why I say it. 'I would have preferred to have had a girl, myself.'

A caramel-blonde lock of hair, the squeeze of a small, narrow palm in mine.

Ingrid doesn't respond, and closes her eyes for so long I start to wonder if she's fallen asleep.

'Maybe,' she says eventually. 'That way, you think you might understand what makes them tick. I don't know.'

She takes a long pause before continuing.

'You haven't met Simon and Petter, Kjell's grandchildren. We have nothing in common, absolutely nothing. They live in a world I don't know the first thing about. But when they visit me, we have a nice time together. Simple. They don't expect anything other than good food, and I have no delusions about getting into their minds. There's no drama, no hopes to be fulfilled. Just . . . a nice time.'

I'm exhausted by this day, my head is swimming and I don't know where Ingrid is going with this. 'Because they're boys, you mean?'

I'm surprised at the belligerence in my own voice.

'Without the feelings . . . and the hopes and dreams – yes, call it drama if you like – there's no *intimacy*!'

A shadow falls over Ingrid's calm brown eyes, and she shakes her head firmly.

'That's not true. I love those boys. I've always been in their life. How many people can you say that about? Love and responsibility, they're intertwined.'

*

The night gives me no solace. I have one of those unbearable dreams where part of me knows I'm sleeping and that it isn't real, but I can't tear the other, terrified part of me out of the nightmare. I'm lying on the beach with my legs in the water, the tide comes in and I can't move. My arms and legs are paralysed, I can't speak, I can't cry for help. The water climbs higher and higher on my body; it's warm and comforting, lapping softly upwards. Still, the terror ripples through me. The only thing I can move are my eyeballs; I roll them from side to side in the hope of finding rescue. Seaweed sticks to my legs, little white crabs emerge from holes in the sand and dart up my body. Now only my face is above water; I inhale through my nose in desperation. A large, shimmering blue starfish washes up on a wave and embraces my throat, as if to console me. But I don't want consolation, I want to breathe, get up, be free! I lower my pupils down towards the pulsating sea creature, flash a signal with my eyes: go away! Leave me alone! Something soft tickles my chin, flows over my face with the water and waves, drowns me in golden-brown curls. The Star of the Sea looks at me with sorrowful eyes and fills my mouth with tears.

192

31

Ateca

Dear God, I know that in Heaven we'll all live in great wealth and glory. It doesn't matter how much or how little we have in this life. Please show me humility, and teach me to appreciate what I have.

But it's so hard to be poor, Lord! You know how much I want to give Vilivo what he wishes for. He never asks for unnecessary things, and it's not his fault that he doesn't have a job. And now that he's got this new chance! To play rugby for Korototoka against Nausori at their away game next Saturday. But he can't play on a real rugby league team without shoes, Lord! He hasn't even asked for the most expensive ones. 'Only eighty-nine dollars, Na, and they're really nice! Black with green stripes. The same ones Salesi has.' But eighty-nine dollars is almost a week's salary, Lord. And Mister Armand did offer! It wasn't my fault that he overheard me mentioning it to Madam Kat. 'Won't you let me be his rugby sponsor?' he said. 'To thank Ateca for securing me such great accommodation?' His smile hung in the air, big and round like a glistening fried egg in a skillet. I saw that Madam Kat didn't like it; her mouth was dissatisfied. But Mister Armand pushed and pushed until I finally said yes and thanked him. Afterwards I couldn't hold back my laughter; it rolled out of my mouth in big gulps. Mister Armand got scared and hurried out of the kitchen.

I don't think Madam Sina liked it either. She looked sad this afternoon, as if she'd heard bad news. Forgive me if I shouldn't have accepted the money, Lord. But it wasn't for me! And I've been thinking that Mister Armand probably has more than enough money.

I told Vilivo tonight that we can never accept anything else from Mister Armand. I'm sure he understood, though all he did was stick the money in his pocket without a word. Please help him, Lord. Help him and let him find work, so he can support himself, become an adult and start a family.

In Jesus' holy name. Emeni.

32

Maya

The strip of sand she's walking on grows narrower and narrower. Tall grass encroaches on the beach from uphill, the houses with thatched roofs grow smaller and disappear behind Maya. The rank stench of piles of sea-weed, half-rotten green coconuts and food waste makes her wrinkle her nose and halt.

She's standing on a beach. Maya looks down at her toes. The straps of her black flip flops are dusted with a fine layer of sand. She stops and removes them. Lifts up the long, floral skirt tied around her waist and walks carefully into the water. Stands there a while and lets the warmth of the white frothy waves envelop her feet, takes a few steps further out. Now she has to hike her skirt up higher. She looks down at her knees; the skin wrinkles over the round knee-caps. Lifts her gaze back out over the water – is she going swimming? No. Maya turns around and wades back to the beach. She lets her toes rest on the firm yet soft surface. The tender prickling under her feet flows up through her legs. She focuses inward, feels how the grains of sand circulate in her body, follow the bloodstream, slink between the cells. Maya sees a picture in her mind's eye: a yellowed chart she's pulled down over the chalkboard many times. The human body stripped of skin, red muscles, pink tendons. The circulatory system, the skeleton. The grains of sand rush through her, dance past the long quadriceps, glide softly up into her hip joint.

She stands perfectly still and shuts out the sound for as long as possible.

'Maya! Maaaya!'

The woman walking towards her has greyish-blonde hair, thin and lank. She shouts, waves her arms and looks agitated. When she catches up to Maya, she stands still for a moment, pulling herself together before she speaks.

'Look how far you've gone! Don't you remember we were supposed to have an early lunch? And go into Rakiraki this afternoon? Now the others have left without us.'

Maya looks at the woman blankly. Lunch? She can't remember whether she's eaten lunch. She just wants to stand here, with the sand and sun rippling through her body. She opens her mouth but the right words won't come. She tries, feels her mind searching, doing sweep after sweep, but no. The confusion upsets her, the sand swishes in her ears, she looks at the grey-blonde woman, pleading with her gaze: Help me!

'Come,' the woman says. Her eyes are kind, and Maya feels the murky wave recede, leaving her head above water.

Sina grabs her hand and turns her around slowly.

'Wait,' Maya says. She bends down and picks up her flip flops before they start walking back in the surf that erases all footsteps.

*

Why is Kat asking her for help? Maya eyes her friend suspiciously. It's evening in Vale nei Kat, and all Maya wants to

196

do is sit here and listen to the comforting sound of the waves. She traces the smoke from the man's cigarette with her eyes. Who is he again? He's pressed up against the thinnest of the women, who laughs loudly at something he says.

'You've taught a few Home Ec classes, haven't you?' Kat says convincingly and tugs at Maya's arm, trying to get her out of her chair. Maya yanks it back, irritated. 'Literature,' she says emphatically. 'Norwegian Literature and History.'

'OK.' Kat smiles. 'But can't you come and take a look with me anyway? I made a dress. It's finished, but I want to fasten some ribbon around the collar, and I can't make it look nice. Didn't you say you used to make a lot of your daughter's clothes when she was younger?'

Her daughter. Evy. Maya can feel her blonde hair between her fingers, thin and smooth, it was a struggle to gather it into a ponytail. The Christmas dress she made for her in the tartan material, green and red, the collar a shiny dark green. Ribbons down the sides for tying up in a big bow at the back. Maya lifts her hands in front of her, ties the bow again. She smiles at Kat and gets to her feet, walking past the man with the cigarette.

The machine is on the table in the corner; Maya knows she knows what it's for. She examines the orange material patterned with big flowers, the white ribbon rolled up next to it. She sits down in the chair and feels Kat's gaze like a murmur in her neck. Her hands pull out a long length of ribbon; she places it on the material, it looks pretty. White on red and orange – the colours fill her with anticipation, something is about to happen. She turns around and looks at Kat, and her friend nods encouragingly. 'Can you sew it on?' she asks.

Sew it on? The ribbon sits in Maya's hands, a twitching, unwelcome animal. She doesn't like to hold it. Doesn't know why she's sitting there. Why is Kat standing behind her, asking questions?

'No!' Maya says and stumbles to her feet so abruptly the chair falls backwards. She strides through the living room, not looking at anyone as she rushes down the porch steps and out the gate. She doesn't know what Kat is after. She doesn't understand what they all want. She can't be here!

The road is bumpy and there are no streetlights; still, her feet keep running. She looks down at them – why isn't she wearing shoes? And where's Steinar, why isn't he here to help her? She has to go home, she doesn't know what she's doing here on this dark road. Where is Steinar? The fear rips through her. She doesn't know why she's running up the hill; has she been here before? She has to stop after a while, her legs can't run any further. She has to rest, and looks around for a good spot. A path beside her leads to a house with a green chair planted outside the door. She can sit there. Maya takes a seat, rubs her feet to get the sand and mud off. Her feet are dirty.

'Is everything all right, Madam Maya? Can I help you?'

The man who comes outside knows her name. She's seen him before, but nothing is certain. There's something that won't quite clear up in her head, everything is murky, loose.

He looks at her a while. 'Wait here, Madam Maya,' he says. 'I'm going to get Ateca.'

As he walks away, she can see his legs are crooked, as if he's walked far. She gets up and keeps going uphill. It's night-time, and the big house at the top of the hill is dark.

A long beam runs across the length of the roof, the straw hangs heavy over the thatched walls. Maya walks right over to the little side door. It's unlocked, she pushes it open and enters. Sits down on the floor. There's nobody home. A large wooden bowl sits against the wall; it's decorated with shimmering shells. The wall above it is patterned with circles and squares in black and brown. Why is this house full of weapons? There are sharp, dangerous things on the floor: axes and rows of pointed spears. Maya stands up; she can't stay here! She stumbles over to the door and gets outside. Her legs hurt.

'Madam Maya!'

The figure standing beside her is short, but her hands are large, with strong, warm fingers. They've grabbed her wrists, hold both her arms in a tight grip. 'Madam Maya! Shouldn't you be at home? It's dark, you could trip and fall. I'll walk you back.'

Maya feels nothing, thinks nothing, just lets herself be led through the darkness. She senses the sharp rocks on the road cutting up her feet, sending an irregular, but not uncomfortable rhythm through her body. She's going home. The woman with the short, curly hair is taking her home.

33
Sina

Sina can feel it right under her collarbone. Something about the muscles there; they had been loosening up, smoothing out, softening. Making her neck less taut, her jaw looser. Now they've knotted up again. Bound back together. The furrows from her mouth down to her chin have been carved another millimetre deeper. The tendons in her neck are tight, her shoulders tensed up to the way they were before she came here. Fiji had been filling her with bula; now it's disappearing, trickling away.

When Ateca came home with Maya that night, she'd been out looking for her as well. When Maya stormed out after the sewing incident, Kat had first told them to leave her alone. 'Maybe I pushed her too hard,' she'd said. 'She just needs some time to herself.'

Time to herself? Sina had been uncertain at first; the old respect for everything Kat says and does is still lodged inside her. But Maya's face on the beach earlier that day — there's something very wrong. She can't fool herself any longer. Can't keep telling herself that Maya's just a little scatterbrained, a little more forgetful and absent-minded than most. It's more than that.

So she'd stood up, sounded the alarm and raised her

voice to Kat. 'She could get lost. Or worst of all, drown. We have to go after her.'

She'd noticed the mocking look Armand shot in her direction, but brushed it off like a piece of lint on her sleeve. Set out running after Maya. To no avail: both paths, up towards Salote's shop and down towards the harbour, were empty. Fear dug its claws into Sina, the thought of Maya's uninhabited, blank face led her further, past the clearing behind the rubbish dump and all the way down to the beach. She'd run and shouted, shouted and run the whole way back, stomped up the stairs to the porch and torn open the door: 'Is she here?'

It wasn't until she saw Maya on the sofa next to Kat that she felt herself heaving for breath and detected the sickening taste of blood in her mouth. This wasn't the time to ask where she'd been found; Maya's eyes were murky and distant, and all Sina could think of was how to make them sharp and unclouded again. So she hadn't waited for a sign from Kat; she'd squeezed herself on to the sofa next to them and taken Maya's cold hand. Stroked her stiff, resistant fingers until they loosened up and her eyelids started to droop. Until Ateca cautiously approached and asked if she should help them get her to bed.

It was only when Sina got up from the sofa that she noticed Lisbeth and Armand still sitting on two chairs at the dining table. In a flash, it struck her how out-of-place they both seemed. Useless and passive, two dolls dressed up for a tea party. Always taking, never giving.

Since that first night, she's been waiting for him to bring it up again. The spark in his eyes when Ingrid mentioned the

201

chocolate was the same old look she knew well; she'd heard the calculator whirring in his head. Armand has had plenty of time to look around; he's inspected the sweet house and has been asking both her and Lisbeth casual questions. What are they planning to do, export? Oh, really, to Norway? How interesting. So it'll be important to have a good contact on that end, right?

'We already do,' Lisbeth responds. 'My daughter knows all about market analysis; she's working on a marketing campaign strategy.'

The words sound completely comfortable in her mouth, Sina has to admit it. Not surprising, since Lisbeth uses them in discussions with Ingrid and Kat almost every day. But Armand isn't so easy to impress.

'That's great,' he says, and Sina recognizes the smile he flashes Lisbeth. Oh, how she recognizes it. 'Of course you need people to handle the marketing. But what you also need is someone who understands how business really works. Someone who'll be ready to pounce when it counts and can make the tough decisions without batting an eyelid. Someone who knows the ropes.'

She shuts her ears. Thinks to herself: Lisbeth isn't the one making the decisions. It's up to Kat. Kat's cocoa, Kat's chocolate.

Maybe she hasn't been angry enough, maybe that's where she's gone wrong. Dismayed, yes. Ashamed, yes. Shattered, exasperated, yes. But not angry enough. Because Sina knows exactly what she wants. She wants Armand to leave. It feels brave, but good, to think the thought and turn it into words in her head. She wants him out of Fiji and out of her life. She wants Maya's eyes to clear and for them to fall back into the synchronized stride they've found down here. And if Maya's step falters, if she grows scared or panicked, Sina's feet will find the way for both of them.

She decides to drive herself to Rakiraki that afternoon. Vilivo is nowhere to be found. He normally acts as driver for them but he's not always at the house, of course. He's probably running around down on the rugby pitch; the black-and-green shoes he thinks Armand paid for are glued to his feet every single day.

She's barely driven the truck before; in irritation, she thinks to herself that Kat doesn't trust her with it. How hard can it be when the highway code is as ridiculously simple as it is here? Squeeze in wherever you can, and be ready for buses and taxis to do whatever they want. She's getting used to driving on the left, and there's only one road that leads straight into town, it's impossible to get lost. Sina has errands to run in Rakiraki, and she prefers to handle them on her own.

She wants to tell Kat that she's taking the truck, but her room is empty. It's neat as always in there: the mosquito net tied up in a knot, book and water glass on the bedside table. Her computer sits on a low table by the window. It's turned on and a geometric pattern in rainbow colours rolls across the screen. It's usually kept on the desk in the living room; Kat's obviously been doing something private. Sina feels a surge of curiosity and nudges the mouse. The sliding pattern of colours vanishes and Kat's inbox fills the screen. Sina leans forward. The latest email is from evyforgad@gmail.com. She clicks it open without hesitating.

Dear Kat,

Thanks for keeping me updated. I'm not going to lie and say I'm not worried, but I'm also full of admiration for the way you're all handling the progression of Mum's illness. We all knew it wouldn't be easy, of course. From the first time the doctor mentioned early onset Alzheimer's as a possibility, he was very clear that there was no cure, and that this would only go in one direction. Branko and I have talked about it often: how outstanding you've all been to take on this responsibility.

It was frightening to read about the incident when she ran off in the middle of the night. Thank goodness you found her before anything happened. I don't know what I can say, except to repeat what I've said before: if you're ever in doubt about whether you want this responsibility, I'll come down and get Mum right away. You've already done far more than can be expected of friends, no matter how close you are. And as I've also said before: you must tell the other ladies how grateful I am for everything you do for her. When they travelled to paradise, I'm sure they hadn't expected that it would also involve playing nursemaid for someone with severe dementia. And it's even harder, of course, when it's impossible to know how much she herself is aware of what's happening.

Everything's fine back here in Trondheim. Work is busy; I often feel I don't get to spend nearly enough time with my daughter. But I guess everyone feels that way.

Sina's heart pounds in her chest; she has to sit down to catch her breath. *Early onset Alzheimer's. Take on this responsibility. Everything you do for her.*

Maya is sick. The doctor in Norway diagnosed her before she left for Fiji. Kat has known all along and hasn't told any of them. While Evy has assumed they all know. Evy has believed they took this on as a group project, some kind of tropical end of the line for her mother. Sina is suddenly furious: who the hell does Kat think she is? Does she think she has the right to manage their lives, just because she can afford to invite them here? To play fast and loose with truth and lies however she wants?

Sina sits on the crisply made bed, her hands folded in her lap. Her gaze falls on the sewing machine in the corner, surrounded by pieces of fabric, spools of thread and a pair of scissors. A brightly coloured bula-patterned garment lies folded up next to it. White, red and orange. The child's dress that sent Maya running out in a panic.

Sina has never deluded herself that she knew much about Kat's peculiar life. The occasional letter, a few short meetings, snippets of things she's heard. Forty years doesn't just shape secrets, she thinks. It also shapes ways to keep them. To deny or embellish. To silence and repress. To explain to oneself why things turned out the way they did.

The anger fizzles out of her like a glass of sparkling water left out in the sun. It's not a burden to be Maya's friend; it's a bonus. Kat hasn't kept quiet to trick anyone, but to shield them. Some secrets are best kept secret. She won't say anything.

Sina closes the email. She retrieves the keys from the

kitchen drawer, goes outside and starts the truck. Kat isn't home, there's no one around to ask for permission.

She had forgotten how liberating it is to view the world through a windshield. Sina drives slowly past the houses that line the bumpy main road up through the village. Salote is out on her steps with a broom; a man sits napping under a plastic tarp in front of a row of pyramids of small oranges. Mosese's wife sits outside their house with the coconut grater between her knees; a young boy waves a fan back and forth in front of her face. Sina cranes her neck to catch a glimpse of Armand in the doorway, but without high hopes: she doubts he spends much time with his host family beyond sleeping there. He hasn't shown up at the house today, and no one's missed him, Sina thinks. She feels the anger towards him pounding in her temples; sometimes hot and throbbing, sometimes a churning desperation. It's what no one wants to think about their child: that no one misses him. Armand is unwanted.

But she *had* wanted him, she had! Sina leans forward and her fingers curl around the steering wheel. The conversation with her mum at her bedside in her tiny room back home remains crystal clear in her mind after all these years: the crying and the yelling, the accusations, the reproaches. The pleading with Sina to come to her senses, to get rid of it. The way that with every one of her mother's outbursts, Sina had grown more and more sure: she wanted the baby. She was going to do it alone.

Sina keeps her gaze fixed on the road; a quick swerve to avoid a cackling hen sends the right front wheel into a pothole and her knee slams into the dashboard – dammit! She drops one hand from the steering wheel and rubs her throbbing knee. Was it really Armand she'd wanted? The baby, the responsibility of bringing up another person? Sina picks at the grazed bruise. She hadn't been prepared for leading and advising someone in the art of living. Her mother's words slice through her: 'And the child, Sina? Do you think it'll be easy for the child here, with all the rumours and gossip?'

At the time, she'd shut her ears, believing that her mother was only worried about her own shame. But she'd seen it since, of course, she'd pieced it together: unexplained bruises, his schoolbooks torn to shreds. The coat she'd bought on sale that he suddenly didn't want to wear any more. The outings to classmates' cabins to which he wasn't invited. They never discussed it, she hadn't known how to help. She'd believed that sometimes, shutting your mouth and staring straight ahead was the only way to get you through. Has he thought the same way? Has it got him through?

Sina turns on to the tarmac road to Rakiraki and finds words for the sadness that's replaced the anger and the aching in her knee. All she had wanted was something that was hers. Something no one else had.

She'd never imagined that Lisbeth would decide to come to her rescue. When her friend was finally done being shocked – 'What have you done, Sina?' – so holier-than-thou – 'I don't know what you're thinking, wanting to keep it!' – it had felt as if she had tried to take this over for herself as well. Offering her a job in the warehouse, donating crumbs from her and Harald's table of bounty: 'At least you'll *have* something, right?'

Sina pushes her foot down on the accelerator. Hears her

mother's nagging voice in her other ear: 'I can't *believe* Høie wants to take you in, with the mess you've got yourself into! You should be grateful you're friends with Lisbeth – look how she's setting it all up for you!'

Having everything set up for her hadn't been Sina's plan. She hadn't had a plan, really. Apart from never again thinking about those few minutes in the boys' toilet in the school gym, when the school dance was over and the only people left were from the clean-up crew. 'You like this, Sina? You think it's hot, right?' The boy's hoarse voice in her ear, the stench of alcohol from his wet mouth. His hand cupping her breast hard, her head thudding against the wall when he pushed himself into her. 'You think this is hot, right?' The way he had inched open the cubicle door when he was finished, the searching glance into the hallway. The schoolyard the following Monday, when he didn't even turn to look at her when she said hi.

Lisbeth and Harald Høie were always meant to be. The prince will always get his princess, that's just the way it is. And of course she needed the job. Needed the money. But she didn't need Lisbeth's pity. Didn't need the condescending mercy mixed with an oh, so poorly camouflaged relief that she had secured her own prize. Safe in the castle on the hill with the king.

But she'd let her friend know it, clear as day, and she knows Lisbeth has never forgotten. *I'm the one who has something, Lisbeth. Not you.*

Sina isn't sure why she never left the store. The job wasn't much to speak of, she could probably have found something more interesting elsewhere, even with just a high-school diploma. But she kept going: the work wasn't demanding and it was a stable job. They've managed, she and Armand. They haven't been a burden to anyone, goddammit.

Sina is done with her shopping. Shower gel and baking powder and potato flour, apple juice for Maya, and a bag of Kat's special rice. Soft toilet paper, white sugar for baking. Now she's strolling around Rakiraki, postponing and delaying her last errand. She stops outside the cinema and looks at the posters of daring Bollywood ladies and leading men in black. Waits outside the open door of the aromatic Hot Bread Kitchen, but resists the temptation to go inside. It smells better than it tastes anyway; the cakes with stiff turquoise frosting just taste of sugar and artificial vanilla.

She pulls herself together and steers her steps towards the side street on the left. The 'Dream Travels' sign is faded and hangs lopsided; the air-conditioning greets her like a wall of ice when she opens the door. The Indian girl behind the desk is bundled up in a shawl, and nods drowsily at Sina to offer her a seat in the chair across from her. She keeps pecking away at her keyboard; her long nails make a clicking sound against the keys, giving Sina goosebumps. Finally, she finishes typing.

'How can I help you?'

Sina heaves a deep breath. 'I'd like to know the price of a ticket from Nadi to Oslo, Norway. One way.'

She puts the slip of paper she is given into the zippered pocket of her handbag. A few options for different routes, different prices for different dates. But they all go the same way. Out.

Sina shoves the thought of money aside and thanks the girl for her help.

34

Ateca

My dreams are so unhappy, God. Is it because Madam Sina is so sad?

I dreamed I was sitting in a bure on the beach with Vilivo in my lap. He was little; a plump baby with wise eyes. Madam Sina was lying beside me; she was young and her big belly was bulging. She was going to give birth to her son, but when he came, he was a snake. Madam Sina was scared, but I knew he was possessed. Just like the child born to the chief's daughter in Rewa, who was cursed from birth and couldn't become a human until he was loved by another woman besides his mother. I told Madam Sina this, but she didn't want to hear it. She just got up and walked down to the beach, and I hurried after her with Vilivo in my arms. The snake stayed there, a newborn, not moving a muscle.

Later on in the dream, Madam Sina was walking down the beach again, with Madam Maya beside her. I was walking behind them; the air was thick and still. I peered down in the sand at the footsteps in front of me, and I suddenly saw Madam Sina's feet were the only ones leaving a mark. The footprints Madam Maya made in the sand were gone as soon as she lifted her feet from the ground. A plane made a wide arc in the sky above me; its white hull gleamed so much it blinded me. I leaned over my son and held his head close to me.

God, you know what we all need. Give me good dreams, give Madam Sina happy thoughts. And let Vilivo find work, so he can support himself, become an adult and start a family.

In Jesus' holy name. Emeni.

35
Ingrid

She can't stand him any more! The fake charm, the arrogance, the looks he gives both Ateca and Lisbeth – *Lisbeth*!

Ingrid shakes her head; she can't believe it. She feels sorry for Sina, who must be so embarrassed about this middle-aged – yes, that's what he is, middle-aged! – idiot. Lisbeth is his mother's friend!

Ingrid is glad Armand's attempts at flirting aren't directed at her. She wouldn't be able to hold it together if he tried to flash her one of the cocky smiles he gives Lisbeth. A bone she snaps up like a hungry dog, Ingrid thinks with a combination of pity and disdain, and lights the citronella candles with a sharp flick of her match.

Wildrid is making more and more frequent appearances on the porch at night. It's as if there's more space for her in the flowery sulu, there's room to breathe on the beach where the wind lives in the palm leaves and gives her voice air and volume. Ingrid often finds herself retreating into the shadows by the hammock and letting Wildrid take part in the conversations when they really start to get interesting. And tonight they reach new heights.

'Well, this is really nice. I have to admit I didn't quite

212

know what to think when Mum said she was moving to a feminist commune on the other side of the world,' says Armand.

Lisbeth laughs as if on cue, and makes sure to turn her smile towards Armand on the good side, the side that doesn't show her discoloured crown. '*Feminist* – as if!'

But it's Maya who takes the bait. 'Well, who did you think Sina was going to be living with? And please, spare us the clichés about bra-burning man-haters.'

Maya's had a good day. Her voice is clear, her gaze is steady, her hands rest calmly in her lap, two birds in their nest.

Armand squirms in his chair, but his voice stays brash. 'Haha, you never know what crazy antics you ladies might get up to, right?'

Ingrid looks at Maya; can she really stomach this crap? She herself certainly has no desire to join in.

But Wildrid does. 'And what kind of crazy antics would that be, Armand? Believing that women should have the same rights and opportunities as men?'

'Yeah, yeah, but that's not what it's about—'

'But that's exactly what it's about! No more, no less. It's not that complicated!'

Kat is startled as well, and Ingrid isn't sure whether she detects affirmation or mockery in her voice. 'Well, how about that? You're still sticking to your guns in your old age, Ingrid.'

Wildrid opens her mouth, but Lisbeth is one step ahead of her; the words slip out past lips painted Coral Pink. 'OK, so I'm not a *feminist* or anything, but of course we should have rights and opportunities.'

'Well, then you're a feminist!' Wildrid retorts. 'Why are you afraid to say it?'

Lisbeth beats a hasty retreat. 'Afraid? I'm not afraid, that's not it . . .'

'Then what?' Kat waves her hand casually, as if asking for the floor. 'Of course you're afraid, Lisbeth, come on! Everyone's afraid to be labelled a militant bitch.'

'Do people really still think that way? For Christ's sake, I can't believe it!'

All heads turn towards Ingrid. The outburst throbs against her temples. Ingrid wants to stay seated but Wildrid jumps up from her chair. 'I'm so offended by this bloody cowardice! Who are we apologizing to? Why should believing in equal opportunity make us militant bitches?'

Maya's voice is still calm. 'Well, that's not exactly how it is. But to many people, the word "feminist" sounds angry and harsh. Not womanly, in a way.'

Ingrid sees that Maya immediately regrets her choice of words. But before she can correct herself, Wildrid jumps in. 'What are you saying? *Femina* is the Latin word for "womanhood"! And you've been in charge of educating young girls for years – I can't believe you haven't taught them what "womanhood" means!'

Maya blinks in astonishment behind her glasses; her hands lift up like frightened birds out of their nest. 'I . . .'

Armand has been sitting there watching them in the discussion he's unwittingly provoked, which seems to amuse him. And now he raises his hand, like a judge asking for order in the court. 'Ladies, ladies! Calm down, please, think of your blood pressure.'

Wildrid is about to snap back at him, but Armand is quicker this time.

'Can't we agree that men and women are born different? That there's nothing wrong with a woman embracing her femininity?'

Born different. Embracing her femininity. Ingrid can't believe her ears. But all Armand can hear is his own resounding brilliance. 'I can assure you that no one appreciates the feminine touch more than I do. After all, what would we men be without you? There's no doubt that you have something we don't. We admire it; we can't live without it, even. But that doesn't necessarily mean we're alike, does it?'

Ingrid feels exhaustion sagging limp and heavy off her shoulders. She can't stomach any more of this rubbish. She shoots a glance in Kat's direction: can't we just ask him to leave? But Armand keeps blathering on, and the fatigue dissipates as quickly as it came – is she really hearing him right?

'This stuff about business, for instance. It's no secret that I have a good amount of experience with these things, perhaps more than . . . hmm, well, you, that is.'

He nods towards Kat. 'Not to discount what you're doing here, but I assume your overseer is doing most of the work?'

Kat furrows her eyebrows; her lips stretch into a narrow smile. 'Mosese? He manages the plantation; he has nothing to do with the day-to-day business operations.'

In her mind's eye Ingrid sees the old plantation manager's uncomfortable shuffle in front of the computer screen when she tried to show him a website – she has no idea whether he can even read. How naive she has been!

'Of course, of course, I have no doubt you're a great CEO, Kat.' Armand's smile is probably meant to be disarming. 'But if you're really planning on going *global*' – he lets the word hang in the air – 'wouldn't it be safest to have someone who knows their stuff on the other end? Someone who can talk dollars and cents, yeah? And it just so happens that I have some spare time in the months ahead. My network is pretty wide, to put it that way, and I could take it upon myself to do some research.'

Kat's eyes narrow. 'What kind of research?'

Armand throws his arms out wide. 'Niche opportunities. Possibilities for profit. Simply put, how the market's looking.'

'We've got that part covered.' Kat's voice is hard; her words curt. 'Lisbeth's daughter is a professional.'

Out of the corner of her eye, Ingrid can see Lisbeth squirming in her chair, her body turning away from Armand, her chin tilting down.

He forces a laugh, readies a new offensive. 'My dear ladies, I'm only trying to help . . .'

Sina has been sitting in silence. Now she abruptly extinguishes her cigarette in the ashtray. 'I think it's pretty obvious, Armand. At Vale nei Kat, we help ourselves.'

The disbelief in his face when he looks at his mother; Ingrid holds her breath. Clouds gather in his eyes; his jaw tenses as he sucks in offended air. For one wild moment, Ingrid thinks he might slap his mother; she readies herself to get out of her chair and shield Sina.

But that's all Armand has to say. His hands shake slightly when he takes a cigarette from the case and lights it. The silence on the porch is broken only by a fat gecko on the wall above the door frame: *tock-tock-tock!*

Wildrid claps her hands over her mouth to suppress a delighted peal of laughter.

*

The air in the plantation is green and moist. Ingrid trudges behind Mosese, trying to follow his steady, undulating gait as she swats at the insects buzzing around her head. Mosese wears an inscrutable expression as he stops to let his fingers slide across a yellowish-red pod and frees it from the trunk with a quick chop of the knife. He slices it in two and lifts the upper half so the shiny, fat seeds are exposed, perfectly braided together in their soon-to-be-interrupted sleep. Ingrid doesn't have to ask; she's been out here with him so many times that she knows a flawless cocoa fruit when she sees it. She smiles at Mosese and lets Wildrid poke her fingers into the moist, white meat surrounding the beans. She digs out one of the brownish-red pearls and rubs it between her thumb and index finger. Drags the sharp bittersweet smell down into her lungs.

'Do you have enough help for the harvest?'

Mosese answers the way he usually does, by lifting his head and tipping it back slightly, a sort of backwards nod. It had taken Ingrid a while to understand that the backwards nod means yes, or at least not no. But then it might also mean he doesn't think the question is worthy of an answer. Ingrid has to be content with the knowledge that Mosese has been harvesting the cocoa crop on this plantation for years. He would let them know if he lacked manpower. He has a big family; Ingrid presumes each and every one of them will show up to help.

She tries again. 'Is it going to be a good crop?'

Another backwards nod.

She gives up. It's one thing to show interest; bothering and nagging Mosese is another. Still, Ingrid knows that *Kat's Cocoa* needs a good harvest; now that she is doing the books, she knows that some money will have to come in soon to make up for all the outgoings. Not least now that they're in an investment phase, ramping up the production equipment, machines and cooling systems. They may be starting small, but these are considerable expenses. Should she consult Johnny? What if she called him? In an instant, it all comes back: the tiny room, the narrow bed. The rich smell of chocolate on their breath.

Ingrid notices Mosese staring at her, and the worry sinks down deep in her stomach: this chocolate business was her idea after all. They'd all been fired up by her suggestion but she's the one who insisted they go ahead. What if it doesn't work out?

And so what? Wildrid quickly retorts. Kat was the one who invited us all here to take new chances. This is what we came here for! Pieces of chocolate, snapping free and easy between our fingers. Pleasure melting on our tongues. Come on!

Ingrid lets herself be convinced. She holds the ripened pod in her hand, envisions the shimmering brown seeds melting and transforming into the product they've discussed: a pure, dark chocolate made with real cocoa butter, maybe a hint of coconut. She can hear Lisbeth's voice: 'It has to be exclusive but not too niche. We should focus on the health message, "a little piece that's good for you". Market the flavonoids in cocoa that keep the arteries healthy and improve the circulation.'

'A little piece that's good for you.' 'Pieces of happiness.' It's a clever sales message. Ingrid is sure the others are just as amazed as she is over Lisbeth's contributions. Not just her enthusiasm, she's done her research, too, and actually seems to have a talent for this. She can't possibly have learned all this from her daughter's marketing lessons? Maybe it's some kind of extension of what she's always excelled at: improving and making the most of her assets. Accentuating the favourable parts and showing them off to their best advantage.

Ingrid really wants – so much that her stomach churns – to believe that *Kat's Chocolate* is going to become a reality, sending aromatic, succulent pieces of happiness across the seas. Little mouthfuls of tropical love from a beach in paradise.

But it's a risk. It's costly and they have to keep their accounts in check. Ingrid knows what she contributes personally to the fellowship every month, and a quick calculation tells her that even if the others are paying the same, it's not enough to cover the big investments they need to make in addition to the daily upkeep of the house and utilities. And paying for Mosese and Ateca and Akuila. And Vilivo. And Armand. She shudders. Kat hasn't mentioned who is paying for the parasite's room and board, but Ingrid is sure she knows the answer.

Maybe Kat has a personal stash, a source of income outside the cocoa business? Could Niklas have left her a ton of money? Ingrid shakes her head faintly as she pictures him: tall, magnificent Niklas. Broad smile and big ideas. Ingrid has visited them all over the world, and his voice rumbles in the background of all her memories: enthusiastic, intense, determined that all problems were there to be solved. Everyone could see he worshipped the ground Kat walked on. Ingrid furrows her eyebrows . . . No, worshipped isn't quite the right word. He brought her in. Counted on her. Yes, he counted on her, one hundred per cent. Through thick and thin. Niklas and Kat were a team unlike any she'd ever seen. Completely united. Wide open, Ingrid thinks. No secrets.

Yes, she decides, it is possible. It might be that Niklas left something behind for Kat.

But Kat doesn't want to talk about money.

'I wouldn't have invited you all down here if I was broke,' she says casually when Ingrid gets her on her own a few days later. She dismisses the offer to go through the numbers and the budget one more time. 'The harvest will be what it normally is; it'll be fine. It's like this every year; it's natural for the budget to swing up and down from season to season. This isn't the County Bus Service, you know!' She laughs and elbows Ingrid. 'Don't be so worried. You're the one who wanted to make chocolate, right? So we're going to have to take some risks!'

Ingrid has no intention of asking, but it just spills out of her. 'Did Niklas leave you some kind of cushion? Before he—'

Something stiffens around Kat's mouth, and Ingrid immediately regrets her question. 'Sorry, I know—'

'That he wasn't planning to drown?'

Ingrid feels the muscles in her throat tense, flounders around for words. 'Kat, you know I didn't mean . . .'

But her friend's gaze is far away. Under her white shirt

her breathing is calm and regular as she gets up from the porch steps they're seated on. 'Come,' is all she says.

The sunset is only a few minutes away; it's low tide and Kat picks up her pace along the beach. Her feet kick up little fans of sand with each step, and she stays silent as they approach a row of boats that sit stranded on the beach, mute and waiting. When they reach them, she turns her back to the water and walks towards the belt of palm leaves, seaweed, plastic bottles and ends of rope that mark the edge of high tide.

Ingrid follows a few steps behind and sees Kat come to a stop in the shadow of the hull of one of the larger boats, lying under a palm tree. She turns around and stands frozen, staring down towards the strip of seaweed and driftwood, or maybe out across the ocean. The sunset gathers itself in an orange bundle of rays, and in the space of a few minutes the day is sucked away, disappearing into a drain of pink and purple.

Kat, still under the tree, waves Ingrid over. 'Look,' she says and points towards the water, which is now just a dark, undulating line across the horizon.

Ingrid squints and thinks she can see the shape of a boat near the shore, a dark, immoveable animal. 'What am I looking at?' she asks. 'It got dark so quickly.'

Kat doesn't respond. She stays still a while before bending down and removing one of her sandals. Clears out some seaweed and puts it back on. 'If we stay here any longer, the mosquitoes will eat us alive.'

After dinner, Ingrid wants to be alone. She shuts the door to her room and finds the light switch on her wall. A movement at the edge of the mirror startles her; a flash of a shadow that halts on the mirror frame when she gets closer. The gecko stands frozen; black, beady eyes, grey-green skin. Revoltingly rubbery, the little lizard hasn't got a trace of anything cute to compensate. Suddenly Ingrid is struck with compassion for the unattractive reptile trying to freeze itself into invisibility. 'Poor thing,' she says softly, and carefully approaches it with her finger. Its lumpy body doesn't move; Ingrid's nail is a millimetre from touching it when it suddenly jumps. It chirps loudly as it vanishes behind the frame. A greyish-green tail is left behind under the mirror, curling in on itself like a newly hatched snake. Ingrid jerks back, but Wildrid leans forward, picks up the squirming tail and cradles it in her palm.

36

Lisbeth

It's ridiculous, of course, and she just knows the others are laughing at her. Maybe they're talking about it amongst themselves, maybe not. Lisbeth hides her head in her hands. Armand's twenty years younger than her, for God's sake! A hopeless slacker; haven't she and Harald called him that over and over? How bad they feel for Sina, that her son is so . . . useless. She even asked Harald if he would give the boy a chance in the store, but he put his foot down there. 'We've helped Sina because she's your friend. Not exactly eye candy behind the counter but at least she does her job. But that layabout son of hers? I won't take him in!'

She doesn't even think about Harald that much any more. She's stopped believing he'll try to get her to come home. The little she's heard from him and about him has been from Linda. *Dad feels betrayed*, her first accusatory emails read. And eventually: *Dad's doing fine*. Not a word about a separation or other formalities, it seems he's pretending nothing is wrong. Lisbeth is surprised at how little it hurts. Anyway, she and Linda have other things to talk about. New things, in a new way.

Still, it's embarrassing, this thing with Armand. Not that anything has happened . . . How inappropriate, oh dear me! But what is she supposed to do? When he sits down beside her in the evenings and winks at her after one of Ingrid's harsh quips, as if the two of them are secretly laughing at the others. Calling them the 'loonies' when they're not there, rolling his eyes so only she can see, when, at 10 p.m., after they've already eaten, Maya asks whether dinner will be soon.

She'd been mortified when Ateca had entered her room without knocking the other day. 'Sorry, Madam Lisbeth, I thought you were out . . .' She quickly retreated, but not before she'd caught a glance of Lisbeth in front of the mirror, in the lingerie set she almost hadn't remembered bringing with her: silky black lace, a push-up bra. What was she thinking? She'd tossed the lingerie back in the drawer at once, and told herself that she'd only wanted to try it on. God knows she's put on weight in Fiji, she wanted to see if it still fit.

Armand is no dreamboat either, far from it. The glimpses she's caught of his belly between the bottom few buttons of his shirt, the reddish-blond tufts of hair she'd rather not have seen. So why does she still bring out her lipstick for an extra touch-up before dinner? Smooth her hair down whenever she hears 'Hey, ladies!' outside the door? She's not sure. But there's something in his gaze when it slides across her, something she has missed. He shows up every morning, spends a few hours drinking their coffee, using their internet, lying in their hammock and commenting on how lucky they are: 'You girls really live in paradise, I hope you know that!' As if he's been sent out as some kind of inspector, who begrudges them their pensions and wants to make sure they're not having too much fun.

The others think she's being foolish, she knows that. But it's the only way she knows how to be; it's not her *style* to reject a man's advances! Lisbeth gets up from the edge of the bed. Armand isn't a *man*, stop it now! He's Sina's son. And that's what makes it so unbearably shameful. The distance, the shadow of hostility in Sina's eyes that makes uncertainty flicker in Lisbeth's chest. Hostility and . . . disdain?

It's not the butterflies in her stomach that makes her wink back at Armand and laugh at his jokes. Or butterflies anywhere else for that matter – that's not it. Just a sadness over the inevitability of years going by. The young mugger who took her money. The smell of sweat and greed, the feeling of his skin beneath her fingertips. Salesi, she knows his name now. Knows that the closest she'll ever get to him is a pair of black shoes with green stripes.

'Where are you going, Ateca?'

Kat's voice from the living room.

'I thought I'd see what Jone caught this morning, Madam Kat. If he has any good snapper, maybe I could bring you some?'

Lisbeth gets up on an impulse. 'I'll come with you, Ateca,' she says quickly. 'You can show me how to pick out the best fish.'

Is Ateca looking at her a little strangely? Lisbeth thinks she can see a glimpse of the black lace lingerie in the corner of her eye, but they're just going to have to get past this. Kat nods in approval, and Lisbeth fetches her white straw hat. The red ribbon along the brim matches her skirt this Tuesday afternoon.

It's as if he's been waiting for them. Armand comes gliding out of the shadows alongside one of the sheds above the pier. 'Hey, girls!'

Without asking he falls into step with them, staying close when they near Jone's boat where his sons are sorting the fishing tackle. It must have been a good morning out on the reef: blue parrotfish, shimmering silver mackerel and a giant red grouper lie in a tub of water. Ateca squeezes the fish with practised hands, checks that the eyes are clear and the gills are bright orange. She finally settles on two medium-sized fish and looks up at Lisbeth sideways. 'Maybe we could make *kokoda*. Has Mister Armand had that yet?'

Lisbeth isn't too crazy about Fijian food in general, but the lime-marinated raw fish in coconut milk, seasoned with chilli and onion, has become one of her favourites. 'But it's a lot of work, isn't it, Ateca? It takes time?'

Ateca smiles. 'Madam Ingrid can grate the coconuts. She's got good feet. And Madam Sina can help me chop up the fish.'

'I can help, too,' Lisbeth hurries to interject. She can at least chop the onions and chilli; Ateca doesn't need to make her sound totally useless!

'*Kokoda* sounds exciting.' Armand flashes Ateca his broadest smile. 'You have to teach me how to make such a specialty. There's way too much tinned food and too many microwave meals in a single man's kitchen, you know.'

Ateca glances at Lisbeth, who suddenly can't help but smirk a little: Armand's request for Ateca's pity has fallen on deaf ears. The image of bosso Armand alone in the kitchen, cooking for himself without a single woman nearby, is obviously not one she can picture.

'I can keep the glasses filled, at least,' he continues and

takes a step towards her. 'And set the table with Maya. Help her count to six.'

Lisbeth can't believe he's winking at her. A rapid little jeering laugh accompanied by a flutter of his eyelid. Something cracks inside Lisbeth's head – a balloon popping, a tiny explosion. Armand's reddish face grows blurry in front of her and her voice quivers, but not from tears.

'Of course you can help,' she says. 'But just leave Maya alone.'

Thankfully he doesn't come in when they return with the fish. Ateca goes straight to the kitchen and Lisbeth stops when she spots Maya standing in the doorway to her room, gripping the door frame. She's wearing a hat and a night-gown, and her eyes are full of fear. Lisbeth understands at once. The afternoon light is telling Maya it's time for her walk on the beach, but she can't find the way and Sina isn't there.

But the Star of the Sea is there. Maraia suddenly appears beside them and loosens Maya's iron grip on the door frame. 'Come on, Nau,' she says, and leads her back into her room. Lisbeth retreats and has taken a seat in a wicker chair on the porch when they reappear. Maya in her old blue dress and Maraia in a bula dress Lisbeth has never seen before. Bright, happy colours; white and red on an orange background. When Maraia puts her hand in Maya's, Lisbeth sees that it fits like a key in a lock.

*

'Sushi,' Armand says and smacks his lips after consuming his third helping. 'Even back home in meat-and-potatoes land, people have started to see what delicacies the rest of the world has to offer. Of course, those of us who've travelled quite a bit have tried more than frozen pizza and tuna casserole, and have a slightly more refined palate, but this' – he flashes a huge grin across the dinner table – 'not many people can say they've tried this.'

Lisbeth looks at him wearily. She can't be bothered to correct him, to point out that kokoda isn't sushi. What would it matter if she said so? Armand will always know best, no matter what.

But Maya's having a good night and, taking a deep breath, she explains, 'Kokoda isn't actually sushi, it's fish cooked in lime juice. Ceviche, which is made in Central and South America, is prepared in the same way. It's a chemical process: the citric acid denatures the proteins in the flesh of the fish so the molecules change their structure, and—'

'Of course I know that!'

His interruption isn't good-natured, it's brusque, and Maya looks confused. She pushes herself out to the edge of her chair and continues. 'It's quite interesting, really. I can't quite remember where the method comes from; I've read about it but . . .'

'No, it's not always easy to remember everything, is it, Maya? But at least tonight you remember where you live and who you're with, and that's nice, isn't it? Shall we drink to that, ladies?'

Armand raises his glass and looks around with a grin, winking at each of them. Something pops inside Lisbeth's head again, the same feeling of something collapsing. Maya sits frozen with her mouth open, a red blush slowly creeping across her face. Sina clutches the edge of the table; Ingrid jumps out of her chair and starts, 'You know what—'

But it's Kat who takes charge. Kat, who sets down her spoon and fork calmly, and looks Armand squarely in the eyes. 'There's an old saying that guests, like fish, begin to smell after three days. It's been three weeks now, Armand, and the stench is pretty strong. I don't know how long you're planning to stay in Fiji, but in any event, this is your last evening in my vale. You'll have to see your mother somewhere else after this.'

As if his mother is the one he's here to see, Lisbeth thinks, and her gaze travels reflexively over to the chair at the end of the table. Sina wears the same expression as always; jaw locked, deep frown lines, corners of her mouth pinched. And now she gets up, shoves the chair hard and storms out of the room. She returns with her handbag, and Lisbeth wonders briefly if Sina has fetched her passport and wallet because she wants to leave the house, too. But Sina walks over to Armand, pulls a light blue envelope out of her bag and slams it on the table in front of him. And it's Maya, not Armand, she's looking at when she hisses through clenched teeth, 'Here's your ticket. You're flying out of Nadi this Saturday.'

37

Ateca

Dear God, I know that children are the greatest gifts you give us, but they're also the ones who bring us the greatest worry. You've created all mothers, Lord, so you understand both me and Madam Sina. Her boy is grown up but she frets about him anyway. What I didn't understand until tonight, Lord, is that she's scared. Just as scared as I am when Vilivo's been sitting up too late around the grog bowl and comes stumbling home in the middle of the night. It was the same fear I saw in Madam Sina's face on her way to Mosese and Litia's house. She said she wanted to thank them for letting Mister Armand stay there, but I could tell what she was actually afraid of was that he hadn't behaved well. Even though he's an old man with white in his hair.

It bothers me that we haven't prepared itatau. Mister Armand is leaving in two days, so there won't be time for a farewell party with a lovo. But I should have thought of the itatau! I tried to explain it to Madam Sina, that it's one of our traditions, a thank-you for the time you've shared. The guest thanks the host for welcoming him with open arms, and apologizes if he has behaved badly. Mister Armand has lived comfortably at Mosese and Litia's. Hot water to shower in and Australian biscuits with his tea in the morning. The custom is that the guest gives thanks and the host wishes him safe travels and welcomes his return. I told Madam Sina we didn't have to make a big deal of it, just buy some yaqona so we could drink kava. But she got upset and thought it was because Mister Armand had done something wrong. 'We'd be happy to pay more,' she said. Pay more! She's a kaivalagi, she doesn't know our ways. How could she understand that offering more money would be an insult?

Madam Sina is the one I know the least, Lord. But I can tell she has the same aching heart that I do. 'Don't worry,' I told her. 'Vilivo can get the yaqona. We'll arrange for the itatau, Madam Sina. Don't worry.'

And you saw what happened, Lord. How her eyes twitched, like a bird blinking, and a drop ran from her nose down to her lips. 'Thank you,' she said. I was looking for a handkerchief, so I didn't see her face when she added, 'But he's not coming back.'

Calm Madam Sina's worries for her child, dear Lord. And calm my worries for Vilivo. Let him find work, so he can support himself, become an adult and start a family.

In Jesus' holy name. Emeni.

38

Kat

The plan has always been to use the first beans that were ready. It would have been best, of course, for Johnny to have been here while we experimented with making chocolate, but he couldn't get away. Jone's daughters and daughters-in-law peel the shells off the dried beans; their conversation and laughter become a billowing background soundtrack of excitement as they sit in the shade, picking and plucking away.

We've harvested, we've fermented and we've dried. The yellow, reddish-gold and brown pods have been cut off the trunks, beans and fruit pulp have been left to simmer in the sun, wrapped in banana leaves until fermented. Mosese knows exactly when the leaves should be opened; he digs out a deep-purple cocoa bean and holds it between his hands, inspecting it closely before he shows me. 'Look at this, Madam Kat. This is just the right colour.'

We've dried the beans on mats in our courtyard and turned them carefully; not too fast, not too slow. Maya has assumed responsibility for the oven and the roasting. 'None of us knows how to do it, obviously,' she rightly pointed out, 'but at least I was once a good baker, and I intend to make friends with this oven!' The oven seems to agree, and we follow the recipe meticulously through grinding and heating, until we end up with a large steel bowl full of cocoa mass. Rich, liquid, strong and bitter – our very own cocoa mass! We look at each other and smile; Ingrid throws her long arms out wide and hugs each one of us in turn.

We make mistake after mistake. We can't figure out how to press out the cocoa butter correctly. We try and fail with different ratios of cocoa mass, fat and sugar. After the tenth or twelfth result that's far too bitter, we even add milk, despite Lisbeth's objections. 'No, it has to be dark chocolate, nothing else! We can't sell milk chocolate as "a little piece that's good for you".'

We grind and roll without getting the chocolate smooth enough. The cooling system breaks down and refuses to keep the temperature in the sweet house sufficiently low.

But no one is giving up. Ingrid is the first one there every morning; Sina and Maya find ways to work together as a team. Lisbeth spends time on the phone and online, but has just as much cocoa powder in her hair and just as many chocolate stains on her clothes as the rest of us. She's bought us aprons – long, green aprons with strings that go all the way around the waist and tie at the front. Ateca has one too; the first time she put it on, she laughed so hard she had to sit down.

The conching is the greatest challenge. I hold my breath and curse my fogged-up glasses when the hot chocolate mass is poured out over the chilled stone plates and the turning begins. Back and forth, back and forth, a never-ending process exuding dizzyingly sweet smells until the mass changes consistency, and a trained eye will be able to see that the temperature is below 33 degrees Celsius. Not our eyes. We push our glasses up our noses, squint and fiddle with thermometers, ladles, measures, and spill the mess everywhere.

But suddenly, one day we're there. The chocolate mass is perfectly silky and stays at the right temperature; it slides soft and supple into the moulds. Smooth, shiny bars of chocolate, eight millimetres thick. They glisten at us, dark and inviting: bite us, taste us, swallow us! Let us melt in your mouth!

The promise-laden snap when I break off a piece of happiness is like music. Chocolate Symphony No. 1. I let it rest on my tongue and wait as long as I can to swallow. The taste of the gods in the brownish-purple beans fills my mouth until it flows over and spills down my throat. I close my eyes and think of Niklas. That he would have wanted this for me.

*

Sina has finally decided to follow the doctor's recommendation. I'd thought she might want to go home to Norway for the surgery, but when I asked, her face fell and she shook her head.

'What would I go home for? Do you think Armand will come running to take care of me? Sit by my bedside and read aloud to his sick mother?'

I would have smiled, had it not been so heartbreakingly unfunny. 'No, you're right. That doesn't sound like Armand.'

All I wanted was to console her and give her courage. Reassure Sina that we'd keep her safe. But before I could find the words, she'd launched into her worries about money again. 'I want to do this here. I've looked into what it would cost, and the insurance will cover most of it. And if there's anything extra needed, I'm sure I'll—'

'Don't think about the money, Sina!'

How many times have I said that since she came to Fiji? The constant, tedious anxiety about money breaks my heart. It makes me embarrassed but mostly just sad. I'm no millionaire either, but it helps to have a financially savvy brother. He's made my inheritance from our parents grow to a nice sum after selling the house in Norway, and even after the chocolate investment, there's a good chunk of money left. Sina, who's worked hard her whole life, who's never bought anything for herself, and has put everything she owns into that perpetual money vacuum who's about to turn fifty – she shouldn't have to worry about whether she can afford to have her uterus removed.

As we sit on the wall outside the cemetery, she tells me the whole story again. About the pains and the tests, the doctor who recommends that she have it all removed.

'He says there may be something that's not quite right.'

She looks at me; her eyes reveal nothing. But her words are steady. '*May* be. He says it's probably not cancer. And Maya had it all removed many years ago; she says it's not a big deal.'

I'm waiting; there's more to come.

'It's just . . .'

Sina's eyes are red and puffy; the lashes are short and blonde. Suddenly, I realize I've never seen her cry.

'I thought that now . . . down here . . .'

I put my arm around her shoulder. Sina's neck tenses but I squeeze harder and her head falls reluctantly on my shoulder. Here in Fiji, Sina was supposed to finally be able to breathe. It was supposed to be her turn to bury her toes in warm sand and fill her mouth with coconut milk. I had promised her that.

'I know,' I sigh and pull her closer, peering down at her scalp, which shines white through the greyish-blonde tufts.

Her shoulder tightens up under my arm; her head lifts. 'I love my son,' Sina says and looks me squarely in the eyes. Her gaze is hard and defiant.

'It was my choice. I'm the one who decided he should grow up in a two-bedroom apartment in Rugdeveien, without a father and with second-hand skis bought at a car-boot sale. No one ever asked him; you have to remember that.'

I know that's true. And I also know this is something I'll never be able to touch.

'I know,' I say again.

I make calls. Make arrangements. Check the surgeon's background and pay the fee to guarantee a private room. If all goes according to plan, Sina's surgery will be on a Monday and, if all the tests are clear, she'll be discharged a few days later. I'll be the only one accompanying her to Suva, although Maya was obviously wounded by this decision. I think she knows why, but I haven't had the energy to discuss it. I'm the one Sina needs most right now.

Maya's journey away from us continues in uneven phases. The repeated questions, the words that disappear for her, the confusion in her eyes when she's looking for her comb and can't remember what it's called. 'I can't find the hair-thing!'

236

But it's not always like that. In between, there are periods when no one can tell anything's wrong. Maya sits with an old atlas, telling Maraia all about the world's oceans. She remembers historical dates and book titles, and which vaccinations her daughter had when she was a child. Then, the next day she will lose track, mumbling slowly and struggling to complete a sentence. It's more than forgetfulness and absent-mindedness; everyone has seen that and understood it. They've absorbed it and seem to accept that no good will come of bringing it out in the open. We don't need to give it a name. We'll take Maya's days as they come. As long as we're able.

I know what lies ahead. I've read about how patients like Maya will eventually become unable to accomplish even simple tasks. Become apathetic and lose interest in all the things they used to enjoy. Act hostile for no reason, when fear and paranoia spread darkness in the mind and the heart. But we're not there yet. Maya still remembers more than she forgets. We don't have to make any big decisions yet.

It's hard to know how to handle Evy – my emails to Norway are becoming more and more evasive. Maya's daughter isn't stupid; I'm sure she understands that things have got worse. But we can still manage it. We can still take care of each other. A game of musical chairs in which some days it's Maya, some days it's Sina who's left with nowhere to sit.

Thank goodness for Ingrid. Ingrid holds down the fort at home in Korototoka; I don't have to worry about that. The plastic chair in the waiting room at Suva Private Hospital cuts into my back; they said the surgery itself would take about an hour and a half, plus time for her to wake up afterwards. But it's been over five hours now since I said goodbye to Sina as she checked in, and a slender Indian doctor – she didn't look a day over twenty-five; how can they all be so young? – with bright-red lipstick had assured me that this was a totally routine procedure. 'You can visit your sister tonight; she'll be awake enough to talk then.'

Could something have gone wrong? The evening receptionist is on the phone; a security guard slouches in a chair by the door with his eyes half shut. I didn't bring anything to read; I know the poster on the wall by heart now. *The balance on your account must be settled on your discharge.* If Ingrid were here, she would've laughed at the wording with me.

Should I ask for Sina one more time? 'Your sister's still sleeping, madam,' is the answer I've received three times now. 'Someone will let you know as soon as she wakes up.'

I must have dozed off, as a nurse in mint-green scrubs wakes me, shaking my arm gently. 'Madam, you can come in now.'

The room is dark; the curtains are drawn and only the light from the bathroom door ajar filters into the room.

'How are you doing, Sina? Are you in pain?'

Her head on the pillow moves slowly from side to side. 'Not much. I'm a little nauseous.' Her voice is hoarse, croaky.

'At least it's over now. They said everything went according to plan.'

Sina gives a little nod. She lies there with eyes closed, and I'm not sure whether she's fallen back asleep. I take her hand. The white palm is soft; it feels intimate, like stroking her across the stomach.

'Sleep well,' I say. 'I'll be back tomorrow.'

I have many friends in Suva. Australians who've hammered down their tent stakes on the island for good, people from NGOs Niklas and I worked with over the years. Many of them diligent and dutiful; some idealistic and indolent. Some have nothing to go home to; others have left far too much waiting for them back home.

I'm staying at Deb and Steve's house tonight. Their passports say New Zealand, but they could have come from anywhere; they fall into the broad category 'landed and stayed here'. They've sailed around the world, travelled and explored and scuba-dived and lived, and ended up here on the outskirts of Fiji's capital, where their *Vale ni Cegu*, Place of Rest, offers plenty of good food, soft beds and calm nights. This is where I usually stay when I visit the city; Vale ni Cegu calls itself a 'homestay' and offers precisely that: a feeling of home, a place where you can wander into the kitchen and peek in the fridge if your stomach begins to rumble before dinner. And I have finally stopped the friendly quarrelling with my hosts about paying. 'Your stories from the bush are more than enough payment,' Steve says as he walks out on to the tiles around the pool, with a bottle and three glasses. The moon is small and new, and the sky above Suva shimmers clear and deep.

'Well, I'm excited to hear the update,' he says as he takes a seat. 'How are the chocolate plans going? Was it useful, talking to Johnny?'

'Johnny was exactly who we needed,' I respond. 'Thanks

for putting us in touch. He's been more important to us than you can imagine.'

'Great!' Steve fills the glasses. 'And can we now make a toast to *Kat's Chocolate*?'

'I hope so,' I say, and picture Lisbeth's smile, Ingrid's face when she threw her arms around my neck: *We did it!* 'We don't have everything figured out yet, but at least we've found the right flavour. And it's good!'

We drink to *Kat's Chocolate*, and I tell them we're targeting the health market. 'That's where the opportunities are, according to Lisbeth's daughter.'

'Health food, yes, that's right,' Deb laughs. 'Kat's deliciously irresistibly sinfully healthy chocolate!'

I agree. 'And now we have to come up with some nice packaging. Something both snazzy and appetizing.'

They nod. Snazzy and appetizing, that's what it has to be.

'And your friends from Norway are happy?' Steve asks. 'Have they managed to cut ties and leave all the snow and doom and gloom behind?'

Doom and gloom? I look at him, surprised. 'Why would you think they're gloomy?'

Steve shrugs. 'I assumed as much. Didn't you say they've all lived their whole lives up in the cold next to the North Pole? From personal experience, I can tell you that the stretch between Northern Ireland and the Scottish islands isn't somewhere I'd ever want to go back to. Grey seas, grey skies, grey outlook, and so bloody cold!'

I smile at him and realize that this isn't something I can explain to Deb and Steve. It's not the dreary weather Sina and Ingrid and the others have travelled away from. That

240

too, perhaps, but I prefer to think they've travelled *to* something: the sulu loosely wrapped around hips that are allowed to grow wide. A fragrant frangipani tucked behind the ear. Laughter for no reason. The freedom that comes with distance.

'They're doing fine,' I say casually and take a sip of my wine. 'Now we just have to get Sina back on her feet, and then we'll head back out into the bush, as you call it.'

'But do they *get* it?' Deb asks and leans forward. 'I mean – they haven't lived like us, and . . .'

And what? Does she mean that they haven't experienced the flipside of our crazy vagabond life, the times when we didn't know where to find the money to pay the project people their salaries? That my friends have never been sick with malaria in a place where they couldn't speak the language? Or that they haven't grasped the unjustness of our having so much, while those around us have so little? Or is she referring to the feeling of vulnerability that's always there for us? The unpredictability people like she and I always feel, as we cling to a way of life we'll never one hundred per cent understand?

'The ladies are learning,' I respond. 'They know it's not all cocktails in the shade and food falling out of the trees.'

She wrinkles up her forehead and shrugs. 'Well, in a way it is almost like that. People here can pretty much fill their stomachs with what they find in their back yards.'

I shake my head, suddenly feeling exhaustion coiling like a steel wire around my forehead. 'That's not what I meant, really. I was thinking of . . .'

It's hard to find the words. 'I was thinking of what many

241

people back home imagine our life to be. That all we do is sit here drinking wine and gazing out over the ocean.'

I wave my hand with a flourish over the glasses on the table, the bougainvillea sagging heavy and violet against the wall.

Deb nods. 'I know what you mean. But your friends, do they get that it's not exciting and . . . *extraordinary* all the time? That we do have a regular everyday as well?'

Do they get that? I picture Ingrid with the coconut grater in her lap. Sina digging up cassava for dinner with Ateca. I nod with certainty.

'Yes, they do. But the freedom we have, the choice we've made – it doesn't come for free, does it? We've paid a price.'

'What do you mean?' Deb pulls her slim calves beneath her on the chair.

'Of . . . not belonging.'

Deb looks as if she's about to laugh. 'Oh, come on, don't give me that rootlessness crap! You've always said that it's narrow-minded and wrong to define roots in terms of geography. That your roots lie in the values you hold, what you cling to when push comes to shove.'

Steve comes up behind Deb's chair, carrying a light jacket, and drapes it over her shoulders. She peers up at him with a quick smile, and I feel the longing like a hollow in my stomach. Deb has someone. Belongs to someone.

What am I trying to say? That the price we pay is a kind of trade-off. Freedom for security, that's the choice we make. We give up the usual framework: family, neighbours, lifelong friendships. Sacrifice a little of one thing for more of the other. The extraordinary.

242

'I don't regret it,' I say to Deb. 'But everything comes at a cost, right?'

'Mm-hmm. The things you can't have. The things you had to give up.'

Deb sees it. Sees the void left by Niklas, sees that I have nothing left. No family, no partner, no children – am I really so conventional after all?

'But you do have the ladies now,' she says, and her voice is soft and consoling. 'The collective. That's an anchor to the past. You have a long history together – that makes for a sense of belonging.'

Steve has gone inside, and Deb and I sit in silence for a while. I think of Sina; the soft, pale hand resting on the blanket. Maya, the knot in my stomach: how long can we manage it? History that gives you belonging. Belonging that brings responsibilities.

I drain my glass and stand up. Time to call it a night. I want to get to the hospital early tomorrow and see how Sina's doing.

39

Ingrid

She's a down-to-earth person, no one can deny that. Ingrid Hagen has a firm grip on reality and has little patience for superstition and silliness. When you find it hard to believe that something is true, it usually isn't.

But something's opening her up, here in Fiji. The chlorophyll that makes the leaves burst into green, the light that pries your eyes open. Wildrid, who will speak up, or break out in a dance, more and more often these days.

When Mosese doesn't show up for three days, Ateca is the first one to mention it. Ingrid's been a little worried, too; the manager is normally the picture of reliability.

'I'll go by his place on my way home tonight, Madam Ingrid,' she says. 'Maybe he's sick.'

When Ateca walks towards the door with her bag tucked under her arm, Ingrid decides on a whim, 'I'll come with you. If Mosese's ill, I might be able to help with something.' She sneaks a peek at Lisbeth and Maya, who are both dozing in their chairs on the porch after dinner. 'They'll be OK on their own.'

Ateca looks at her with an inscrutable expression before nodding softly and opening the door. They walk quickly up the road. Ateca shouts 'Bula!' when they arrive outside the little house with two plastic chairs on the front steps, and Mosese's daughter-in-law ushers them inside. As they greet Litia, Ingrid is surprised to see Mosese sitting by himself, watching the small TV in the far corner of the room. The volume is turned all the way up. Mosese makes no sign of turning around and Ingrid's attention is caught by the flickering images on the screen. The prime minister sits listening to a speech in an assembly hall with a *salusalu* around his neck. The honorific garland, made of dried banana leaves and fresh flowers, looks as if it's making his neck itch; he scratches himself and looks impatient.

At last, Mosese turns towards them. 'Bula.' He lifts himself halfway out of the chair, and that's when she sees the bandage on his shin, a large piece of gauze wrapped just below his knee. Ingrid feels her stomach churn; something about the stained, white dressing against his dark kneecap makes her feel unwell.

'Mosese, what happened to your leg?'

She can't hold back her astonishment. Something in the way Ateca shuffles quickly to the side vaguely signals to Ingrid that she has shown a lack of respect, but she doesn't take the time to assess it fully.

Mosese slumps back in his chair; he obviously can't stand without support. He mumbles something and looks away. Litia comes closer and speaks only to Ateca. 'He burned himself.'

'Burned himself! On what?'

Litia looks encouragingly at her husband, but he keeps his eyes glued to the TV screen.

'The lovo.' Litia almost snorts the word, and Ingrid is

amazed. If there's anything Mosese's surely done a million times, it's making a lovo.

'We'd prepared the food, and he was going to open it to check that the stones were hot enough. He opened it way too fast and carelessly' – Litia shakes her head and shoots her husband a reproachful look – 'and a red-hot piece of wood sprung out and seared his leg.'

'Isa!' Ateca claps her hands together in an outburst of sympathy.

'Does it hurt?' Ingrid can hear how dumb her question sounds right away. Mosese wouldn't have shirked his duties if he'd been able to walk at all.

Litia keeps her gaze fixed on Ateca as she speaks. 'It won't heal, and it keeps oozing.'

'Have you tried *domele*?'

Litia gives Ateca an offended look, as if the juice of crushed basil leaves hadn't been the first thing she tried. 'Of course. And I put *tavola* leaves on the wound right away. But it's not working.'

Mosese moans softly in his chair, and Ateca kneels down in front of him. 'Can I see the wound?'

He leans forward and loosens the soaked bandage. Ingrid shudders. The burn wound is severely infected, with greenish-yellow scabs. Clear pus oozes from the thin membrane that can't cover up the blood vessels underneath.

'You have to—'

'Find someone from Beqa, I know!' Litia's tone is curt as she interrupts Ateca. 'We know. But it's hard to go any-where when he can't walk.'

Ingrid doesn't understand: Beqa? The little island off the

coast of Suva is five or six hours' drive plus a boat ride away – why in the world would they go there? She wants to ask, but Ateca stops her.

'There's a woman from Beqa married to a man in a village not far away. The problem is how to get Mosese there when he can't even stand on his leg.'

'I could drive him in the truck.' Ingrid says it without a moment's thought. 'I'll go down and get the key.'

She heads towards the door, hears the start of Ateca's protests and ignores Litia's distrustful stare. She doesn't know what Beqa has to do with all of this, but giving Mosese a ride in the truck is the least she can do to help him. The image of the oozing wound is fixed in her mind's eye as she hurries down the road.

The nausea has loosened its hold by the time she pulls up in front of Mosese's house.

The old man's sons help him out to the truck, where he's hoisted into the back seat with his foot outstretched while Ingrid, Litia and Ateca squeeze in the front. One of the sons insists on coming along, and has to sit on the truck bed. He pulls a jacket over his head to shield himself from the dust.

Ingrid looks at Ateca; it seems like she's going to have to ask for an explanation. 'What is this thing with Beqa? Are we going to some sort of healer?'

She feels Litia's eyes on her – *what does this kaivalagi know about anything?* – but puts the car in gear and tries to avoid the worst potholes in the road.

'People from Beqa,' Ateca begins, leaning back in her seat, 'have power over fire.'

Ingrid glances at her quickly. 'Power over fire, how?'

Ateca hesitates a moment, searching for the right words. 'People from Beqa, Madam Ingrid—'

'From Navakeisese,' Litia cuts in. She keeps her gaze fixed out the window. 'Those who are Sawau.'

'People from the Sawau clan,' Ateca corrects herself quickly, 'they can take away the pain. From burn wounds. They can stop fire from burning the body.'

Ingrid turns her head and stares at her, and Ateca quickly points at the road. 'Madam Ingrid, watch out . . .'

Wildrid takes over inside Ingrid. Her whole body is tingling. Stopping fire. Spirits and supernatural powers. Whatever this is, she is ready! 'What do you mean, Ateca?'

The story unfolds in the darkness of the front seat. Of how long, long ago, a Sawau warrior stuck his hands under a stone in a gushing waterfall. He thought he had caught an eel between his hands, but discovered that it was a small spirit. The spirit begged for its life and offered the warrior all kinds of gifts to be set free, but everything was turned down, until he proposed the gift of power over fire.

Ingrid's eyes dart away from the road again. 'What does that mean?'

'The spirit dug a hole that he filled with red-hot stones,' Ateca continues. 'Then he walked across the stones without getting burned, and invited the warrior to follow him. He did, and he didn't get burned either. Not a single scorch mark on the soles of his feet.'

'And so . . .' Wildrid grips the steering wheel harder.

'That's why people from Beqa have power over fire. They can walk across white-hot rocks without getting burned, and they can help people who have been burned.'

'Help Mosese? How?'

Ateca shakes her head. 'You'll see when we get there.'

The woman opens the door when the truck stops in front of the house. She's probably accustomed to sudden visits late at night, Ingrid thinks. Mosese's son jumps off the truck bed and greets her politely. 'We come from Korototoka; my father needs help.'

The woman nods silently and nudges the door open; they help Mosese inside. Her husband mumbles a quiet greeting and leaves the room. The woman sits down on a stool and pulls Mosese's leg on to her lap. Without a word, she removes the bandage from the weeping wound and strokes her hand slowly back and forth across it. Her lips move, but it's impossible to hear what she's saying. The only sound is the rustling of an animal running across the roof of the house, and the sharp chirp of a gecko in the corner.

They sit there for a long time. The hand slowly pulls the fire and pain from Mosese's leg, gliding back and forth in the half-light. Ateca sits by the wall and appears to be asleep; Litia's eyelids are drooping. Only Ingrid is wide awake. Her gaze follows the hand pushing and pulling, the smoke from the kerosene lamp coats her tongue. The voices of Mosese's son and the woman's husband float past the open window.

After what feels like several hours, the woman from Beqa gets up from the chair. Mosese lies on his back on the floor, his arm draped across his face. Ingrid leans forward to look at the wound. It looks pale and pink, covered in a dry, smooth membrane.

The car is quiet on the way back to Korototoka. Mosese sleeps the whole way home.

40

Ateca

Dear God, please make Madam Sina completely well again. She and Madam Kat have been gone for five days. Now Madam Sina just has to rest for a while in Suva, then they'll be back. Thank you for making the doctors' tests come out clear. And thank you for letting the woman from Beqa help Mosese with his leg last night. You know our names and make sure we have what we need.

But Madam Maya isn't doing well, Lord. She's restless and scared because Madam Sina is away. But it helps when Maraia comes to visit. Today they played ocean. Madam Maya held a pillow in her arms while she nodded to the rhythm of a song she heard inside her head. Maraia sat on the floor, surrounded by the shiny pink shells that usually lie on the window sill.

The ladies in the house are like a necklace made of shells: from the same beach, but all of them a little different. Each one worries for the next one on the string: Madam Lisbeth worries for Madam Sina, Madam Sina for Madam Maya, Madam Ingrid for Madam Kat, and Madam Kat for all of them.

I worry for all of them, too. How can I not, when the air in Vale nei Kat is as thick as thunder? As if the house is about to burst.

When Madam Kat comes home, it'll be easier for all of them. Dear Lord, hold your hand over the ladies until she returns.

In Jesus' holy name. Emeni.

41

Maya

She wonders when Evy will get here. It's been a while since her daughter was here, hasn't it? 'You have to come and visit us, Mum,' she always says. But Maya can't stand the long, boring train ride, the trip across the mountains to Trondheim in the overcrowded car where the heater never works very well. It would be better for Evy to come here. Maybe she doesn't have time. But it's been a while since she was here, hasn't it?

Maya pushes open the door to her room and stays still, frozen to the spot. Something is wrong; she doesn't recognize this. Is it her eyes? She covers them with her hands, uncovers them again. Still the same. She struggles to bring the words to the front of her brain, the words that will tell her what's wrong. They're there, she can feel it, just out of reach. Without the words, she doesn't know what she's afraid of, but that's what she is. Cold and mindlessly afraid.

Dark. It's definitely dark. Her feet refuse to step off the black precipice, her stomach convulses – she doesn't want to fall! She holds on to the door frame with both hands, there's a void in front of her, the dizziness surges through her body. She can't move her legs, she doesn't know what this is. With a shriek, she lets go and falls back into the hallway.

From the chair by the table under the window, Ingrid scrambles to her feet. 'Maya, what is it? Did you hurt yourself?'

She quickly tears down the blanket she's draped across the window to shut out the sun, which is causing a glare on the computer screen. 'Did you open the wrong door? Let me help you.'

*

From: kat@connect.com.fj
To: evyforgad@gmail.com
Subject: Maya

Dear Evy,

I'm sure you're wondering why your mum hasn't been writing. I'm sorry to say it, but I don't think you can expect any more letters or emails from her, if the situation doesn't change. And I'm afraid it's not likely to. Maya has good days and bad days, but I have to be honest and tell you that she's spending more and more time in her own world. Except for a few truly difficult days here and there – and I think those happen when she momentarily realizes that there's an enormous, unconquerable distance between who she was and who she is now – she still seems to be doing well; she's calm and peaceable. I don't like to use that word, and I don't mean to be condescending: even as a quiet, introspective soul, so far from the active, energetic friend I knew, Maya's still a wonderful person to be around.

I've mentioned before that, medically speaking, we don't have much to offer her here in our village in Fiji. She doesn't have any medications other than the ones you left, and we don't have access to any Alzheimer's specialists. We can see that forgetfulness and dreams occupy more and more of Maya for each month that goes by, and here in the house, all we have to offer is the love we have for her. She doesn't always remember our names, but for the most part she trusts us and knows that we have her best interests at heart. On the bad days when she cries because there are big black holes all around her and inside her, one of us holds her hand, or we take her down to the beach to listen to the ocean.

There's a little girl named Maraia who visits us often. Maya is always happy to see her, and they sometimes go for walks together. Otherwise, Maya mostly spends her time with Sina. Having known them both since high school, it's good to see that the old bonds of friendship still hold – even though those two weren't the closest back then, if I remember correctly. In any case, everyone needs someone, and this is a place where we can each be 'someone' for each other.

I know it must make you worry to read this. I don't want to brush under the carpet the fact that Maya's dementia is worsening, but I also want to assure you that we're taking care of her the best way we know how. I do think her experience of everyday life here is mostly good, and that's what I mainly want to convey to you. She's doing well physically, although you'd probably notice that she's lost weight since you last saw her. She doesn't always remember or want to eat.

You know you're more than welcome here whenever you'd like to visit. Maya asks about you sometimes, but never in panic or dismay; I don't want this email to scare you or make you feel guilty. If you want her to come home, we'll understand, and we'll find a way to make that happen. But I want to emphasize that Maya isn't a burden to us, even in the reality she now lives in, which we can't share with her. And if the road should end here in Korototoka, we'll be ready to hold her hand down the last stretch of it, too.

Best wishes to you and your family,
Kat

42

Sina

She still feels awful. The wound aches, she walks hunched over like an overripe plum tree in autumn and moves her legs with slow, tiny steps. And the others don't seem to care much, either. Sure, Ateca starts every day by asking how she's doing, and Lisbeth does cast her anxious looks. Kat has brought her home again, so she probably thinks her job is done, Ingrid pulled her aside the moment they walked in the door with a story about Mosese who'd been ill, and how they were behind on the packaging and preparation of the cocoa. And Lisbeth's daughter in Norway wanted to know when she could expect the first chocolate delivery. Sina understands that, of course; after all, this is supposed to be their new livelihood, and Kat obviously needs to get back to business. With all the back and forth, this hospital ordeal has wasted over two weeks of her time, Sina thinks dismally. Not to mention how much it must have cost.

'The most important thing is that they didn't find anything wrong,' Kat says, and shoves aside all talk of money. 'We'll deal with that later. They'll send a bill.'

Sina knows that's a lie; she saw with her own eyes how Kat took out her blue credit card and spoke quietly to the man behind the counter while she was filling out her own discharge papers. But what can she do?

Sina drags herself the last couple of steps across the rough wood floor and sinks down into the wicker chair in the corner of the porch. She can't even go for a walk with Maya; the doctor has ordered rest for at least three weeks.

'How's it going? Are you in pain?'

Lisbeth has followed her out and sits down on the edge of the top step, her cigarette case in hand. Her meek, nervous voice scratches and claws in Sina's ears. Her slender bum looks as if it's ready to jump up and run away at any moment. Sina feels her irritation growing.

She digs deep inside herself: is it jealousy she feels? Because Lisbeth has suddenly been given a starring role in Vale nei Kat's new business venture? Because she has connections and knowledge while Sina will never be anything but unskilled help? Or is it just the discomfort of seeing how Lisbeth is obviously so awkward around her?

'Can I have a cigarette.'

Not a question, more of a short message between spouses who have been around one another for fifty years. Why can't I stop being so grouchy with her?

Lisbeth throws her the case, so quickly and eagerly that she misses the table and the cigarettes spill out on the floor. 'Sorry . . .' She jumps up and starts gathering them again, gives Sina a cigarette and fumbles to find the lighter.

Sina leans forward to take it, and feels a jolt of pain in her wound. 'Ow!'

Lisbeth jerks back and Sina suddenly feels tears pressing

257

against her eyelids – dammit! Why can't she just act normal, without fluttering around the house like a moth.

'Sit down!' she says brusquely. 'Stop fussing so much, for goodness' sake!'

'I'm not fussing, I was just going to . . .'

'Yeah, yeah.'

They smoke in silence for a while. Ateca comes around the corner with a laundry basket under her arm, and Lisbeth jumps to her feet. 'I can fold those for you!'

But Ateca shakes her head. 'That's OK, Madam Lisbeth. I can do it myself. It's better if you keep Madam Sina company.'

Lisbeth's hand is shaking when she sits back down and retrieves the cigarette from the ashtray. She's afraid of me, it occurs to Sina. The thought hits her like a lighting bolt: Lisbeth's afraid when I talk to her!

The tears are there, a throbbing lump in her throat. The surgery, the painkillers. The aching wound. She's so tired. She just wants to be done with all of it.

Sina takes a long drag on her cigarette and looks Lisbeth square in the face.

'It's Harald who's Armand's father,' she says.

It's as if she's dreamed it. Lisbeth's white, frozen face as she got up and walked away, down the stairs and along the road. Maraia, who suddenly appeared below the porch and looked at her wordlessly before turning around and following Lisbeth. Ingrid and Kat, who helped her inside and into bed: 'Sina, sweetie, you have to take it easy. Don't you know you need to rest? You're exhausted!' The tears that kept running. For Armand and his pathetic life. For Lisbeth and for herself. For everything.

258

Sina lies on her back, breathing with her mouth open. She must have slept; through quivering eyelids she can make out the half-light in the room. She has to pee but doesn't have the energy to get up.

Ateca cracks the door ajar. She's holding a bowl in her hand. 'You have to eat something, Madam Sina. Here's some soup.'

She lets Ateca prop her up in bed, tries to avoid putting pressure on her full bladder. Has Lisbeth come back? Has she talked to the others? She's going to have to talk to the others. The betrayal, her own, Harald's; it's too big to be contained in Lisbeth's skinny body.

'Eat some soup,' Ateca repeats and holds the bowl out to her. 'You have to regain your strength, Madam Sina.'

Her strength. She's completely drained. Her blood runs thick and sticky through her veins, like an infection. She pushes the bowl away. 'I have to go to the toilet,' she mutters.

Ateca waits inside the door as she sits down. Turns away and rearranges the soap on the edge of the sink as Sina pees, a long, steady stream. Sina's eyes linger on her belly when she looks down to pull up her underwear. The pale, wide stripe of skin, like a long, unbaked loaf of bread resting on her thighs. The wrinkled, vertical dressing. She gets to her feet and lets Ateca help her back to the bedroom.

The door is open and Maya's sitting in the armchair, on top of a pile of clothes. Ateca helps Sina into bed, takes the soup bowl and closes the door behind her. Sina leans back against the wall and shoots Maya a weary smile. What she really wants to do is sleep. But Maya's gaze is fixed on her face, surprised and patient all at once. Her fingers fiddle with a long, white strip of something or other.

'The dress,' Maya says. 'I made it.'

Sina recognizes the ribbon. 'Kat,' she says reflexively. 'It was Kat who sewed Maraia's dress, you remember.'

'I made it,' Maya repeats, louder. She drops the ribbon and ties an imaginary bow with her hands in the air. 'Green and red.'

Sina doesn't argue any more. The insects outside buzz the minutes away. She slumps down into bed and closes her eyes. Everything that kept us so busy, she thinks. Everything that mattered. And all we have left is the colour of a dress.

When Sina opens her eyes again, the door is half open and two black silhouettes stand out against the light. Lisbeth's thin shoulders and Maraia's curly mane. Sina is about to open her mouth when Kat's voice echoes down the hall. '*There* you are, Lisbeth. And Maraia, what are you doing here so late? Your mum must be worried about you.'

The big calm in the little voice. 'I was just helping her find her way home.'

All her other feelings have blended into this one now. Sina has never realized that this is what sorrow feels like: a sticky, greyish-brown toothache. A fog that never lifts, just envelops her like a mountain of hard work piling up on all sides. It has become everybody's sorrow. Not just hers and Lisbeth's, but Maya's too, even Ingrid's. And Kat's. Nothing exists or is felt before it's gone through Kat. A filter they all have to pass through.

'Does Armand know?' is the only question she had asked Sina.

Sina had shaken her head. 'No one,' she'd said. 'No one's ever known.'

'Not even Harald?'

She hadn't responded. She's sure Harald knows. He can count too, dates and months. But they've never spoken a word about it. And that the company should have been called Høie & Son Building Supplies by now? She never thinks about that. Never ever.

Lisbeth hasn't asked a single question. Not of her. In the murky slow-motion film the days have now become, that's the worst thing of all. She has told Lisbeth, and everything is different now, though nothing has changed. She hadn't planned on saying anything; she didn't even know that the unspoken sentence still lurked somewhere on the back of her tongue. What good would it do? It's all in the past, lies abandoned by the side of the road behind her, used up and paid for.

'So why did you tell her now, then?'

Sina doesn't even have the energy to get annoyed at the fact that it is Ingrid who asks the question. She can't bring herself to search for the words that could explain the most tormenting of pains: to be in possession of the power to crush another. And to know that you have it in you to use it. Realizing that the only way to soften the pain of having the upper hand is to lay down your weapons.

She shrugs and looks over at Maya sitting in the chair at the head of the table. Her clear blue eyes are completely void of history.

43

Lisbeth

She just can't think. Lisbeth is fully aware that she's never been in the same league as Maya, or Ingrid for that matter, when it comes to being smart. She's never cared; she's always had other things they envied her for. But none of that counts any more, and she doesn't know what to do. She's helpless when the mirror stares back blindly without telling her how things are supposed to get better. And her head is empty. Sina, Harald, Armand; she doesn't know where to begin. Where to dig a sharp finger-nail into the thick shell of the throbbing sphere of her head and start to peel everything away, piece by piece.

The worst part is Sina. That she had insisted on getting Sina a job in the store. That she, Lisbeth, was the one who had made sure Sina and the boy had a roof over their heads and food on the table all these years.

The worst part is Harald. Picturing him and plain, flat-chested Sina. His disparaging comment about Armand: 'That layabout son of hers? I won't take him in!'

The worst part is Armand. That she got all dressed up in her green silk blouse. His winking across the table. A red-hot wave constricting her throat: standing in front of the mirror in lacy black lingerie.

Lisbeth's never had much use for God. Never needed anything that couldn't be fixed with her make-up bag or paid for from her wallet. She has looked down with a condescending smile on Ingrid's enthusiasm for exploring all sides of village life in Korototoka, including the religious part. Hymns and after-church coffee have never been Lisbeth Høie's style.

For Lisbeth Karlsen, a lot of things are different. One of the strangest consequences of Sina's revelation was that she immediately changed her name inside her head. Took back her maiden name to turn herself back into the person she was before Harald. She has to get away from his name. Is it possible to become who you were before?

Lisbeth Karlsen takes back her evening prayers too. She's not sure whether she's ever really believed in God, and she's not too worried about it now. But when she lies in bed at night, she folds her hands and repeats to herself the prayer her mother would read to her and her brother every night. 'From sorrow, sin and deepest fear, protect me with your angel near.' It's a little too late for sin and sorrow. But maybe she can at least sleep through the night without fear. Lisbeth Karlsen is free and wide open, free as only someone who's lost everything can be.

Now she understands the hostility, the resentment in Sina's voice, the glimmers of something like scorn. Or does she? *She*, Lisbeth, is the one who was betrayed; if anyone has the right to be bitter, it's her. Disgust bubbles up like green bile in her throat – she's been the one walking around feeling sorry for Sina this whole time! Walking on eggshells around her to avoid rubbing salt in the wound of how pathetic she was. Her sad little life. That *she*, Sina, could take that nasty tone with *her*! With what *she* had on her conscience!

But Harald's face is always there. His condescending tone whenever he talked about Sina: 'Not exactly eye candy behind the counter.' The slap on her backside, her fiftieth birthday present: 'Guess I'll have to buy you an ass job.' The compliment, the most loving words she could expect from him: 'You know you're a hot piece of ass.'

She stands in front of the mirror. Her mascara-free eyes are dry and the grey roots along her centre parting stare straight at her, mocking her. Hot piece of ass. That was always enough for her. And Sina never even had that. Just some genes from Harald in a son who loves her about as much as he loves a cash machine with insufficient funds.

It hits her like an explosion, bursting in her head: is this about the family business? Høie Building Supplies, which has provided for all of them for so many years: her, Joachim and Linda. Sina and Armand. Harald is the third generation. The fourth generation, Linda and Joachim, don't want to take over the business. But Armand! Is that what Sina wants? To throw Armand into the ring to fight for control of the family business? He is Harald Høie's eldest son. The birthright of the firstborn, is that what Sina's after? A whirlwind chaos in her head: paternity test, living will and testament. If this inconceivable thing is true, it will tear the safety net out from under Linda and Joachim. Has Sina told him? Does Armand know who his father is? His wide, gleaming smile. 'You hens really live in paradise. No rooster to bother you.'

She has to talk to Sina. Must ask her if this is what she has planned. If what she and Harald did almost fifty years

ago – she can't bring herself to picture it, can't stomach it –
is going to shatter her own children's future.

Suddenly she longs for Joachim. How has she managed
to let her son slip away? How did she allow Harald's con-
tempt – *'Well, if that's all he wants to do with his life!'* – to
shove her out of Joachim's life? Her quiet, considerate son.
She's let him disappear, into a different life and a family she
doesn't know. His daughters, Viva and Sara, do they even
remember who she is?

*

The little weekend bag looks silly at her feet. It sits on the
ground, silver-grey with a stylish retractable handle, a perfect match for her lightweight linen trousers over freshly
painted toenails. Ingrid has driven her to the bus station in
Rakiraki; she's insisted on taking the bus alone from there
to Denarau. The luxury dreamland bubble of Denarau,
where the hotels sit side by side along the white, newly
combed beaches. The artificial island just outside Nadi, a
mere fifteen minutes from the airport, where Australian
tourists stream in every week to hotel rooms with just-made
beds with masi-patterned bedspreads, and yellow blossoms
adorning the sides of the bathroom sinks. Manicured
lawns, swimming pools with scrubbed tiles and striped
beach towels, spas with hot-stone massages, foot massages,
coconut-milk massages. Chiffon-draped wedding chapels
with ocean views, golf courses, torches, and kava cere-
monies every afternoon at five.

Lisbeth needs to be alone. Everyone gets that, no questions asked. When she'd gone over a week without speaking

to anyone, it was Kat who finally suggested it. 'Why don't you take a few days away for yourself, Lisbeth? Go to Denarau, soak up the sun by the pool. Visit the spa, use the gym, watch the sunset from the bar.'

She'd only nodded. She hadn't even asked how much it would cost. And now she's climbing aboard, sitting down in a window seat on the bus to Nadi and Denarau, with three days at the Royal Davui Plaza ahead of her. She's not going to think. She's not going to cry. She's not going to do anything at all.

The cool, dry air envelops her when she enters the room. Her suitcase is already perched on the bench by the wall, and she turns to the young man who has clicked her key card into the slot on the wall. '*Vinaka vakalevu*, many thanks!' He observes her for a brief moment, just enough for her to wonder whether he's waiting for a tip – but hadn't Kat said they don't do that here? – before he bows hastily and shuts the door behind him.

She sinks down on to the bed, fixes her gaze on the bamboo blinds in front of the balcony door. Through the glass she hears the noise from the pool: a whining, roaring jumble of voices over a background of music. Her eyes glide across the room. The fruit bowl packed in cellophane on the table. The carved wooden turtle on the wall above the minibar. Armand would have liked it here, it occurs to her. The cool, soft whisper of luxury. The polite bows of younger, more handsome men further down the ladder.

Armand. She examines her thoughts. What is that taste in her mouth: nausea? Embarrassment? Anger? She has the vague sense that there's something wrong with her internal circuitry. She should feel something; the thought of Armand should spark some sort of reaction, but she feels nothing. A mild discomfort but nothing that riles her up, pokes her, strangles her. She prods further, testing herself: Sina. What does she feel for Sina?

It's as if she's left it all behind outside the door of room 206. Sina and Armand, the betrayal – she says it out loud to herself: 'She *betrayed* me!' – but nothing happens; it's been left out there, as distant as the shrieking of the children in the pool. Her friend's colourless gaze, the emptiness in her voice when she said it. As if the words meant nothing at all. Lisbeth lifts one hand from her lap, traces it slowly upward and places it over her heart. Strokes back and forth over her linen blouse with slender fingers. But she feels nothing. Nothing broken in there. No raging tears yearning to burst out.

Lisbeth gets up from the bed. Opens the dewy-cold bottle of white wine in the minibar and begins to unpack.

It's not the least bit difficult going to dinner alone. She knows she looks good. The white dress she hasn't worn since she came to Fiji swishes airily around her legs, and the large bejewelled necklace lends a touch of artistic free spirit to the outfit. She sits down at an empty table with four chairs, and has barely ordered a drink before she is joined by a couple, quite a bit younger than her, who ask whether the seats are taken. Alan and Donna are from Sydney, they tell her. This is their third time in Denarau, their first time here at Royal Davui. 'And it's so *cheap* now in the off-season!'

Alan smiles at her, and Lisbeth feels an old reflex kick in: is there something special there in the corner of his eye? A little glimmer as he turns his head partly away so his wife won't see?

But Donna sees nothing. She's already hung her hand-bag over the back of the chair and is heading for the buffet, the long table where the food spills out towards the guests in two tiers. Grilled fish. Steaming pasta, a boatload of shrimp. Lamb chops accompanied by asparagus glistening with butter. Chicken curry, beef rendang. A dedicated bar-becue station where chefs with tall white hats carve out your favourite cuts. 'Roast beef, ma'am? Some pork?'

The woman in the white dress has a great time at the table with her new friends. They don't know her, she doesn't know them, they've never been to Reitvik and they've never been shopping at Høie Building Supplies. They have no idea how many children Harald Høie has. When they ask whether she's on holiday alone, she nods without volunteer-ing any more information. 'Let me treat the ladies to a glass of champagne,' Alan says gallantly, and Donna and Lisbeth smile as they accept. And when the dessert bowls are empty – Lisbeth is satisfied with a small portion of fruit salad; kiwi and passion fruit – she gets to her feet and smiles. 'I think I'll have to retire a bit early since it's my first night,' she says casually, and thanks them for the great company. 'Have a lovely rest of your evening!'

The dress flares out a little more around her legs as she walks towards the exit; she can feel Alan's gaze on her back. She follows the flagstones around the pool and up the footpath towards the hotel building. Behind her, she hears the waves patiently washing up on the beach. It suddenly strikes her how harmless the whole thing is. I'm just myself, Lisbeth Karlsen thinks. And everything is fine. I can eat dinner with friendly people I meet at a hotel. I can look forward to going to bed alone.

She wakes up early the next morning. Savours the quiet in the room, the pale shimmer through the blinds that tells her the sun has begun its daily march across the sky. Lisbeth opens the sliding door to the balcony and leans against the railing, delighting in the luxurious plushy bath robe. Royal Davui Plaza slowly comes to life beneath her. A man in a beige hotel uniform stacks fresh towels on the shelf by the pool; an older woman shoves a cart with a mop, broom and bucket down the path. Gardeners reposition sprinklers around the lawns. They wear soft fabric hats the same colour as their uniforms; they move around down there like little worker ants, trimming an unsightly branch here, moving a few decorative stones there. Two of them work side by side, kneeling on the ground, half concealed in the shadow of a big bush. One of them laughs at something the other one says and punches him playfully on the shoulder. Lisbeth admires him, watches the muscles move under his cotton shirt. He removes his hat and wipes the sweat off his brow. When he turns his head and the sun strikes his face, Lisbeth gasps. It's him! Him, the mugger, Vilivo's friend! The young boy for whom she had ached with desire as she stood there with his knife in her hand. It's Salesi with the rugby shoes, on his knees on the lawn down there.

Blood rushes to her head, the cigarette drops out of her hand on to the balcony floor. Now the second gardener emerges from the shadow, and Salesi gets up. They gather their tools and walk towards a side door of the hotel. Lisbeth hurries to retreat into her room; her pulse throbs in

269

her neck. She slams the balcony door shut and just stands there, gasping for breath. Then she whacks the door frame with her palm. 'Bloody hell!'

Her voice is hoarse and unrecognizable, and she looks around, afraid that someone might have heard her. Why is she swearing? It's a good thing that Salesi has got a job at a hotel in Denarau! One less unemployed youth in Korototoka. One less person throwing his life away, idly sitting under a tree and waiting for something to happen.

She lets the bath robe drop to the floor and gets in the shower.

At breakfast, she meets the couple from last night again.

'We've already secured our sunbeds by the pool,' Donna says with a satisfied smile. 'You know what the trick is? You have to claim them with towels that are different from the ones they hand out down there.'

'Oh?' Lisbeth looks at her, surprised.

'Yes. That way, people will see that they're taken, you know? We brought towels from home just for that reason,' she says and drags Lisbeth over to the window. 'See?'

Sure enough, there are two lounge chairs side by side in a prime spot on the long edge of the pool, with lemon-yellow and dark red towels draped across them.

Lisbeth nods, full of admiration for her new friend's resourcefulness.

'You're more than welcome to settle in next to us . . . Did you bring anything you can run down and leave there?'

'Thanks so much,' she quickly responds. 'But I was thinking of checking out the spa after this. I might book an appointment for later today.'

They walk out of breakfast together and stroll through the airy lobby that opens on to the ocean; the sound of trickling water from a fountain, the aroma of coffee and frangipani. They take the stairs down to the ground floor, where Donna turns right to head towards the pool, Lisbeth left to follow the sign with the carved words 'Heavenly Bliss Spa'. As she raises her hand to wave goodbye, a door to the stairwell behind her opens. A gardener in hotel uniform comes up beside them, smiles politely, and is poised to deliver his standard 'Bula!' when he freezes, his mouth wide open. Salesi's eyes are just as clear, his features just as soft and young as they were that night. And he sees who she is. The recognition spreads across his face like a curtain being pulled back, and he mumbles a confused 'Ma'am? Bula . . . ma'am!'

She instantly feels her face flush and a prickling sensation rise in her throat. Lisbeth senses Donna's eyes on her and knows she must look breathless and flustered. She tears her eyes away from Salesi and quickly tosses a 'Bula!' out in the air. Donna furrows her eyebrows, perplexed – *she can tell we know each other!* – and looks from one to the other without saying a word. And before Lisbeth can piece together a single sentence, the moment has passed. Salesi pulls away, throws her an uncertain look before turning his back and shuffling down the footpath in his cheap, worn-down rubber sandals. She can barely make out a few bluish-green curved lines on his arms under the edges of his shirt sleeves, like animals trying to escape.

'I'm sure I'll see you later today,' Lisbeth says and nods away Donna's wondering gaze. She doesn't know what the taste in her mouth is. Something akin to embarrassment. Mixed with the glimpse of the stooped shoulders hurrying around the corner far ahead, it turns into a chewed-up wad of disappointment and shame.

She noticed it when she arrived. The poster in the lobby that read 'Free Wi-Fi', and something about the business centre opening hours. Lisbeth's thoughts slowly ripple back and forth under the massage therapist's skilled fingers. Up along her temple, charting a steady course back along her skull, she gasps as they reach the tender spot on her neck. One little pressure point and violet lightning flashes behind her eyelids. Oh!

'Does it hurt?'

Lisbeth nods into the hole on the massage table. 'A little, but keep going.'

She's convinced herself that she's not hurt by how rarely she hears from Joachim. Part of her had felt as much disappointment as Harald back when their son decided not to follow in his father's footsteps, yet she had known, deep down, that Joachim was making the right choice for himself. He is compassionate, her son. Gentle. A care-giver. Completely different from his sister. Linda has never denied that her own needs and wants come first.

Their emails show them just as they are, Lisbeth thinks as she stands in the shower and lets the hot water rinse off the last traces of coconut oil. Linda has hinted several times over the past few months that she wouldn't mind a trip to Fiji. If Lisbeth could find her a good hotel. And, since she lives down there, maybe she could get her the local rate? She and her boyfriend would like 'one of those bungalows all the way down on the beach, the ones with the thatched roofs, you know.' But with air-conditioning, of course, and the hotel has to have a proper gym. Linda doesn't envision visiting her

272

mother in Korototoka: 'It would be so complicated, and we can't take more than a week off work,' but maybe Lisbeth could come to Denarau and spend a few days with them?

Since she's been in Fiji, Joachim's emails have been few and relatively short. No outbursts or accusations when she left, no mentions of Harald. He has only enquired how she's doing, whether there's anything she needs.

Joachim's emails have been about Lisbeth. Linda's emails have been about Linda.

As she dries off and pulls her clothes on, she thinks about Joachim's daughters. He's barely mentioned them in his messages to her. Such a distance between them, she thinks, and pauses in front of the mirror with her hairbrush in her hand. Her grandchildren. She doesn't know much more about them than their names and how old they are. Suddenly it hits her: he thinks I don't care. Harald rejected him and I turned my back to all of it.

She tucks the brush into her handbag and walks towards the lobby with quick steps. 'Could someone show me how to use one of the computers in the business centre?'

From: lisbeth.hoie@hotmail.com
To: joachim.hoie@telia.com
Subject: Hello from Fiji

Hi Joachim and the whole family!

I'm writing from Royal Davui Plaza Hotel on the holiday island of Denarau. I know that sounds luxurious, and it is! I've just come back from a spa treatment after a beautiful breakfast buffet, and I'm about to head down to the pool. There are no fewer than three pools here, one of them has several water slides and a wave machine. There's entertainment every night: meke (Fijian dance), and sometimes a lovo, where they bury the food in a hole in the ground. It might sound weird, but they wrap the food in palm leaves so it's all clean and safe. The meat comes out incredibly juicy and delicious!

There's a gorgeous beach just below the hotel, and every day there are young boys who walk by and offer horseback rides. It's mostly little kids sitting in the saddle as the horses are walked up and down the beach, but I'm sure it would be easy for an experienced rider to set off on her own.

I don't know if you guys have any interest, but it would be really great to have you come visit me here. I think Viva and Sara would love the beach and the pool and the horses. It would be nice if you could visit me at home too. I have a pretty big room in Kat's house, and maybe it wouldn't bother you to be a little cramped for a few days?

I know plane tickets to Fiji are expensive, but I can help you with that. I don't know if you have time either, but maybe next year? It would be so great if you could meet my friends. I would really love to show you what my life is like now.

Lisbeth pauses. Deletes the last sentence. Puts it back in. Signs off, *Hugs from Mum*.

Then she hits 'send'.

44

Ateca

Can you please watch over Maraia, Lord? There's something special about Sai's little girl. She's always willing to help, and easy to love. No wonder Sai would rather keep her at home and hasn't sent her to school yet.

You know it's been hard for Sai, Lord. Her husband is gone, no one's seen him since he went to Suva to find work. Sai does what she can with her vegetables and her chickens, but she can barely scrape together enough for school books and a uniform for one of her two daughters. The older girl is the smarter one; Sai says she's going to be a doctor. Maraia is thoughtful and wise. As if she knows the secret of the sea turtles, or why the tagimoucia flower is the colour of bleeding tears.

I'm a little scared to take her with me down to the ladies too often. They all like her, that's not the problem – Madam Lisbeth has even given her a gold necklace! And when Madam Maya gets lost in the dark, Maraia takes her hand and shows her the way out.

But do you see that she can get a little cheeky, Lord? Like today, when Madam Sina and I were making roro and Maraia was helping us rinse the leaves. Madam Kat came in the kitchen and her face lit up when she saw the girl. But when she asked if it was her mother who had taught her to rinse roro, Maraia brazenly shook her head. 'I just know how,' she said.

Madam Kat didn't get annoyed, Lord. She just stroked her cheek and let her hand rest on top of her curls, without touching the human head, which is pure and sacred. 'Tulou,' she said. Forgive me.

Bless Maraia, Lord. Let the Star of the Sea shine for all the ladies of Vale nei Kat.

In Jesus' holy name. Emeni.

45

Kat

It was a good idea for Lisbeth to take a few days in Denarau. Ever since Sina made her revelation, the roles have changed; the balance in the house has been thrown off. Sina is still pale and washed-out; she lurches when she walks, like a ship in a storm. But she's assumed a kind of dignity, too; the confession has straightened out her stooped shoulders. And Lisbeth, dear God, she was completely bowled over; she needed to get away for a while.

If we're going to survive, this is how it will have to be. Lisbeth will have to live with this new truth and Sina will have to accept the rest of us looking at her differently.

We have each taken in the news about Armand in our own way. His father is none other than Harald! I have a thousand questions I'm never going to ask, and I'm sure the others' heads are buzzing with them, too. Ingrid's reaction was typical Ingrid: a mixture of astonishment and indignation, as if the revelation of Armand's paternity only confirmed the negative impression of him she already held. Reasonable, practical Ingrid was also the one to bring up the question of whether he had a claim to any inheritance. Without warning, she raised the subject unceremoniously at breakfast one day.

'So, they'll have to share it between the three of them now. Harald's estate, when the time comes.'

Lisbeth stiffened in her chair; her hand holding the mug jerked so hard the coffee spilled over the edge. She stared blankly at Sina. I held my breath and swore silently at Ingrid. For Christ's sake, was that really necessary? Sina was the only one who wasn't fazed. She just kept chewing, and swallowed her mouthful of bread before she replied, 'Armand doesn't know who his father is. And he's never going to find out either.'

To be honest, I wasn't surprised. Sina has been carrying this around for almost fifty years; I highly doubt she has some secret plan to throw down Armand like a trump card in the very last round of the game. But for Ingrid, her reply wasn't good enough. 'Surely you don't mean that! He's going to get what's rightfully his, isn't he?'

Had I been able to reach her under the table, I would have kicked her in the shin. This is none of Ingrid's business! Sina may be poor but she's not greedy. Armand is both, but this time Sina doesn't want to give him the opportunity to demonstrate that.

It was like a well-choreographed dance: Sina reaching for another slice of bread, Lisbeth slowly placing her mug down. The confusion in Lisbeth's round grey eyes; the relief shuddering through her slender body. Her shoulders quivering as Sina shaved off a piece of cheese without looking up: 'We've always managed. I've supported both Armand and myself. Now it's time for him to support himself, goddammit.'

But Ingrid wouldn't drop it, her eyes flickering back and forth between Sina and Lisbeth. 'But we're talking about a lot of money here! Høie Building Supplies is a hugely successful company. He has a *right* to part of it, after all.'

Then Lisbeth finally opened her mouth. Her face was flushed, and her voice was breathless. 'Fairness isn't all black and white. You don't have a *right* to something you've never been part of!'

Ingrid quietened down after that, but it was Sina's face I noticed. It was wide open and full of wonder. And something else, too. Respect.

It's hard to tell what Maya thinks of all the commotion these past few weeks. She stays by Sina's side as always, but hasn't shown any sign of understanding this business with Armand. Or maybe they discuss it on their walks, what do I know? Not that their relationship is based on conversation.

And Ateca? I'm not sure whether she's registered it either. She didn't ask any questions when Lisbeth packed her suitcase to go away for a few days, at least. But I'm sure Ateca has her own thoughts on the matter, she always does. Her own thoughts and her own conclusions.

A walk by the shore is always calming. The sand is warm and inviting; I stop for a moment and scoop up a handful. Let it run through my fingers before continuing down the beach, which is almost completely deserted this early in the morning. But Jone's awake. I wave to the burly figure on his way down to the boat.

'Bula, Madam Kat!'

'Bula, Jone. Going out so early?'

The laughter bubbles out of his mouth like liquid brown sugar. 'I'll have to if I want to catch anything.'

I hang around for a minute while he preps his fishing equipment; after a while one of his sons shows up to help. They work in silence; the sun already quivers with heat some distance above the horizon. Jone raises his hand and waves goodbye before they shove the *Vessel of Honour* into the waves and jump in.

I trace the path of the red boat as it bobs up and down on its way out to sea. The moment stands still around me: the reflection in the water, the wind barely rustling the palm trees. This is what we are. Everything we say, everything we do to each other, it's all nothing in the end. All that matters is having your feet planted firmly on the earth. Feeling your breath move in and out.

A sound by my side, a tiny movement. Through my sunglasses I peer down at the girl with the caramel hair. 'You're quiet, Nau,' says the Star of the Sea. Her serious face sends a ripple of joy through me.

Maraia walks on without another word, and I follow. Her feet know where they're going. We wander past the other boats ready to set sail, towards the place where the row of coconut palms is broken by a dark, swampy stretch of mangrove forest. Over to the spot under a tree where a larger boat was docked that night, shored up, with a scratched-up hull. A boat that cast a shadow long enough for a person to disappear in, even though the moon shone balolo-big and the beach was full of people.

Maraia comes to a stop, and squats down in a position my knees recognize. This was where I didn't sit. This was where I didn't see Niklas lean forward with his camera.

This was where I didn't shout out when he stumbled and fell. This was where I didn't cry for help when his body sank into the water and remained there.

Maraia's eyes glitter with grains of sand that glow in the sunlight. When I hesitate, she pats the ground next to her, and I sit down. We say nothing to each other. Behind my open eyes the film reel starts playing again, the man with the camera bag on his back. Ateca's babbling voice: *He would have shouted if he needed help, right? But no one heard anything. You have to believe it was his heart.*

Beside me, Maraia draws in the sand with a twig. A heart, she carves the lines deeper and deeper. I watch her fingers grasping the stick, the motion of her delicate wrist. Suddenly she turns to me with a knowing look. 'No one heard anything,' she says.

I keep my gaze fixed on the heart in the sand and feel the sun burn my back.

We walk back to the house together, a narrow, strong hand in mine. My head is numb, the thoughts spin around in there without shapes or words. Maybe this is how it is for Maya? The intense feeling that something is happening; you know, you want to, but you can't quite grasp it. Most of all, I feel the need to cry. As if something between Maraia and me has been established and destroyed at the same time. As if we know something about each other that we'll never discuss.

We stop for a moment at the bottom of the stairs leading to the porch. 'Do you want to come in?' She nods and we walk hand in hand up the four steps. I don't want to let go. I want her tiny, warm fingers to remember the pressure of mine. Ours. Mine and Niklas's.

I take her to the office nook in the living room. It sits on the corner of the table, the paperweight that held his days together: a five-armed starfish made of blue-painted wood. The arms with soft and rounded tips, worn smooth by his fingers. Patiently guarding inflow and outflow, everything that comes and goes. Five fingers on a hand, five women in a house.

I place the star in Maraia's hand. 'It's yours,' I say. Her fingers close around it, embracing its sleek, comfortable shape.

'Yes,' she says. 'I'm the Star of the Sea.'

We find Maya in the kitchen. She has a mug sitting on the work surface in front of her and is slowly and deliberately removing all the contents of the lower shelf in the pantry. Tea bags, sugar, spices. Honey, salt, oatmeal. Ateca brushes the floor in careful sweeps, keeping an eye on Maya, who is totally consumed by what she's doing. The shelf is empty now, everything's lined up on the counter.

I ask Maya whether she's looking for something. 'Is it the lemon tea you want? I think we ran out.'

Maya looks at me and shakes her head. 'No,' is all she says. She turns back to the work surface and stares at the items she's removed. Ateca has stopped sweeping. Everything stops as we wait for Maya. She places the empty mug back on the shelf. Then she turns towards Maraia and smiles. 'I can show you something,' she says. 'I'm a teacher. I can show you something.'

She walks out of the kitchen and Maraia follows. Her small hand keeps a tight grip on the blue starfish. I peek over at Ateca, but she doesn't return my look. Simply puts down her broom and starts cleaning up the tea and bags of spices.

I head back to the office nook. The pile of papers, letters and bills, spills across the desk. I gather them together, retrieve a smooth, white stone from below the porch and place it on top of the stack.

Ingrid has printed out a few articles she thinks I should read; I unfold the top one. *Reduces the risk of blood clots!* she's written in the margin in her large block letters. It is a piece about flavonoids in cocoa, how they increase the oxygen supply to the brain, making you more awake and alert. I crumple up the piece of paper and toss it in the wastepaper basket. Lisbeth has already noted this.

I pick up the next article but put it down again without reading it. I feel the restlessness prickle in my body. Where was Maya taking Maraia?

The door to Maya's room is half open. The two of them are seated on the floor in there. A large atlas lies open across Maya's lap; her strong, crooked index finger traces the outline of Viti Levu on a map of the South Pacific.

'The ocean is big,' Maraia says.

Maya nods solemnly. 'The island is only a little bigger than my finger.'

'And we're even smaller.'

Maya agrees. 'We're smaller than a tiny dot.'

'Is that because the ocean is so big?'

Maya contemplates the question. 'Yes,' she says at last. 'We're so small because the ocean is so big.'

The shuffling footsteps behind me tell me it's Sina. I quickly pull back from the door frame, as if to shield the

283

pair's solemn game. But Sina isn't as fiercely protective of Maya as she once was. The revelation, the confession, the announcement – however she chooses to think of it – has made her less fierce. Or, not fierce . . . less sharp, maybe. Not as brusque and as prickly as before. It's most obvious in her relationship with Lisbeth, of course. The balance between them has shifted. But Sina doesn't act like a repentant sinner. To the contrary, it almost seems as if she's relieved – maybe that's what happens when old secrets are set free? Her jaw is unclenched, the frown lines on her forehead are less deep than they were.

I turn towards Sina and, to distract her from the two behind me on the floor, I ask her whether she wants to sit outside for a while. 'Do you know where Lisbeth is, by the way?'

She shrugs, and there's no edge to her voice. 'On the computer, I think. She was going to write to her son.'

Maybe it's the thought of Niklas's blue starfish in Maraia's hand. Or maybe it's because Sina sits down in the chair closest to the door, where he always sat. Whatever it is, he's there; his presence stronger than I've felt it in a long time. My nose tingles, liquid pools in my eyes and in my throat, and I can tell I'm going to cry, right there, in front of Sina.

She leans towards me, shocked. 'Kat, what is it? Kat?'

I shake my head, force my throat open. 'It's nothing, I . . .

'I miss Niklas,' I finally say. It feels safe, like a line from a movie. I'm allowed to say that I miss Niklas.

Sina nods. 'I miss Armand,' she says. I think to myself,

284

That's not the same thing. 'And now he's not just mine any more.'

In a flash, I see what she means. Now that everything's out in the open, he belongs to everyone. I think that I should say something consoling, but Sina continues. 'I wish I had another child.' She reaches out her hands and grabs my knees. 'Do you? Do you wish you had children?'

I stare at her, stunned. Did she actually say that? Grumpy, crusty Sina entering my most intimate and private territory. Do I wish I had children? Maraia's earnest face flickers before my eyes, the sound of her silver bell voice rings in my ears. *No one heard anything.* My Star of the Sea.

Sina continues frantically, far beyond tact and sensitivity now. Her eyes are feverish and distant all at the same time. 'For years I thought Armand was enough. Everything he was going to become.'

She pulls back her hands and places them on her stomach, which bulges out under the loose-fitting shirt. 'Maybe, if he'd been a girl.'

'If I'd had children, I would rather have had a girl,' I say, struggling to keep my voice even. 'Someone to see myself in, somehow. A reflection of my face in the mirror.'

Sina looks straight into my eyes. 'Was it Niklas who never wanted it?'

Is she really asking me these questions? I look at the hands of this new Sina, and my own palms fold over my belly in the same way, resting on the muscle in there that never got to show how it can contract and stretch. *Was it Niklas who never wanted it?* There are so many things wrong with the question that it's impossible to even search for an answer.

He never said it, that he didn't want children. He didn't have to, it was clear it would never make it far enough up the list. It would always be at the bottom of the agenda, not a priority. I've often thought that my own weakness was to blame. My need to be the person I thought he wanted: the patient, compassionate, selfless Kat. Was I afraid to lose my status as equal partner in Project Save the World? Could we have become parents, together, if I'd been brave enough to say it? *Niklas, I want children. I want to have children with you.*

How can I answer Sina's question? 'I don't know.' That's the truth. I don't know the answer, because I never asked.

How can I tell her about the suspicion that grew in me, slowly and reluctantly, about the man I'd risked everything for? For whom villagers in Malawi and women's associations in Pakistan gave speeches, and to whom they had waved tearful goodbyes when he left? A certainty that grew out of tiny pieces of evidence: her strangely narrow ears, almost without earlobes. The caramel-golden shimmer in her hair; the short, wide nose. Her mother Sai, who never came near our house. When was it that the pieces fused together into a kind of conviction? One that placed the words on my tongue, ready to be hurled at him: 'Maraia is yours, isn't she?' Or was I enjoying the fact that I was the one who knew? That was something I could explain to Sina. The power of being the one to know and not say. She'd understand that.

But that's not how it was. I wasn't out for revenge, I didn't want to wound. Not Niklas, not anyone. It was the disappointment. The sorrow that he knew, and turned away. The pain in seeing the pitiful side of the big

Mister Niklas. That he was no better than any other Harald Høie.

Didn't he trust me enough? We could have made it work! Couldn't he have allowed me that, allowed *us* that? The joy over the Star of the Sea — we could have made so much room and time for it. Why didn't he trust me?

'It's best for everyone this way,' was the answer I got the night I finally asked. No, I didn't ask. I just told him that I knew. And that all I wanted was for us to share it. Share Maraia, like we'd shared everything else.

At first he looked shocked, almost scared. Then embarrassed. Defensive. I was astonished by my own reaction – I felt myself wanting to stroke his hair, cheer him up, tell him it was all going to be OK. I had to shove the lifelong team-player Kat aside, and heard my own voice, shrill and unfamiliar: 'How could you not *say* anything? I could have lived with it, Niklas, I could have turned it around! We could have been ... godparents, *something*! Instead of this ... cowardice!'

He still could have saved it. Could have stood up, could have said he would try, that he would talk to Sai. We could have discussed it, continued to be Team Kat & Niklas. Found solutions that worked in the light of day. We could have turned it around. It could have become something good.

But instead he left. Stood up from his chair and spoke right past me. 'You're hysterical and exhausted. We can't talk when you're like this. I'm going to bed.'

'You robbed Sai of her husband!' I wanted to scream. 'Do you think it was a coincidence that he left? You robbed Maraia of a father! You robbed me of—'

But he had already closed the door behind him. His backpack with the camera equipment stood ready in the corner. And that night the balolo arrived with the full moon.

I fold both hands across my stomach again. A mirror image of Sina sitting across from me, who stopped waiting for an answer long ago.

46

Ateca

Dear God, I can't sleep tonight. The nuts on the vonu tree are as hard as turtle shells and slam when they hit the ground. Vilivo hasn't come home tonight, and the screech of an owl makes my heart grow small and tight with fear. Help me watch over everything. Tell me what to do.

Aren't all waves part of the same ocean, Lord? The ladies' village lies by another sea, a much colder one. But all stories mix together in the water; they all share their secrets. So the waves off the coast of Madam Kat's village must know what's happened on a beach here in Fiji. Everything is connected, and the ocean doesn't lie.

Balolo will come in three days, when the moon is full again. Madam Ingrid wants to come out to see it; she's the only one in Vale nei Kat who wants to go. It was easier last year: the ladies were new to Korototoka and they didn't know what balolo was. But now Madam Ingrid thinks she knows everything. I've told her that iTaukei don't like to have kaivalagi with them when the balolo comes. I know you'll forgive me for that lie.

I've asked you many times, Lord, whether it was a dream I had that night. The balolo night two years ago, when the sea was rainbow-coloured under the boats and the women ran around on the beach with buckets and pots and pans. I meant what I said to Madam Kat, that no one had seen anything. That no one had heard Mister Niklas cry out, that he must have fallen, his heart must have stopped. But it's in my dreams that I see things most clearly, Lord. What has happened and what must be done. And it's not always that we hear with our ears or see with our eyes. Sometimes the waves wash away what we see; it doesn't have enough soil stuck to its roots to stay planted.

Was it real, Lord? Or was it a spirit you showed me in a dream? A shadow of a figure in a checked shirt disappearing into the darkness behind a boat.

Was it you who gave me a sign? Should I tell Madam Kat about it? Please, Lord, show me what to do.

In Jesus' holy name. Emeni.

Ingrid

Ingrid's always been good at accepting the facts and moving on. She registers that the equilibrium in Kat's vale is disturbed but keeps on with the daily life she's built for herself: tending to the vegetable garden, pouring the chocolate into moulds in the sweet house and driving the truck – she's become the regular driver in the house now that Vilivo is gone. Ateca was beside herself with worry the morning after Ingrid dropped the boy off at the bus station in Rakiraki. How could Ingrid have known he hadn't told his mother he was leaving, before getting a ride with her? He'd chatted away, told her about the job opportunity he'd heard of, something about a bridge-building project. It didn't occur to her for a moment that he hadn't told Ateca.

Of course she's noticed that the balance of power between Sina and Lisbeth has shifted. One is more even-tempered than before; the other holds her head up high in a new way, as if the judgement of others no longer concerns her. Best not to remark on anything, Ingrid thinks. Just let things be.

But Wildrid inside her wants more. The drama, the undercurrents of shock, betrayal and shame, it energizes her and makes the thoughts swarm in her head. She keeps a close eye on Sina, delighted that her sullen scowl is gone, and feels a pang of joy to see that Lisbeth appears not to give a hoot. Wildrid wraps an orange scarf around her head and removes the bra under her T-shirt before strolling out to the porch in the night air. Offers up a bottle of wine she's brought from her trip into town.

'Are we celebrating something?' Kat asks and reaches out with her glass.

Ingrid pours and shrugs. 'That we've come this far, maybe? *Kat's Chocolate*. We've created something here. Isn't that worth celebrating?'

Kat raises her glass. 'It is,' she says. 'It definitely is.'

'A toast to the chocolate ladies!' Lisbeth chimes in. 'Plain and simple!'

Her tone is so carefree that Ingrid has to look at her twice.

Sina looks as if she's about to speak, but shuts her mouth again.

Wildrid spots Lisbeth's cheerfulness and slams the bottle down on the table. 'We have to have a taste!' she says exuberantly. 'A little piece of happiness right now, we've earned that much!' She scurries across the courtyard, opens the door of the sweet house and returns with a tray of small, elaborately wrapped packages in shiny cellophane, which she sets down in the middle of the table. 'Eat, drink and be merry!' she says gleefully, and puts a piece of chocolate in her mouth. She closes her eyes as she devours the sweet delight, lets it flow through her whole body. Licks her lips and lets out a sigh. 'That delicious feeling,' she says. 'Again and again.'

Kat unwraps a piece, folding the cellophane between her fingers as she chews slowly and thoughtfully. 'Who would have thought,' she says, 'that we could make this happen? It tastes like . . .'

'Success!' Lisbeth chimes in. 'It tastes like success!' She puts a shiny dark piece in her mouth and smacks her lips as she tastes with an expert's tongue. 'Round and deep,' she says. 'With a trace – just a tiny hint – of coconut. The sound of crashing waves and wind in the palm trees.'

'You can *hear* the chocolate?' Sina teases her. She pops a piece into her mouth. Something gentle spreads across her face; the tense frown lines soften. 'It's good,' she says. There's surprise in her voice, as if it's a discovery she's making in this very moment. 'Damn, it's good.'

Maya sits with a wrapped piece of chocolate in her hand; her fingers can't quite remember how to unwrap it. Wildrid grabs it and quickly rips off the cellophane. 'Here, Maya. You have to celebrate a little, too!' Maya carefully closes her mouth around the aromatic piece; a tiny quiver in her lips as she lets it melt on her tongue. The chocolate leaves brown smears at the corners of her mouth as she smiles. 'It tastes like happiness,' she says. 'Like everything we ever wanted.'

Kat looks at her, smiling with her whole big mouth as she lifts her glass anew. 'Yes, it does,' she says. 'Everything we ever wanted.' She lets her gaze glide across the room. 'What do you think, ladies? Did everything turn out the way we wanted?'

'Well, I wouldn't trade it for anything,' Lisbeth responds without missing a beat.

Wildrid thinks she hears a challenge in her voice, and picks up on it. 'You mean, for the big house on the hill?'

Lisbeth looks at her, astonished. 'Yes . . . That's what I mean. And for a bastard of a husband who thinks only of himself.'

Sina's head jerks up; Wildrid sees that the guarded look in her eyes has dissolved into a kind of amazement. The tension sparks along the walls, shoulders are squared, and Wildrid feels a delighted rush in her stomach. She throws the ball to Maya. 'And you, Maya? Would you trade it in? Would you rather be in Norway? With Evy?'

She doesn't know why she added that last part. To insinuate that Maya needs a babysitter no matter where she is? She wishes she could take it back.

Maya holds her glass in her lap, clutching the stem with both hands.

'I was good at drawing,' she says. 'And painting. Branko paints. Evy's husband. He's a painter.'

Ingrid looks at Maya, astonished. Had she had dreams beyond her teacher's desk? She pictures them clearly, Steinar and Maya. Goal-oriented, unwaveringly clear on what they wanted. Stability all the way. Could it be that Maya didn't get everything she had wanted?

Wildrid understands, a small triumph behind the orange bandana. 'Colours, right, Maya? That's what we're missing back home, colours?'

She gets up and takes a few quick steps into the garden. Disappears for a moment and returns with a yellow flower, which she tucks behind Maya's ear. 'It's not too late, you know. Never too late.'

She leans forward and gives Maya a hug. Ingrid feels Maya jerk backward and spill red wine in her lap, but Wildrid squeezes her harder. 'You're allowed to draw,

Maya.' The words follow on their own accord: 'Maraia can draw with you.'

Her gaze involuntarily travels over to Kat. Looking for Kat's approval. Kat's blessing. No conversation is over before they hear from Kat.

But there's no reaction from the wicker chair by the stairs. The forehead under the fringe is wrinkled, the gaze fixed on the horizon. Kat is somewhere else.

'And you, Kat? Is there anything you'd change? Anything you'd do differently if you could make the journey all over again?' Ingrid hears her own voice but it's Wildrid who asks. Kat and Ingrid have known each other for ever; Ingrid would never have asked her that. She's seen Kat with Niklas, seen what they've accomplished together. Seen them passionate, ecstatic, exhausted, resigned. Seen them fight so the sparks flew, heard them make love through thin walls. Ingrid is sure Kat wouldn't change a single comma in her story.

But Wildrid gets another answer. Kat pulls her gaze back from the beach. 'You can only see one step at a time,' she says. 'Never the whole journey, and then suddenly, it's over. But I'm happy. It's been wonderful.' She smiles softly, as if at her own secrets.

'But it's not over!' Wildrid objects. 'I still have so much I want to do.'

Kat nods slowly, as if she agrees, and Ingrid feels something gnawing at her: is Kat sitting there so self-satisfied with her colourful, exciting life that all she can do now is lean back? Enjoying the memories of her dramas and triumphs as she feels sorry for those who have lived their lives in the background, applauding from the sidelines?

'You've never seen it, have you?' Wildrid says sharply. 'Never understood how you were the yardstick for everything; how we all strove to be just a tiny bit like Kat, a fraction of what you were! And don't you see it now, with your loyal subjects gathered around you once again?'

Ingrid is horrified. She wants to get up and wrap her arms around Kat, tell her she doesn't mean a word of what she just said. That Kat has been an inspiration for her always, that there's no one she loves more. She wants to say that she's tired, she's had too much wine, she didn't mean it!

But Wildrid holds her back. Wildrid throws her arms open wide and turns to the others. 'Lisbeth! Sina! Tell me you don't know what I'm talking about!'

Sina lifts her head, looks from one to the next. 'If that's how it was, I had no idea,' she says. 'I was just grateful.' She blows out a big cloud of smoke and turns to Lisbeth. 'If I had to do it all again, I'd be much less grateful.'

Lisbeth shrugs. 'I always knew,' she says. 'That I wasn't like you, Kat. No one could be like you. But I didn't care. I had other things.'

Ingrid wants to stop them all, stop herself. That's not how it was! There will always be a leader. Someone to look up to, someone to write the rules. Someone the others are eager to please. That doesn't mean she's . . . some sort of tyrant!

No? Wildrid asks. Hasn't it been convenient for Kat that you've always been there, ready to praise and admire her? To follow close behind her, camera in hand, ready to document her and Niklas's amazing accomplishments? Why couldn't it be you in the centre of the frame? Why weren't *you* allowed to shine?

Ingrid shakes her head. No one shines when they wear a

size eight shoe. When your hands are wide and knobbly and you earn a solid B+ average, you're trusty and reliable and you rise slowly through the ranks. But trusty and reliable doesn't catch anyone's eye. Solid and patient doesn't send anyone's pulse racing.

She can feel Kat's eyes on her. Turns towards her and meets her gaze. 'I've loved so little,' she says.

The silence hums in their ears, tightening like a coil around Kat in the centre. She opens her mouth at last.

'It's not too late,' she says. 'You just said it yourself. You can always find something. You can never know what form it's going to take.'

Wildrid grabs Ingrid's hand. 'That delicious feeling,' she whispers. 'Again and again.'

Ingrid doesn't draw the curtains in her room at night. She likes the shadow play of the branches on the speckled brick wall outside, and the window is too high up for the guard to peek inside.

She sits on the edge of the bed, unwraps the orange scarf loosely tied around her head. Checks whether Wildrid is still there, hammering away in her chest, but no. The house is quiet around her, even the gecko on the wall above the light switch is frozen still in the moonlight. I've loved so little. She pictures Kat's face, Sina's. Has Sina loved? Has Lisbeth? *You can never know what form it's going to take.* Maya and Steinar. Sina and her son.

Ingrid searches her heart. She retrieves what's inside with trembling fingers: Simon and Petter. Kat. A pair of surprisingly young eyes looking at her through a wreath of laughter lines: *I've been waiting. I thought you would come.*

She lies down on the bed, feels the familiar aching in her back. Thinks to herself that she'll take Sina out to the garden tomorrow. They have a glut of beans right now, okra too. Maybe Sina could plant some flowers? Ginger flowers and yellow allamanda. Bird of paradise. Delicate frangipani. Ingrid knows the perfect spot. In the right-hand corner just below the porch, with enough sun, not too much shade. Sina can make something beautiful there.

Ingrid turns towards the wall. Tomorrow she'll write to Kjell and ask him to sell her apartment.

48

Ateca

Tonight I dreamt of black clouds, Lord. They burst with roars of thunder, and the water flowed across the earth. The ocean rose to meet the rain, and the waves crashed in over the land. The fields drowned and villages were washed away. Afterwards, the ocean lay calm and quivered with lifelessness. Only a few twigs floated on the surface, and an empty red boat. When I awoke, I knew something important was going to happen.

I said nothing to the ladies. Kaivalagi don't understand dreams the same way we do. For them, a dream is something the heart doesn't dare to remember by day. Something old that you can't let go of. For us, it's about the future. A hope we can build something on.

I was afraid when I received the next sign. It's been many years since I've heard the death drum, but I recognized the sound at once: the slow, heavy thud is impossible to miss. When the lali beats the rhythm of death, it's not intense and passionate like a meke, or light and dancing like when a baby is born. It's deep and dark, and lets the echo from one beat reverberate completely before the next one comes.

I knew it was the death drum because Akuila didn't hear it. He stood beside me outside the house, and as the heavy rhythm sang in my head, he was talking and laughing as usual. I turned away from him and listened for the sound. But it grew weaker and weaker, and finally turned into silence.

You've said that we should trust you, Lord. That you'll lead us safely through the storm. Help me to be brave and strong.

And Vilivo, Lord. I don't know where he is, but I know he'll come back. Watch over him in the meantime. Help him and let him find work, so he can support himself, become an adult and start a family.

In Jesus' holy name. Emeni.

49

Maya

She doesn't remember what Evy said. Evy is her daughter. There was something she said. I should have written it down, Maya thinks. What Evy said.

The kitchen around her looks familiar. The thing on the work surface that you put bread in; when the slices come out of there, they're brown and slightly burnt. The creaking noise when the door swings open behind her reminds her of birds. The woman with the dark curly hair who always makes her tea smiles and hands her a cup. Maya smiles back – who is she again?

'Evy said it's your decision,' Kat says. 'Whether you want to keep living here with us or go back. She said she could make up a nice cosy room for you in their house in Trondheim.'

'Trondheim,' Maya repeats. Evy lives in Trondheim.

Kat nods. Maya nods back. She likes that they're nodding together. Something on her chest makes a clicking noise. She looks down. Every time she nods, there's a clicking noise when the seeing-thing she wears on a string around her neck hits a button on her shirt. She keeps nodding, click, click, click, click.

'Maya,' Kat says and grabs her arms. She's stopped nodding. What is she saying now? Her mouth is very close to Maya's face.

'Evy loves you very much. We do too. It's your decision where you want to live.'

It's your decision. It's your decision. It's important that she hears what the mouth is saying. She has to remember it. She should write it down.

A very old woman stares back at her in the mirror, surprised. The strange thing is that when she blinks, the woman in the mirror blinks at the same time. Maya tries to blink with one eye to make sure she's seeing correctly, and the woman does the same. She has a seeing-thing hanging on a string around her neck, too. Maya turns away from the woman in the mirror; she looks cross. She wants to find the woman with the curly hair who always makes tea. Has she eaten dinner yet? She can't remember.

'Maraia's here to see you,' Kat says. A small child comes in and sits on the floor.

'We can look at some books,' the child says. 'I'll find one.'

They look at the big book with flags and oceans.

'There we are,' the child says, and points to a little speck in a big blue field.

'Yes,' Maya says. She doesn't know what the child means, but she understands that it's possible to be a speck. Be like a speck.

'I knew someone who painted pictures,' she tells the

child. 'Specks of colour on top of other colours. I don't remember who it was.'

The child gives her a long look. 'Do you get scared when you don't remember?' she asks.

Maya doesn't know. Is she scared? What was she supposed to be scared of again? She stares at the mosquito net hanging like a white, rolled-up cloud above her bed. She's supposed to be scared of mosquito bites.

She looks at the dress the child is wearing. Orange, with red and white flowers. She opens her mouth. 'Bowl,' she says, and looks at the girl with her eyes full of wonder.

She doesn't know why she said it. But the girl smiles. 'Bula,' she responds and smooths the dress down with her fingers. 'Bula dress. Madam Kat made it for me.'

Maya shakes her head. She's the one who made the dress. She's sewn all of Evy's clothes. They don't have a lot of money, Steinar and her, and it's useful that she can make what her daughter needs. 'I can teach you to sew,' she says in Norwegian.

But the girl shakes her head. 'Now I don't know what you're saying,' she replies. She speaks a different language, and Maya is glad that she can understand it. She wants to respond, but the words glide away, like ice skates on the frozen-over lake at Reitviksletta in the winter. She opens her mouth and closes it again. Strokes her hand over the flowers on the girl's dress. She's not Evy after all.

'Bula,' the girl says again and smiles.

From: kat@connect.com.fj
To: evyforgad@gmail.com
Subject: Good to see you

Dear Evy,

It was good to see you. I know it wasn't easy to leave here last Sunday, and I think you've made a brave and compassionate decision. I feel sure that letting Maya stay here with us will give her the best days possible. We don't know how many more of them there will be, but we'll make them as good as we possibly can for her.

Maya still enjoys spending time with us in the sweet house, and I honestly believe that a piece of chocolate or two a day is good for everyone, no matter the state of their health! She likes painting; she often sits on the porch with watercolours and paints together with little Maraia, whom you met. It's become harder for Maya to speak English, it seems, but she and Maraia understand each other anyway.

Let's keep in touch.

Warmly,
Kat

*

She walks beside the child along a beach. They hold hands and walk towards a red boat pulled ashore under some palm trees. A large, broad-chested man spreads out his net across the boat to dry, a spider's web with glittering drops of ocean.

'Bula, Jone,' the child says to the man.

'Bula vinaka, Maraia.'

Maya takes off the head-thing that makes her hair sweaty. She looks at the child, who nods to encourage her to say something. 'Bula vinaka,' Maya repeats.

The man laughs; the child laughs, too. Maya stands still and absorbs the laughter, a warm, gentle wave rolling towards her. She can't remember what was so funny. But the laughter is round and comfortable, a song through her head. She shuts her eyes to picture it. A red stream behind her eyelids, a trembling. She feels the wind lift her hair from her head, feels empty and light. There's something she should remember. But the sand under her toes is cool here in the shade; there's a taste in her mouth of something sweet. Maya draws a deep breath in through her nose, hears a startled cry from somewhere far away. A feeling of gliding slowly through time, arms holding her tight as the big song breaks through and fills her to the brim.

50

Sina

She walks past Maya's room. Peeks in through the door that's ajar and sees a book with large maps laid on the floor, a pile of ironed clothes on the bed. The afternoon is hot and sticky, and Sina wonders whether she should walk over to the sweet house. There are moulds to be washed, cardboard boxes to be folded, tinfoil and cellophane to be cut. It's cooler in there and probably empty; Kat's in the kitchen and Ingrid's in the garden. In a few hours, when the day begins in Norway, Lisbeth will get on the phone with potential customer contacts. Maya's gone for a walk and Maraia is with her. Sina decides to glance around the corner below the porch, where her Vanda orchids and copperleaf are now thriving in full bloom. Thanks to the compost Ingrid makes out of their food scraps, the bearded irises seem to be doing especially well.

She takes the four steps down into the garden before she sees him. Jone comes walking along the beach, carrying something in his arms, something heavy and limp. A small person walks beside him. From their rhythm, the slow steps without haste, Sina can tell right away that something's too late.

The worst part is Maraia's huge, black eyes. She just stands there, doesn't cry, doesn't say anything. It's worse looking at her than at the lifeless bundle that is Maya; the hat Sina carefully strokes off her, the shell that is her body. Kat tries to talk to Maraia, ask her what happened, but she gets no reaction. It's Jone who speaks. He tells them Maya looked completely normal when she and Maraia came walking along the beach, before she suddenly stopped and collapsed.

When the doctor arrives, Sina hears something about 'a massive stroke' and 'there most likely wasn't time for her to feel anything'. But she's not interested in the why or how. It's over, it's finished; she knew it the second she saw Jone's big dark shape coming into focus from the backlit shadow.

Sina wants to bathe and dress Maya, and she wants to do it alone. She rejects Ateca's offer to help, and gets a basin of water and some washcloths from the kitchen. She places the green plastic tub on the stool Maya used as a bedside table. Yesterday I was rinsing rice in it, she thinks. She sits on the edge of the bed, on the sheet that still smells of her sweat. One of Maya's hands lies facing palm-up, gaping like a hungry animal. Her fingers are dry and cold to the touch when Sina turns it around and lays it to rest alongside her body.

She makes sure the water is lukewarm. Pulls the dress over the head of the deceased, strokes her hair. It feels withered, like old grass. She loosens the underwear and carefully pulls it off.

She's never seen Maya naked. The white folds of skin, veins and brown spots on a silent map of sixty-seven lived years. The soft cloth caresses her slowly, bit by bit, rinsing, concluding. Over. Our time on earth.

In a soft background hum, she can hear Kat on the phone with Evy, Ingrid out on the porch greeting those who have come to offer condolences. All of Korototoka knows by now that one of the ladies in Vale nei Kat has breathed her last breath. The mats will be here soon, Sina thinks.

Lisbeth pushes the door ajar. 'Can I help you?'

She opens her mouth to rebuff her, but instead hears herself saying, 'I can do it by myself. But you can come in and sit for a while.'

Evy wants Maya's coffin to be sent to Norway; she'll be buried at home in Reitvik. The daughter wanted to jump on the first flight to Fiji, but Kat convinced her it wasn't necessary. 'We can arrange the transportation home from Nadi.'

At first Sina doesn't know why Ateca looks relieved, until she explains. 'It gives us time to have a *reguregu*.'

Sina has never heard the word before. 'Is that a kind of funeral ceremony?'

Ateca thinks for a moment. 'It's more than that,' she says at last. 'It's saying goodbye.'

Sina has so many questions. 'Cremation is quite common in Norway,' she says. 'You don't do that here?'

Ateca nods her little backwards nod. 'Not too often, but sometimes. The most important thing is that Madam Maya has a place with God, with the angels. It doesn't matter whether she goes in a coffin or in ashes.'

She's dreading it. She doesn't want her farewell to Maya to be something foreign and unfamiliar, an incomprehensible ceremony that feels alien. Sina's grief is restrained, almost wary, as if she has to protect Maya through this, too.

The reguregu is indeed foreign, and a bit strange, but not inappropriate. Not frightening. Since Maya doesn't have her own family here, the mats are laid at Kat's feet. Akuila has brought a big tanoa from his house for the kava; the little bowl they keep on their own shelf is for decoration only. The porch fills up with people, a silent procession pours into the house and passes around the dining table where the coffin is laid. Bilo after bilo is drunk, many kind words and prayers are said for Maya. Sina thinks of Evy, of the rest of the family, and of Maya's friends back home in Reitvik: they won't get to experience this. A crowded and heartfelt farewell from those who were there when the journey suddenly came to an end.

Father Iosefa is about to lead everyone in a hymn in the living room, and Sina walks out to the porch. Her gaze is fixed on the waves, and she doesn't notice Ateca until a hand takes hers. She jerks back, but doesn't pull her hand away. Not until the song in the house reaches its last verse, and Ateca sings along.

> And when at last the mists of time have vanished
> And I in truth my faith confirmed shall see,
> Upon the shores where earthly ills are banished
> I'll enter, Lord, to dwell in peace with thee.

Something explodes inside Sina. Suddenly she's furious: at Ateca, at the ridiculous lyrics of the hymn, and she tears her hand away in anger. 'Dwell in peace?' she shouts. 'Maya didn't go to dwell in peace. She had a stroke. And now she's dead!'

Ateca stops singing, but doesn't answer. Just sits calmly with her hands folded in her lap until the hymn is ended.

'Grief makes our thoughts dark, Madam Sina,' she says when it grows quiet. 'I don't know how they do it in your village. But here in Korototoka, no one ever forgets. We'll remember Madam Maya again in four days. And ten days after that. And a hundred days after that again. Even if her body is somewhere else.'

Sina nods, and her anger dissipates as quickly as it came. She thinks of something she once heard Ateca say. *When you say something in Fijian, it belongs to you.* Maybe that's how it is with grief, too? That you have to mourn in a way that your heart understands? So that your grief can find the right place to rest?

'When Madam Maya gets home to Norway,' she begins, 'her daughter will be there to receive her, and there will be our kind of reguregu – a memorial service in her own village, according to our custom. It's different from your way, but it's where everyone who wants to can come to say goodbye.'

'Can everyone speak and say what they want?'

Say what they want? What does Ateca mean?

'Yes . . . anyone who wants to, can give a speech in remembrance.'

'Can they ask for forgiveness, and be forgiven in turn?'

Sina doesn't get it. 'Forgiveness? If they've been on bad terms with the deceased, you mean?'

310

Ateca sighs quietly, and Sina gets impatient. What is this about?

'There can never be peace,' Ateca says, slowly articulating each word. 'Not for the departing, and not for those who remain, if bad blood and harmful deeds aren't resolved. Without one asking for forgiveness and the other forgiving, the departing one can't leave. And the remaining one can't say goodbye with their whole heart.'

A shadow moves beside them, and Sina and Ateca turn towards the narrow, quiet face of the Star of the Sea.

'We're small,' Maraia says. 'We're so small because the ocean is so big.'

It's the first time Sina has heard her speak since Jone brought Maya's lifeless body up from the beach.

The crowd in the living room chimes in with a new hymn, but Sina doesn't hear it. All she can hear are deep, heaving sobs. Kat is standing right behind her, crying so hard her body shakes.

51

Ateca

I wanted to say goodbye to Madam Maya alone before I left. The coffin was so beautiful, Lord. Covered by a tevutevu and beautiful masi. The white shells had been placed there by Maraia.

I wanted to sing the farewell song to Madam Maya. Isa lei. Oh, such sadness. No one can leave us until we've sung the song of parting ways.

> Isa, isa, most welcome guest,
> Your going fills me with sorrow.
> Whatever the reason you came,
> I feel bereft at your leaving.

My heart quivered when Madam Kat started to sing along. Our voices were as light as the wind as we stood there together with Madam Maya in the last big white song.

> Isa lei; oh, such sadness!
> I will feel so forlorn when you sail away tomorrow.
> Please remember the joy we shared,
> And in Korototoka you will always be remembered.

Dear Lord, thank you for welcoming Madam Maya when she gets there. She's travelling alone, but you'll be waiting for her.

In Jesus' holy name. Emeni.

52

Ingrid

They haven't done anything with Maya's room. As Ingrid walks past the closed door, she thinks that perhaps she should go in and open the window. Air out the smell of loss, let in the joy of the bird of paradise flower. But she can't bear it, knows that the atlas is still laid out on the table in there, opened to Maya's and Maraia's dreams.

There's mail on the kitchen counter. It took Ingrid a while to understand how the postal service in Korototoka works: if there's a letter for someone in the village, it ends up either at Salote's house or in the little booth they call the police station. One way or other, the mail will find its way from there to the addressee. Letters usually come to Vale nei Kat via Ateca or Akuila.

But this letter is addressed *to* Ateca, and it's been opened. Ingrid picks up the envelope curiously; the pencil handwriting on the front is in large, grey block letters. No sender. She pokes two inquisitive fingers into the envelope, but drops it back on the counter in a flash when she hears Ateca's footsteps outside the kitchen door.

'Madam Ingrid.' Ateca nods and puts down her basket of groceries.

Ingrid feels the almost-caught-red-handed flush stinging

her cheeks, and hurries to take charge of the conversation. She picks up the letter and casually remarks, 'I was just putting your mail up on the shelf, the worktop tends to get so sticky.'

The embarrassment gnaws a little deeper when Ateca doesn't look suspicious at all; her smile radiates towards Ingrid as she takes the envelope and holds it up like a gold medal. 'Madam Ingrid, it's a letter from Vilivo! From my son. Madam Ingrid, he's found a job!'

Her missing canine creates a wink of a dimple in the corner of her mouth, and Ingrid has to smile back. The laughter pours out deep and rumbling from between Ateca's lips, and she has to lean on the kitchen counter before she can continue.

'It pays well, Madam Ingrid. They're building a new bridge over the Waimakare River. Listen to what he says.'

Ateca's reading voice is slow and solemn, as if she's reading from her worn Bible.

Dear Na,

I'm sure you're mad at me for leaving without saying goodbye. But I knew Madam Ingrid would tell you what I said to her in the truck, although I didn't tell her where I was going. A friend of Salesi's had heard they needed people to work on the bridge construction up in Drokadroka, and I decided to go. On the bus from Rakiraki up through the valley, I met some guys who were working on the new bridge over the Waimakare. They brought me to the bosso of the project, and he let me start working that same day. The pay is good, Na; I'm sending you some money with this letter. There will be more later. There are many of us working here,

*from different villages, but no one from Korototoka. Bosso is
from China, so are many of the others.*

*I do what they ask, it's mostly digging and hauling
rocks. I've told bosso that I know a lot about machines, too,
and today I drove one of the steam rollers. It's good work,
Na, I'm glad to be here. I liked helping Madam Kat with
the chocolate, too – she's always been good to me. But it
wasn't strong work for a man. I am happy for the job up here
in Drokadroka. I want to work hard, build a house, marry
a nice girl and have my own family. And when you're too
old to work for Madam Kat, you'll come live with us.*

*I'll be back, Na, though it could be a while longer. My
house will be in Korototoka. My vanua is there.*

*Please tell Madam Kat that I've found a job. And may
God protect you in Jesus' name always.*

*Your son
Vilivo Matanasigavulu*

'Are you, Ateca?' Ingrid doesn't know why she asks the
question in such a backwards way.

'Am I what, Madam Ingrid?'

'Mad at Vilivo? Like he says in the letter?'

Ateca claps her hand over her mouth, horrified. 'Oh, no,
Madam Ingrid. I'm happy. This is what I wanted.'

'For Vilivo to leave?'

'I wanted him to find work. So he can support himself,
become an adult and start a family.'

Ingrid hesitates. 'Mm-hmm. I mean, he did have work here,
too. But, what was it he said . . . *it wasn't strong work for a man?*'

Ateca nods. 'He was happy to have work, and for

everything Madam Kat tried to do for him. But he was ashamed that there was no use for his good hands and his strong back.'

'He wanted manual labour? It wasn't manly enough, working with chocolate?'

Ingrid can hear Wildrid's voice grow sharp around the edges, and wants to shush her: Ateca can't tear up roles and social rules as old as the gods that inhabit her dreams.

But Ateca simply shakes her head. 'My heart was heavy when he left. But he had to. And when he comes back, it will sing again.'

It takes time to fill a void. And some shouldn't be filled, either, Ingrid thinks as she observes Sina from the porch. Sina's folded a towel to cushion her knees as she crouches down on all fours facing the flower bed. The yellow allamanda has started clinging to the net she's affixed to the wall; the funnel-shaped flowers are blooming in magnificent clusters. Her face is shaded by a flat, bulky hat; Ingrid hasn't heard any-one comment that Maya's frayed headgear is still being worn daily. I guess that's how it is, she thinks. Each one of us takes with her what she needs to move on.

She wanders back inside, feeling the restlessness that's been there all afternoon. It's just a few days since she and Kat sent Maya out on her last journey; a quiet trip to the airport with heavy baggage. When everything had been arranged and the coffin was waiting to be loaded, they sat down in the coffee shop outside the departure lounge and suddenly, there he stood. Ingrid relives the moment again. Her hand jumps to her throat; she feels the way her blush spread, the warm joy that flowed through her body when he materialized in front of their table with a cup of coffee in his hand: 'Ingrid?'

317

She'd risen out of her chair; the surprise made her throw open her arms to give him a hug. Kat's smiling face in the corner of her eye, the rush of people around them that made her sit back down. She can't remember what she said, maybe just an 'Oh!' or a 'Hello!' What she does remember – yes, she's sure of it – is how Johnny Mattson's face lit up when he caught sight of her. As if he saw something he'd been longing for.

He sat down with them, said something about picking up parts for a boat engine. She doesn't remember much more about what was said, only his smile, and his hand waving goodbye as he left. Rough and wrinkled, but strong. And warm, she'd thought.

She doesn't check her emails every day. Kjell doesn't write as often any more, after a nasty exchange when she asked him to put her apartment up for sale. It was Wildrid who wrote the email.

> I've decided to stay in Korototoka. To be honest, I decided it long ago – the first night I saw the red and yellow flames across the sky at sunset. There's nothing I miss back home, nothing you have to arrange. I've contacted the bank in Reitvik – they know me well and they'll put the money from the apartment sale into a mutual fund. A low-risk one, don't worry! We make do with very little here in Fiji; I go barefoot now, saving money on shoes.

Wildrid had laughed as she wrote the last sentence; Ingrid had almost deleted it, but ended up leaving it in.

But there's no word from Kjell in her inbox. Not from Simon or Petter either; they sometimes drop her a line, but not very often. Yet there is a new email for her. In the top row of her inbox, in bold and unopened letters, the subject line reads 'Hello from Labasa'.

Hi Ingrid,

I said I was going to write, but as you've gathered, I'm not very good at correspondence. I also said I would come back and visit, but I haven't done that either. Now that Kat's Chocolate is in full swing, my work is done. But I'm not sure that you and I are done, although we haven't even really started yet.

I was happy to see you at the airport, and I think I sensed you were, too. We don't know each other well, and for all I know, this note might hurt you or frighten you. I hope it doesn't. But I'm done not taking chances, and I won't waste any more time.

I think you and I could understand each other. We're only accountable to ourselves, and we know what it means to go it alone. That knowledge brings peace and lets you look yourself in the eye. But the older I get, the less time I have to wait. I want to grab life with both hands, like we did that night in Korototoka.

I want us to get to know each other better. Do you like fishing? I spend more time on the boat than at home, and I'd be happy to bring an extra crew member aboard. If you're willing to take a trip out in deep waters, I promise to bring you safely back to shore.

Wildrid feels the fishing pole jerking between her hands. The ocean dances around her with silver glimmers, the burning sun sparkles high in the sky, and the boat springs

319

fast and easily from the crest of one wave to the next. The deep-water pole bends, she leans back and battles the reel, giving a little slack, then pulling it back in. Johnny stands behind her to help, his arms wrapped tightly around her. His breath is warm against the top of her head, a drop of sweat drips from his chin and hits her forehead. Wildrid plants her legs wide and leans back as she pulls with all her might, screeches with delight when the giant mackerel flails and resists as she drags it in over the railing.

'There you go!' Johnny says and laughs. Removes his cap and dries the sweat off his face. 'Give it everything you have; don't hold back!'

He puts his big, rough hands around her upper arms. They're smooth and slender.

If you think I'm being too forward, just don't write back, and that'll be that. I'm too old to take offence. But if I'm right about what I think I sensed at the airport, let me know when you might consider a trip to Labasa.

All the best from Johnny,

who looks forward to seeing you. If you want.

Ingrid stands up from her chair. If she wants! Is this really happening? But she doesn't need to read the message again. Yes, it's happening. She looks down at her feet: her toes are curling up and willing her to start dancing. Ingrid Hagen has danced far too little, but she intends to do something about that. Wildrid throws her hands up in the air and laughs from her belly. A big and powerful laugh she didn't know she had in her.

53

Ateca

Dear God, you know it's often hard for the kaivalagi to understand the simplest things. You told me long ago that I have to talk to Madam Kat. But first I had to talk to Sai, so last night I went to her house.

'Maraia knows the song of the women in Namuana,' I said. 'When they sing to the princesses so the turtles come up from the sea.'

Sai wasn't surprised, Lord. She just nodded. 'It brings them to the surface,' she said. 'What's no longer here has simply taken another form, elsewhere.'

I could hear that she wanted to say more, so I waited.

'Everything becomes clear in the end,' she said. 'Even for those who don't want to see.'

I understood at once, Lord. She was thinking of Madam Kat. Madam Kat, who hasn't wanted to see.

I was completely unprepared, I swear. When she continued, the sky pushed the clouds aside, and the moon stood blank like a lie exposed. 'Mister Niklas knew,' she said. I squeezed my eyes shut; I couldn't look at her when she told me. About her husband, who had always thought their daughter was too pale-skinned. About Mister Niklas, who had the truth in his eyes from the day Maraia was born. About Madam Kat, who knows in her heart.

Was I too harsh, Lord? I didn't know any other way to talk to Madam Kat. 'You were angry at Mister Niklas when he died,' I said to her. 'That's why you stayed in the shadows and didn't see.'

I didn't want to hear her answer, Lord. You know I don't want there to be any shame between us. But Madam Kat had to say what she had to say.

'Yes, Ateca, I was angry at him. My heart was burning with fury, and do you know why? Because he wouldn't even look at her! Because he wouldn't open his arms to his daughter and let her in with us. That was what I couldn't forgive,' she said to me. 'That was why. Do you understand, Ateca?'

I understood; I've understood for a long time. You understand, Lord. And now Madam Kat understands too. That she has to perform bulubulu. Ask for forgiveness.

'You're not the one who has to forgive Mister Niklas,' I told her. 'You have to ask Mister Niklas to forgive you.'

Have I done the right thing, Lord? Madam Kat is so much more than my bosso. She's my friend who helps and protects me. But now I'm the one who has to help her.

Bless both Maraia and Madam Kat, Lord. Let their shadows always be still in the moonlight.

And thank you for Vilivo. Thank you for finding him work. Now he can support himself, become an adult and start a family.

In Jesus' holy name. Emeni.

54

Kat

Ask for forgiveness? Is that what I have to do?

I've taken off my flip flops; there's sea foam on the water lapping across my feet. The sun is almost down, so I'll have to walk quickly to get there before dark. The doubt churns in my stomach, I feel stupid and false. A *bulubulu* reconciliation ceremony involves speeches and costly gifts. I don't have a *tabua*, a big expensive whale tooth to offer; I haven't prepared a speech. There are no solemn men sitting there in ceremonial positions waiting for me at the spot under the tree where the boat lay ashore.

It was very hard for Ateca to come out with it. She never hides her opinions, but it's still rare for her to try to pressure me into something. I asked if she wanted me to do it for Sai's sake. 'Is it for Sai? For her to forgive?'

But Ateca shook her head, and for once there was no laughter in her mouth. 'Sai has nothing to forgive. She hasn't lost anything. She has Maraia. She's been given plenty.'

She insisted I had to do it for my own sake. 'The one who doesn't ask for forgiveness can never find peace.' And that I had to do it for Niklas. 'He can't leave your unsettled heart, Madam Kat.'

I don't know how I'm going to do this. The sun has hit the horizon; it's being swallowed by the sea in one giant gulp. A pink shimmer dances around the palm trees for a few seconds before the beach settles down in the quiet of darkness.

Ateca was widowed long before we came here; I never met her husband. But she often has opinions about marriage and relationships. 'The reasons for disagreement between man and wife are as many as there are leaves on the trees and fish in the sea. But luckily the wind blows, the waves crash, and leaves and fish are swept away.'

The wind blows and the waves crash. I stop at the water's edge and stand still. For a long time – until I feel the water lapping right under my knees. The ocean has turned; the tide is coming in. I retreat further up the beach and keep walking. The moon catches up to me, hurries my footsteps and casts white, crackling flashes in the sand.

I didn't know whose boat it was that night, and I don't know now. But it's there, the outriggers mounted on both sides like arms. Come here, they say. Come, sit down. The shadow lies there waiting, a triangle of refuge between the boat and the trees. I glide into safety behind the silent hull, into a salty smell of sun-dried fishing nets.

I haven't brought any offerings, and the one I bear bitter thoughts towards is gone. The appeal for forgiveness must be addressed to the family members of the one who has suffered unjustly, but Niklas's parents are long dead. I'm not fulfilling any of the other ceremonial requirements either, and the insulted party isn't here to give me the absolution I seek. Still, I am here to ask for forgiveness. Bulubulu means 'to bury'. Bury resentment and put an end to bitterness.

Should I speak out loud? Whisper? If I say it in my head, it will be no different from the endless conversations I've had with myself every night since it happened. I must say it out loud.

The words flicker uncertainly around me in the dusk. 'Do you understand that I could hardly see anything?' I begin. 'It was dark and chaotic and the beach was full of people, and I thought you were out in a boat. The shadows in the mangroves kept moving, and everything was a blur.'

I wait a moment, but Niklas doesn't respond.

'You know who I was focused on, right? My eyes, my mind, I had everything fixed on your daughter. *Your* daughter, Niklas. The Star of the Sea glowed and sparkled right in front of you, and you turned your back on her. Couldn't you see that you were turning your back on me, too? On the joy and the magic we could have shared with her?'

I pause, hearing my own voice. How it chops and carves angrily at the silence. This is all wrong, I didn't come here for demands or accusations. I bury both of my hands in the sand, let the damp ashes of the sea cool my palms.

'Ateca says you can't get to where you're going if I don't ask you to forgive me. For being blind to everything but my own disappointment and resentment. For not catching you when you fell.'

The wind makes the wooden boat creak; a dry, wailing sound.

'I wanted you to hurt. I wanted you to feel the pain that you had caused me. The betrayal, that you didn't honour

325

your daughter. That you didn't celebrate her and have her join our journey.'

I raise my hand, remembering the feeling of Maraia's hair under the thin skin on my palm. Maraia's head, for Fijians the most sacred part of the body, so warm under my fingers. '*Tulou*,' I said to her. Forgive me. For my big rough hand touching your inviolable head. A breath of light against my life line.

'Forgive me,' I say to Niklas. I need to say it, and I try to mean it. If I don't, I'll never get out of the shadows. 'Forgive me for letting you die.'

Forgive us our sins, as we forgive those who trespass against us.

Ingrid is sitting alone on the steps when I return.

'You were gone some time,' she says.

I nod. 'I had something I needed to do.'

'Maraia's mother was here.'

Maraia's mother.

'What did she want?'

'I'm not sure. She said Maraia's going to start school after Christmas. She was asking for you.'

I make a sudden decision. 'I'm going over there to see her.'

Ingrid stands up. 'Do you want me to come?'

'If you want.'

'She's big now,' Sai says when we've taken a seat outside her house. A small bowl of mussels sits at her feet; she opens them with a knife as she talks. 'She'll be seven in August, when the ivi tree blooms. She has to go to school, to learn things.'

I feel the sadness settle in my stomach, flat and grey.

'Yes, I guess she has to,' I say.

No open atlases and shiny shells, no tiny footsteps across the floor: 'I'll help you, Nau.'

Ingrid asks the question before I realize it's on the tip of my own tongue. 'And the school fees, Sai? Are they . . . Will they be a problem?'

A pair of brown eyes settles on mine. 'I think it will be fine. There are many people who love Maraia.'

I understand right away. Ateca has been here. Ateca has spoken to Sai and told her everything will be OK. Told her Madam Kat has done her bulubulu and is moving on.

'I'd like to help with the school fees,' I hear myself say. I take a deep breath and make the words come out. 'It's what Mister Niklas would have wanted.'

Only a memory, deep in Sai's gaze. No bitterness. No sorrow, only a past.

'Star of the Sea,' she says. 'He was the one who said it. That night. He held a blue starfish in his hand and said it bore the name of the holy virgin. So I named her Maraia.'

I wait; there's more.

'He didn't want to hurt anyone,' she says. 'He was just searching.'

'For what?' My voice is a whisper. Do I want to know? But now I've asked.

Sai takes her time to answer. Meticulously, she wipes the knife blade clean against her sulu without looking at us.

'A place to pull his boat ashore,' she says. 'A beach.'

A koki bird twitters hysterically behind the house. Sai

327

plunges her hand into the bucket and pulls out a new mussel, twists the shell open with her knife. A laugh clucks in her chest and trickles out in bubbling giggles.

We take the long way home. Past the school, up to the chief's bure, and down past the rugby pitch, where the dust has settled for the day. Just three or four teenagers sit in a clump under a tree, their laughter rolling towards us.

Ingrid looks over at me. 'You know, I still don't get it.'

'What?'

'Why they laugh.'

'Why they laugh?'

'Yes – at all kinds of things. When you and I would cry, or apologize, or whatever – they laugh. They roar with laughter and slap their thighs. What *is* that?'

Humility, I want to say. Everything we don't know how to express; what's bigger and mightier than any words we dare put in our mouths. What embarrasses us because it exceeds what we know or what we see. That's what they laugh at, or laugh about. There's no denial, no mockery. Instead of analysing or discussing the unmentionable, they've united around a way to express it that neither wounds nor offends.

Words, words, words. They don't provide any answer that I can give Ingrid. My babble of words is the opposite of Ateca's belly laugh, of Sai's soft mussel-cleaning chuckle.

'They laugh about what life brings,' I say instead. 'The things that are too big. Too beautiful. That words are too small to convey.'

Ingrid gets it. 'Yes,' she says. 'What we think we can

conquer by talking about it. But it's not about winning, is it?'

No. It's not about winning.

On the porch at Vale nei Kat, the largest wicker chair is pulled up next to the hammock, where Sina's foot dangles over the edge. Lisbeth sits in a light blue sulu, flipping through a pile of papers. I crane my neck over her shoulder. Fish and shells. Boats in colourful brushstrokes. Waves in daring surges over the edge of the page.

Lisbeth looks up. 'They're Maya's. I thought we could frame a few of them.' She hands me the pile.

'Yes, of course.' I take them from her, slightly over-whelmed. 'I didn't know she painted so many.'

'I was keeping them safe.' The voice comes out of the shadow between the chair and the hammock.

I'm startled. 'Maraia, I didn't see you there!'

Golden grains of sand flicker in her brown eyes.

I flip through the pictures, stopping at one where the paintbrush has dripped out a mosaic of green and brown dots. 'What's this?'

Maraia reaches out her hand and points. 'She painted this one for me. We were playing ocean. Can't you see what it is?'

Two dark oval shapes in the middle of the page; hard, glittering shells. Two turtles stretching their heads towards the shore. The translucent sea above the flickering seabed. Brownish-black mangrove trees against warm sand. The figures on the beach are tiny, with long, flowing hair. The song floats away from them, out over the ocean; in gold and lurid pink it strikes the dark shape of the creatures in an extravagance of light.

'Those are the princesses,' I say.

Maraia nods. 'The big song is taking them up into the light.'

She gets up and stands right in front of me.

'I'm going to go to school,' she says. 'But not for a while. First I'm going home. And then I'll come back.'

'Yes,' I say. 'Then you'll come back.'

Between a Moon and a Sea

'Madam Kat!'

Ateca's voice is loud and excited. 'It's happening now! The time has come for Nunia! Can Vilivo take the truck to the hospital?'

I stand up so quickly I feel a pang in my lower back – that damned hip!

'Of course. Go right ahead! And good luck!' I call after Ateca as she scurries down towards the gate. 'Let me know as soon as anything happens.'

I carefully shift my hip back into a comfortable position in the wicker chair on the porch. It's finally happening. Ateca's dream of becoming a grandmother is coming true. The young woman her son brought back from the Drokadroka valley six years ago is mild-mannered, with a sweet smile. She's worked alongside him as they built their house on the vacant plot behind the sweet house and cultivated a small but fertile patch of cassava and sweet potatoes. Along the side wall of the house, a paradise of colours: tender pink hibiscus, fiery flamingo flowers, delicate purple orchids and plump, juicy red protea. On their knees by the flower beds, Nunia and Sina haven't needed many words to

331

get to know each other over yellow pincushions and speck-led heliconia; their hands in the damp earth have done most of the talking. Sina advised, encouraged and admired, and the flowers from Nunia's little garden are now in high demand all the way to Rakiraki, Ateca says.

But there haven't been any children. Vilivo and Nunia had been living in Korototoka as man and wife for less than a year when Ateca came to Sina with the problem. Sina consulted me in turn. 'Ateca wants me to bring her daughter-in-law to the woman doctor. For goodness' sake, just because I had that surgery . . .'

She didn't finish her sentence, but the meaning behind her words was clear: 'Because I had that surgery, there's someone who thinks I can help. Someone who needs me. I'd be happy to take Nunia to the doctor, but I need your approval.'

'Of course, it would be great if you could take her to the doctor,' I told Sina back then. 'It would put Ateca's mind at ease. Nunia's too.'

But the woman doctor found nothing wrong, and Nunia waited. We all waited. At one point the hope was lit and her stomach grew, but something went wrong. So when Nunia got pregnant again last autumn, Ateca didn't say anything. She went about her work as usual, but I'm sure she said her prayers even more intensely, asking that the baby live this time. She often visits the grave of the little girl who didn't survive the last month in her mother's womb. After the funeral, she and Vilivo both kept watch at the cemetery for several nights; no one talks about it, but everyone knows there are practitioners of black magic about. This time it *has* to go well! Nunia and Vilivo would be outstanding parents, and Ateca longs for this grandchild so much. She deserves it. We all deserve it. A baby, the icing on the cake.

If something happens in the maternity ward today, we'll have to call Lisbeth tonight, when it's morning in Gothenburg. She won't be back for another couple of months; her split lifestyle, with a long summer in Scandinavia and the rest of the year in Fiji, suits her well. She still looks ten years younger than the rest of us, but not because of the make-up. It's her role as chocolate ambassador that makes her skin glow and puts a spring in her step, I'm sure of it. That, and the time she now has with Joachim and his family.

I've never seen a more nervous grandmother than when they came to visit the year after Maya died. And I've never seen a stranger welcoming committee than the one that stood waiting for the car with the white-haired twin girls from the other side of the world: a suspicious Sina in the shadowy far corner of the porch, an excited and worried Ateca in the window, Ingrid on the stairs with a huge grin. And Maraia. On the bottom step, holding a basin of water containing a blue starfish, glittering on top of a bed of sand and shells and stones.

Linda and her boyfriend have visited us, too. They stopped by Vale nei Kat for a brief afternoon before traveling on to the Denarau Hilton in their rental car. Maraia was part of the welcoming committee then, too, walking forward to greet them when Lisbeth waved her over.

'Maraia, this is my daughter. Her name is Linda. That means "beautiful".'

The sun glinting on the gold necklace around Maraia's neck, Linda's surprised glance at her mother. 'Isn't that . . . ?'

Lisbeth's calm reassurance: 'Maraia is the Star of the Sea. She shines for all of us in Vale nei Kat.' Linda's sharp mouth softening into a smile.

Lisbeth and her daughter have worked out the best relationship they could have: personal enough to enjoy seeing each other, professional enough to ensure respect. Linda is competent; it's largely thanks to her that our chocolate is now being sold not only in the B FIT chain of fitness centres, but also in health food shops in both Norway and Sweden.

Sometimes I listen at the door when mother and daughter meet on Skype: they're efficient and to-the-point, but every so often you can hear them indulge in small talk and even in cackling laughter of Fijian calibre. Perhaps something loosened a bit for Linda when Harald died a few years ago? A tricky game of loyalty she no longer has to play?

Lisbeth went home for the funeral as the widow, since they never actually divorced. And to give Harald some credit, all the money went to her, not to anyone in the series of younger female companions who came and went in the years before his high cholesterol and narrowed arteries got the better of him. And there was nothing for Armand. When she got back, Lisbeth announced to no one in particular that there was no will and that everything would be divided among the known heirs. Sina didn't even blink. Armand and Harald were never part of each other's lives. The only thread that linked them was spun here in Vale nei Kat, and it never stretched out of the door.

Sina hasn't gone back to Norway. Armand hasn't come back here either. But they keep in touch, and the last news

Sina told us about him was a catering project operating from the home kitchen of a woman he's seeing. Sina has mentioned her name several times with hope in her voice: could this be a decent, down-to-earth girl at last? Someone who could love the Armand who might be there somewhere behind the silken smile, and still stand up for herself. Someone who could keep an eye on the money he got from the sale of Sina's apartment, which she had entrusted to an estate agent. A portion of Armand's inheritance had been paid out in advance, and Sina's frown lines grew a little softer when she transferred a sum into my account as well. 'Overdue rent', the bank reference read.

She now has the title of supervisor and is in charge of the daily overseeing of the sweet house, where four women from the village work day in and day out in green aprons, rolling, conching and pouring the chocolate into moulds. Two of them belong to Mosese's extended family. It makes me happy when I see him occasionally limp down the hill to make his meticulous round of the drying plot, peeking in to observe the chocolate-makers and finally coming up to the house. He still stands on the porch steps and refuses to come in; Ateca still calls me over when she spots him through the window. But now Vilivo usually shows up too, and keeps his predecessor company, answering his questions, taking his time. Our new plantation manager has an 'office' now: Vilivo built a small extension to the toolshed, where he keeps a desk, a chair and an assortment of pipes, pulleys, stamps and tools he uses to improve and repair our machines.

'My son went to school,' Ateca says whenever the opportunity presents itself. 'That's why he has a good job and can support himself.' And then she laughs so hard the sun bounces off the window glass and the hole left by her missing tooth winks gleefully.

If the baby comes today, I know Ingrid will hurry over right away. Madam Ingrid, who even in Ateca's eyes needs no wedding ring to be considered Mrs Mattson, calls to check in almost every day when she's in Labasa. Johnny has a satellite phone aboard the boat, and I can feel the wind on her face when Ingrid reports from the deck: 'Three gigantic tuna fish! Over sixty pounds each! We don't have enough freezers on board, so we'll have to go back in tonight so the fish won't spoil.'

The laughter, the breathless, short sentences; I picture her wide feet firmly planted in cut-off rubber boots among seaweed and fish scales. Her sulu has been replaced with a pair of shorts, her grey hair grown long and gathered in a ponytail under a worn bucket hat. As far from the fastidious, bookkeeping Ingrid as you could get. It's as if an inner alter ego has been set free and is now dancing her own meke on the deck of the boat in Labasa.

When Simon and Petter came to visit last summer, it was quite touching. Like doting grandparents, but without anxiety, Ingrid and Johnny took them out in the boat right away, and later we all sat together and spent a whole evening looking at Petter's photos. Sunsets, big catch, close-ups of a sea snake he'd bent over the rail to get shots of. The joy on the faces of those boys from the country at the top of the world when they raved about lines and hooks, waves and weather. Ingrid's face, beaming with pride over a passion she found and is passing on.

She's a master of the art of balancing, both on deck and

of the books, regularly swapping her salt-streaked sailor's life for a visit to scour the account books of *Kat's Cocoa* and *Kat's Chocolate* with sharp eyes. At least once a month Ingrid comes to stay in the room she still keeps in Vale nei Kat, and she goes through the debits and credits line by line. Vilivo sits in the chair across from her, a giant step forward from when his predecessor insisted on standing on the stairs with his head bowed. I take part too, of course, but it's nice to know the business is in good hands as far as management and accounting goes. These days, it's mostly about the chocolate and the solid brand we've created, although we still make some deliveries of raw cocoa beans to a few of my oldest customers. We use most of the harvest ourselves to produce *Maya*, the signature product of *Kat's Chocolate*. A little piece of happiness. The taste of Fiji, wrapped in shiny cellophane with two glittering turtles on the label.

Sometimes I feel as if Ingrid has taken over the freedom I used to have. Had, and took for granted until the ridiculous, unhappy accident. Fall down the stairs – me? After sitting on the roofs of buses along dizzying mountain roads in Pakistan and battling wild currents aboard tiny boats in Malaysian rainforests? To fall down the stairs at home! The four steps my feet could take in my sleep! Until I tripped one morning three years ago, somehow letting one foot step on the other, and so lost my balance. A femur fracture, weeks of clammy sheets and a bedside table with vases full of limp bouquets. Surgery in Suva, weeks and months of slow recovery, aches and pains, and finally resigning myself to the fact that my hip will always be a little creaky. I guess

I can't complain; many of us have it much worse at this age. But I'll never be best friends with my walking stick, an invaluable but far from beloved appendage.

Ateca followed a few steps behind me the first few months, indoors and outdoors, until I had to ask her to stop. Madam Kat has gained an extra accessory, I told her, but I'm otherwise the same. She doesn't quite believe me, and insists on following me when I take a walk on the beach; sometimes I have to use a sharp voice to tell her I don't want her to come. Some walks I have to take alone. Making my way through soft sand is harder than before; it goes slowly, but I have time. Time and joy over the things that haven't changed: the sunshine that mellows and softens. The boats that bind the days together. The waves that don't exist on their own, but are always part of the rumbling sea. The light that forgives, time and time again.

*

What does it mean to look back? Is it the same as looking forward? I think to myself that it must be. Because she is what's yet to come, while she's also what came before. She stands there in the doorway, a beautiful young woman, fifteen years old. Her long hair in waves more dreamy than the ocean, her gaze ever patient and wise. Free as the wind that brought her here, loyal as the earth that keeps her grounded. Maraia lives here whenever she wants, comes and goes as she pleases, returns when our hearts call out to her. Her footprints in the sand are as big as mine now. Clear, deliberate impressions, with strong toes pointing forward.

I won't follow her the whole way; her time is separate

from mine. I'm going to listen now, feel the waves underneath the boat. Think of the hope that was born that night, between a white balolo moon and a sea that was waiting and watching.

*

The phone that rings inside the house. The gentle footsteps across the floor. The light in her eyes when she comes back.

'That was Ateca. It's a little boy. They're going to call him Niklas.'

Acknowledgements

Many calls for help have been sent across the seas over the course of working on this book. The biggest thank-you goes to Salote Kaimacuata in Suva, who has wisely and patiently guided me to an understanding of everything, from the mystical meaning of kava to rites for funerals and forgiveness. Language and religion, myths, beliefs and modes of address: the possibilities for missteps are endless. If I've avoided the pitfalls, it's thanks to Salote; where I've missed the mark, the fault is mine alone.

Anne Moorhead and Richard Markham have let me participate via email in the start-up of their own cocoa plantation in Savusavu on Vanua Levu, and have generously shared their knowledge of plants, crops and production methods. Without them, Kat and the others couldn't have grown their cocoa.

Thank you to my editor Kjersti Herland Johnsen in Norway, who had faith in the story from day one, for her cheerleading and savvy guidance. Enormous gratitude to my daughter Marie Ostby, who translated every word and nuance perfectly.

Marianne Velmans and her excellent team at Doubleday fine-tuned the manuscript for English readers and gave the book its beautiful design: Alice Youell, Poppy Stimpson,

Becky Jones, Vivien Thompson and Sarah Whittaker, I am indebted to you all.

Huge appreciation also goes to my agent Chandler Crawford, who has brought so many pieces of happiness to so many audiences.

And all my love and gratitude to Knut, who believes in me every day.

Glossary

Brief definitions of the Fijian words that appear most often in the book. The explanations below relate to the context in which they're used in the text, although many of them can also have several other meanings.

balolo	A small sea worm that lives on the ocean floor, which rises to the surface one night every year; considered a delicacy
bilo	Drinking cup made of coconut shell, typically used for drinking kava
bula	Hi, hello; also used in conjunction with other words to describe something typically Fijian, colourful and floral: bula shirt, bula-patterned, etc
bulubulu	Traditional ceremony, usually carried out between families or clans, to ask forgiveness for an insult or crime committed
bure	Traditional Fijian house or hut
dalo	A root crop, which is a staple of the Fijian diet
drua	A double-hull canoe, traditionally considered sacred in the sense that only aristocrats could own one
Emeni	Amen
Isa!	An expression of pity, regret or dismay
Isa Lei	Fijian farewell song, lamenting a sad goodbye

itatau	A ceremony of 'thank-you and farewell' concluding a lengthy visit
iTaukei	The indigenous people of Fiji, i.e. those of Melanesian descent
kaivalagi	Foreigner, stranger
kava	A mildly sedative drink made of dried and ground yaqona (the root of a plant in the pepper family) mixed with water. Kava is the most widely used recreational substance in Fiji, and is drunk both privately and at official ceremonies, where it is accompanied by an elaborate ritual
lolomas	Loving greetings
lovo	An underground oven consisting of a hole dug in the ground, heated by large stones
masi	Cloth made from dried bark, used as a canvas for decorative pieces. In Fiji often painted with geometrical designs
meke	Traditional Fijian dance
na	Mother
nau	Auntie
palusami	Fijian dish in which packets made of roro leaves are filled with coconut and tinned meat and boiled in coconut milk
sa qase	Old, advanced in years
sulu	A skirt-like garment worn by both women and men. Can also simply be a long piece of fabric wrapped around the waist
tanoa	A large, often elaborately decorated wooden bowl used for mixing and serving kava
tevutevu	Collection of woven mats given at special occasions like births, weddings or funerals

tivoli	Traditional root crop, a kind of wild yams
tulou	Forgive me
vale	Home (n.)
vale nei Kat	Kat's house/home
vanua	Literally 'earth', but with an added meaning that encompasses both emotional and familiar/traditional attachment to a place or area
vinaka (vakalevu)	(Many) thanks
vosa vaka-Viti	The Fijian language
yalowai	Muddled and confused, as associated with dementia

ABOUT THE AUTHOR

Anne Ostby is a journalist and novelist who has lived all over the world, including four years in Fiji. She is the author of a number of novels published in her native Norway, and one other novel published in English, *Town of Love*. She now lives in East Timor with her husband.